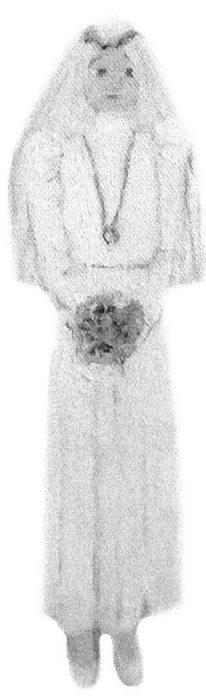

PLURAL BRIDE TO BE

A NOVEL

Cheryl Vaught

Andrew Benzie Books
Walnut Creek, California

A few things didn't get done at my house the last two days because I couldn't stop reading your book. I treat sexual abuse victims and survivors of dysfunctional families and boy, you really nailed it. Glad you released it when the Me Too movement has gained notice. Hope this finds a very wide audience.
  —MnRN

Wow, nice work! I just read the first chapter, and like that the story started out in a baptism-for-the-dead setting! And also captured the "shame" of something natural and completely beyond someone's own control.
  —Nomonomo

Very moving and captivating.
  —Deja Vue

Tuesday was very nonproductive due to your page turner (screen swiper?)! I love so many things about it, not the least being how transportative it is. You perfectly created a microcosm.
  —Ohdeargoodness Nli

Bravo Cheryl, bravo! I just finished reading your book in one sitting. I feel both triggered and unfettered… I loved it!
  —gOrgone

Compelling prose, my friend.
  —[Author] Donbagley

…this is a must-read. Not only does it give nevermos like me an idea of what growing up in polygamous circles is like (spoiler: it's horrible ;-), but Cheryl has a real talent for drawing the reader in—I couldn't put it down.
  —Soft Machine

Wow. Just wow. Very Brave and very raw. It blew me away actually.
  —Gemini

This is certainly a riveting and harrowing novel.
  —blindguy

Published by Andrew Benzie Books
www.andrewbenziebooks.com

This novel is based on the 1953 police campaign against polygamy and events in the author's life. This fictional story and characters reflect my insider's view of mainstream Mormon and polygamous cult life and rituals.

Printed in the United States of America

First Edition: April 2018

10 9 8 7 6 5 4 3 2 1

ISBN 978-1-941713-67-9

*Cover art by Sandra Maresca, Guerneville, California
Author photograph by Lois Tema Photography, San Francisco, California
Cover and book design by Andrew Benzie*

To Sondra Klein, my ex-Mormon younger sister
August 23, 1953 to November 3, 2015

HISTORICAL FACT

Two hundred law enforcement officers arrested the heads of 36 polygamous households and nine women on July 24, 1953 in the town of Short Creek (currently called Hildale, Utah and Colorado City, Arizona) on the Utah/Arizona border. Instead of making direct allegations of polygamy, they used extensive charges of conspiracy to violate laws from statutory rape to misappropriation of school funds.

This raid was the climax of "Operation Seagull," planned for 26 months and included investigations of a host of Mormon polygamy splinter groups in both states.

*   *   *

Most of the history of human experience is lost, like the sounds of acorns rustling through leaves to the forest floor. Fictional twelve-year-old Karen Hardy's summer as a plural bride to be is a whisper as soft as a falling acorn, but not lost. Her story is alive in these pages.

The only men who become Gods, even Sons of God,
are those who enter into polygamy.
—Brigham Young

Journal of Discourses, vol. 11 p. 269

August 19, 1866

TABLE OF CONTENTS

CHAPTER 1

CLEANLINESS IS NEXT TO GODLINESS

Deep in the basement of the Salt Lake City Mormon temple, the doors parted into a gold and white marble palace as blinding as sun on new snow. Karen and Amy along with the other Beehive girls crept into the opulence, shamefaced, hiding behind arms crossed against their breasts, shivering and buck naked beneath the cutoff long johns.

"Sit along this bench," Sister Viva directed them. The slick stone protrusion was like satin over ice against Karen's legs.

Also wearing short granddaddy union suits and looking like a row of rag-tag seagulls on a window ledge, the Deacon boys skittered along an adjacent bench.

Sighs and squeaks of bare feet on glossy stone echoed in the otherworldly ice cave.

Thousands of chandelier crystals caught and sprinkled lights on the water in the gold baptismal font which rested on the hindquarters of twelve life-sized oxen, also of gold. The statues stood guard in a pit, rumps bumping center, metallic faces nosed out, blind to linked spears corralling them.

Karen's knees trembled between the goose-bumpy girls on either side of her. Nervous energy drenched the air and filled Karen's lungs, probably causing her bellyache and Amy's earlier shushing, also the boys' wild antics to let off steam. Any blunder at a time like this would feed the ward gossip mill back home and result in surefire humiliation. Most frightening, what if unseen spirits were watching, ready to spread rumors to the Celestial Kingdom, and ultimately, to Heavenly Father, the Lord God Almighty of the universe!

Youth leaders whispered in a knot and cast stern glances at the kids who assumed an outer calm as brittle as ice crust on a water bucket.

Three fatherly Melchizedek Priesthood holders made their entrance, not wearing the ugly skivvies, but decked out in stark white slacks, shirts, and slippers. Their faces radiated practiced humbleness yet, they strode with absolute authority across the hall. Two of them shared Karen's bleached coloring. The third was bronze skinned and toothy with black bramble hair and a similar wild overgrowth bristling from his neckline and crawling down his arms. Karen concluded he must be a blood thirsty cannibal witchdoctor, converted from some exotic island like those in National Geographic photos.

She clutched her writhing belly.

The two palefaces assumed command posts above the pit next to a marble throne fit for Goliath. The bronze savage peeled slippers off monster-sized feet, then crossed a bridge and waded into the font waist-deep.

Brother Dale beckoned to Enoch. "You're first." The frozen hall amplified the brother's murmur, echoing it into a ghostly moan, and sending shock waves over the gooseflesh on Karen's arms and legs.

For once Enoch didn't have a finger up his nose or poking anyone's ribs. His normal deviltry drained from his face, darkening his freckles against pasty skin and lips. He winced with each movement as he sidled over the gold oxen. The boys' suits were worse than ugly, they must also be painfully cramped in the crotch. Karen smiled to herself.

In spite of loathing Enoch, she almost pitied him on show as the prime example everyone must follow. Thankfully, she wouldn't have that privilege.

The cannibal raised one hand to heaven. The other reached for Enoch's warty hand. Knowing the flesh eating man would soon touch her, maybe even pass on a wart outbreak from Enoch, Karen gagged.

The island witchdoctor prayed aloud in a sing-song chant, "Brother Enoch Zurflew Brown, having been commissioned of Jesus Christ, I baptize you, for and in behalf of, Lorenzo Thadias Ackerman, who is dead, in the name of the Father, and of the Son, and of the Holy Ghost. Amen."

On hearing Enoch's name, *Zurflew*, girls giggled behind their hands, and boys chuckled and hissed. Brother Dale nosed in for a stare-down with one mocking boy who had elbowed those on either side. The boys' shared smirk wilted.

Karen knew the bratty boy's name *Zurflew* sentenced him to a lifetime of ridicule and she silently cheered her own middle name, Ellen.

The cannibal braced Enoch's spine while the young Deacon pinched his nose and tipped back into the water. Quickly, the man jerked him upright. Enoch sputtered and mopped his face. Youth leader monitors nodded confirmation that every hair and thread had been submerged. Enoch would not require a re-dunking for the deceased Brother Ackerman.

Karen remembered jeering tales of kids sticking out one toe and having to undergo multiple humiliating re-submersions. She must stay completely immersed for the spotters' benefit when her turn came.

The savage in the pool shoved Enoch like a chunk of driftwood at the stairway. The boy emerged from the water, gauzy fabric stuck like wet tissue to his shivering behind, exposing a startling purple handprint birthmark which cupped one beefy cheek. Spectators gasped before he turned the birthmark around, plopped it on the edge of the giant's throne, and folded his arms.

The paleface officiators pressed hands to his bent head while one belted out a prayer. "Brother Enoch Zurflew Brown, in the name of Jesus Christ, we lay our hands upon your head, for and in behalf of, Lorenzo Thadias Ackerman, who is dead, and confirm you a member of the Church of Jesus Christ of Latter-day Saints, and say unto you, receive the Holy Ghost. Amen."

The words "Receive the Holy Ghost" thundered throughout the stone walls like a commandment from the Lord's own lips.

Enoch bumbled and half slid down the watery staircase to be baptized for another dead spirit. That baptism was followed by another and another, each dunk picking up speed. The procedure replayed itself like film flopping in a malfunctioning movie projector as Enoch staggered up and back, gasping for dear life between dousings. In all, he provided salvation for ten dead males before Brother Dale aimed the dazed boy back toward the dressing room.

Next, Dwayne made his way to the font. Thanks to Enoch, he knew what to expect. The rite for each dead soul took only minutes, but to Karen names dragged on forever. Once, the hurried baptizer sloshed him so quickly, Dwayne failed to pinch his nose. He flailed wildly. Then his face popped out of the water, snorting and strangling on bodily fluids and spitting font water. Monitors shrugged off the close call. To Karen's count, Dwayne had provided the path to glory for ten more dead old-timers with funny names. But none was as peculiar as the one for Dwayne's present-day best friend, Enoch Zurflew.

Karen memorized each word and gesture. The breakneck speed didn't quell the epidemic of tics and twitches among the long suffering Beehive girls and Deacons. Brian was the last boy, not a shrimp like all the rest, but actually taller than Karen, an absolute dreamboat despite the frightful outfit. Prayers for his dead spirits pattered faster than the auctioneer in Phillip Morris tobacco radio advertisements.

Feeling doomed, Karen clenched her jaws. She ordered herself to follow the procedure to perfection, particularly, pinching her nose.

Boys finished, girls were next. Karen stiffened her body in an attempt to control her trembling limbs and chattering teeth.

Nancy was baptized and confirmed into the Mormon Church for Mildred Elizabeth McCovey and at least nine or ten other dead women. Her bare feet skated through puddles back toward the dressing room. At seeing the men monitor every move through Nancy's drenched suit, Karen choked.

"Next, Karen Hardy." She hurried forward. At least the cool water might soothe her stomach. Too close she saw the cannibal's gruesome buck teeth, his Mormon undergarments, and the thin wet shirt stuck to bristles poking out around dark nipples. She recoiled from the mat around his belly button and hairs curling through buttonholes.

He gripped Karen's hand and raised his other arm. "Sister Karen Ellen Hardy, having been commissioned of Jesus Christ, I baptize you, for and in behalf of Hazel Harriett Wilhelmson, who is dead, in the name of the Father, and of the Son, and of the Holy Ghost. Amen."

He supported her back, and she pinched her nose. Sinking into the pool, she opened her eyes and seeing the water above her face reminded her that immersion represented her death.

She rose, wiping her eyes, reborn as a dead Mormon female from long ago. No ghosts appeared. She sighed, relieved.

But a flustered Sister Luetta bustled over. She babbled to the men behind the confirmation chair, who beckoned to the cannibal. Karen shivered while the four adults conferred. Restrained anger rumbled through their murmurs. Luetta's head hung with some unexplained shame. The other adults joined in the hand-wringing. The grownups pelted Karen with glares. She stood alone in the watery golden bowl, waiting, wondering what was wrong.

Karen heard girls gasping, but didn't risk a look at them.

Sister Luetta jerked a finger at her and rasped, "Come with me."

Somehow, she'd caused a disaster. The cool water turned icy. She waded out and crossed the bridge.

"Girl, we're going to the dressing room."

As if in a nightmare, Karen forced her brain to interpret Luetta's stern words. Although her legs balked, she willed herself to shuffle after the woman. Luetta stopped outside the door, then jammed her face an inch from Karen's, and seethed. "Why didn't you tell us it's your period?"

Karen flinched. She still shivered, but her cheeks burned. She felt like she was swirling down a drain and longed to give in to it, to disappear. "But… but I've never had a period. I d-d-don't have them yet."

In the dressing room, Sister Eldritch was thumbing through her LDS *The Improvement Era* magazine. "Oh, no, not that girl full of questions." The elderly lady grimaced. "What's she done? I hope not desecrate the baptismal font!"

"She said she's never had a period before," Luetta answered. "She may have just started and didn't realize."

"I have Kotex." Sister Eldritch's voice was blade-sharp. She brought out a pad from under her counter. "Get your clothes and go into a dressing room."

Karen's head pounded. She had to think hard to understand. Tears blended with baptismal droplets on her cheeks. Inside the cubicle, she peeled off the wet jumpsuit and examined a red streak along the crotch. A spot had seeped to the outside of the flimsy fabric. In spite of knowing about periods, seeing her blood like this was a shock. The temple matron had said, "One drop of blood would desecrate the font."

Luetta brought a towel and hung it on Karen's shoulders, handed her a wad of tissues for her eyes, and held out two safety pins. "Use these to attach the pad to your underpants."

Her voice had at least turned more kindly.

Karen forced her fingers to comply. She leaned against the cool plaster wall of the dressing room and struggled to control her breathing, but only managed to cry.

Nancy peeked in. "I don't know what to say." She had heard everything. She twisted a dripping ponytail with one hand and patted Karen's shoulder with the other.

Karen wept.

Sister Viva returned with the other girls. "Sit along the aisle until we can go back."

Karen heard familiar voices chattering. Sister Viva lifted the curtain. "Karen, I know you didn't mean any harm, but they'll have to drain and rededicate the font. This is unfortunate."

She crowded into the hideout with Karen. "You and Nancy will wait on the bus until all of that is done. The other girls still have to do their baptisms and now yours."

Karen's tears flowed as Sister Viva rattled on.

"The boys are in the lobby. All of this means there won't be time for our picnic. We'll have to eat our lunches in the Temple cafeteria." Viva brushed her hands in a that's-that gesture. "Go onto the bus with Nancy, now."

Karen thought, this must be the worst day of my life in the worst summer of my life. Summer only started two months ago but it seems like years. I was just a little girl then, but no more.

CHAPTER 2

BETRAYAL

On the first day of summer with school out, Karen had been stuck in the nursery making beds. A morning breeze wafted in through the open window and blended with sounds of Father's clippers biting into currant bushes outside. She edged closer to hear an approaching voice. Bold for a girl of nearly twelve, Karen double-dog dared herself to eavesdrop. Barely breathing, she crouched, straining to hear and peek out through a rip in the pull-down shade.

Karen squinted at Father's broken-down work boots strewn with clippings and the Prophet, Brother Hyrum LeGrande's spit-polished jackboots crushing weeds along the path. "Let the stirrings of your loins be your guide, Brother Edward. Be heedful of the Lord. He speaks to worthy men through these urgings. If called, you must accept a second wife with a grateful heart. As you well know, exaltation requires every man to acquire at least three plural wives."

What, thought Karen? Heebie-jeebies raced up and down her spine. Father might take a second wife and then a third?

She flattened out on the chenille spread of the lower bunk bed for a clearer peek. The word "loins" bothered her. It was a cut of pork, not a word for a family member.

She shifted her gaze upward to Father with clippers in one hand, a currant vine in the other. She angled to see the prophet's ruddy features, heaped with billows of white hair. "Brother Edward, you have the power of the holy priesthood coursing through your veins."

"I admit to worrying about Hosannah." Father tossed aside the clipping and nudged up his rimless glasses. "The commandment of polygamy can be a bitter pill for a woman. She honors the word of the Lord, but might not have the will to take on a sister wife."

"Indeed, women are the weaker sex. You're aware that my own dear but stiff-necked wife, Miriam, is not yet accepting of her sister wives. Her advanced age is her downfall. It's a travesty she was an only wife for fifteen years. If I'd harkened to the Lord's urgings years earlier, she'd be as compliant and content as my four teenaged wives."

"The Allred Group," Father said, "waits until at least sixteen to marry off their girls. Seems reasonable to me."

Karen craned as Brother LeGrande's voice swelled. "Roland Allred speaks as a mere man. He is not the true ordained prophet of the Lord as I am. Heavenly Father has called me to lead His chosen group of favored saints, including you and your dear family. I took two of my wives at age seventeen. Then Rhonda gave herself to me at fifteen, Millie, fourteen. They've acquiesced to the challenges of plural marriage far better than Miriam.

Father grunted acknowledgement and the prophet continued. "Unmarried females are easy prey to the temptations of the outside world. Exposure to its evil influence makes them less fit as wives in Zion. Any worthy man can control his wives if they marry before they're set in their ways. I assure you, my greatest pleasure is molding a pure sweet girl who is still as supple as potter's clay."

"I'll take your counsel to heart." Father jabbed the clippers into the shrubs.

"Plural marriage makes or breaks a man." Brother LeGrande cleared his throat. "I've heeded the Lord's commandments and so far He's rewarded me with five delightsome wives. That's only the beginning. Have faith and you shall be so blessed. But the subject at hand is your daughter."

Daughter? Karen flinched.

"Well," Father said, "Rosemary is still only fifteen. She's my firstborn and prettiest daughter, and I hope to see her hold out as a first wife when the time comes."

What a horrid thing for Father to say! Karen and little Judy were at least as pretty as their snooty older sister.

"I understand what you're saying about Rosemary." Brother LeGrande chuckled. "I can't abide a man who exerts unrighteous dominion over the females in his charge. But you must steer Rosemary away from non-believers and worldly ways. In these latter days, time is of the essence. Hasten her into a suitable marriage. Young brides are needed as vessels to bring down spirits from the preexistence and build His kingdom on earth."

The time called preexistense before mortal birth on earth gave Karen the willies. She suffered feelings of inferiority from lectures about how her unfortunate headstrong nature stemmed from bowing to temptations back in the murky spirit world.

"I see what you mean," Father said.

"But I'm not speaking of Rosemary's hand," the prophet said. "I'm inspired of the Lord to seek out Karen as my plural bride to be."

Karen's hands clamped over her mouth to quell a cry.

"Karen? But she's just a child."

"I understand," Brother LeGrande answered. "It's difficult to give up a daughter when the time comes. That's why I'm advising you now. I recall her to be almost twelve, so age fourteen, fifteen, even sixteen isn't so far off."

"Yes, she is only eleven." Father's voice rose. "Won't be twelve until next month. How the heck can you be considering her for marriage?"

"Calm yourself. I agree. But young as she is, you must be mindful of her future."

"I admit to worrying about her some."

Inches from Karen's head, father's gloved hand clunked the clippers onto the windowsill. She jolted and barely stifled a shriek. What if they caught her listening? Father would holler into her face. He'd bellow insults like "sneaky little brat" and "lowlife belly crawling snake in the grass." Her face stung remembering how he'd slapped her silly when she'd spied on her sixteen year old brother, Richard, and he was just a dumb lug, a kid barely out of Aaronic priesthood and beginner in the grown-man Melchizedek Priesthood.

"Karen questions everything," Father said. "What's worse, she's willful, and has a sly troublesome streak. But at heart, she's a pretty good girl. Shouldn't she stick around until she's full grown?"

"Marry her off to me. I promise you, I'll cure that head-strong attitude in no time. When she's ready, that is. Edward,

I'll quote our first prophet, Joseph Smith. 'If you take this step, it will ensure your eternal salvation and exaltation and that of your father's household and kindred.'"

"Those were Joseph's words? My bosom burns with their truthfulness." He thumped his chest.

The prophet gave an exaggerated shrug. "As you know the official Utah Latter-day Saint Church is in apostasy. True revelations from God rest with me now."

"So," Father asked, "if a man gives a daughter to the one true living prophet, that guarantees celestial glory for himself and all his family?"

"Exactly. Such a man is deserving of the Lord's highest and most cherished reward."

"In that case no faithful saint could deny such a request, could he?"

"You'll see. When the Lord reveals it's time for Karen to marry me, both you and she will meet the challenge. We are never tested beyond our endurance."

Father used his plaid handkerchief to blow his nose. "I never thought the Lord would speak through His One Mighty and Strong prophet about one of my daughters. Makes a man humble, somehow."

No, no, no! Karen screamed inside her head. This can't be true. Had she misconstrued the prophet's words? Father must be confused. He'd have to protect her. He had no choice.

"And Edward, giving Karen in plural marriage would be an earthly benefit to your good wife, Hosannah."

"What? How so?"

"Sister Hosannah can't fail to see herself as a plural wife after she sees her young daughter reaping the blessings the Lord bestows on me and mine."

"Hmm, I hadn't thought of that. I'll pray for greater wisdom and redoubled faith in the principle of plural marriage."

"Mere mortals need time and the love of God to acquiesce to His will." The prophet squeezed Father's shoulder. "I'll leave you to your thoughts," he said. The prophet's staunch form turned and marched off as Father grasped the clippers.

Karen was winded like yesterday, the last day of school, when Enoch had accidentally on purpose pitched a baseball into her belly. She struggled again to catch her breath.

In a frenzy of choking and gasping, she gulped in the ancient smells permeating the mattresses, the army blankets, the mothballs in the closet stacked with worn clothing saved for quilt blocks and rag rugs. She gagged on the dust ground into floorboard crevices and along baseboards. She smelled dust on door edgings, and imbedded in carvings on the mismatched chest of drawers and dresser, all layered with peeling varnish and furniture wax. For the first time, the comforting old smells smothered her and reminded her of rot.

Father felt flattered? How could he sound convinced to sacrifice her? Would he actually marry her off to buy favor with the prophet? Would she have to live in misery to provide exaltation for her family?

No, that didn't make sense. This was only talk and Karen remembered how Father often said, "Talk is cheap."

She hugged herself and rocked until numbness enveloped her like an eggshell holding in yoke and white. She was only eleven and safe for now. She mustn't be caught spying on adult priesthood leaders, but if father wouldn't protect her, she'd have to keep her ears open and watch out for herself. The cheap talk she'd overheard had hit harder than the baseball slammed into her belly.

CHAPTER 3

OUTSIDE AGITATOR

In Ogden, Utah, eight miles south of the Hardy farm, a dark stranger squared his shoulders under his starched white shirt and looked down at the prim police department secretary behind her desk. "I'm Ben Wolfowitz," he said. "FBI from Colorado. The chief is expecting me."

"Please have a seat." She shrugged behind her pre-World War II Smith Corona typewriter. "Chief Walker is a busy man." The woman's lips and long nails flashed crimson, the only splashes of color against her carved ivory features, beige sweater set, and hair.

Ben took a chair and let his eyes dart from one dinged oak desk to the next between a hodge-podge of filing cabinets. He heard a rumble of two or three male voices, paltry compared to the exuberant hubbub of his Denver FBI office. After surveying the squad room his focus returned to the secretary's sweater. I've been in this pit less than a day, he thought, and I already miss Sylvia.

Impatient, he glanced at the wristwatch his grandparents had given him for his Bar Mitzvah. Across the room, he noticed a disheveled police detective rummaging through heaps of papers. The man gulped from a mug, and choked. Dark liquid spewed from his lips and spattered his jacket sleeve and the clutter around him. He gagged. "Holy shit! Julie, this stuff's Postum."

"Sorry, Jack." The blond secretary called to the slovenly cop, who wiped his mouth. "You're the only guy who drinks actual coffee, and the pot's dry. Won't Postum do?"

Dumbfounded, Ben averted his eyes. Other FBI agents landed assignments in glamorous New York City or Washington D.C. He worked harder than any of them. His first assignment was in this backwater Podunk town where hicks spit all over their paperwork.

Jack's chiseled face and strong build would suit a Viking, as would his crude manners. He strode to Julie's desk and clunked down the offensive mug, splashing his thumb, which he dried on his pants.

Ben picked a stray thread from his creased trouser leg and decided the Viking's slacks must double as professional wear and pajamas. Ben saw him as too uncouth for proper work habits, and too handsome to bother with grooming. If he had a mind hidden somewhere, it likely wouldn't be worth the search.

"Coffee and Postum," Jack said, flicking a blond curl off his sun scorched forehead, "are as different as rain water and pond scum." Bending over Julie, his breath ruffled the blond spit curls along her cheekbone.

The intense masculine presence brightened her cheeks from a toneless frost to pulsing pink.

He reacted with a lavish grin. "Sorry, honey. Don't mind me. I skipped my break. I'll just step out to Lil's and grab me some real java."

Jack turned his smile on Ben. "Hi, you're not from 'round here. Do ya need help?"

"How do you do?" Ben answered. "FBI, from Denver."

Jack's swagger and deliberate tone contrasted with the humdrum personality of other Utahans Ben had met who prattled with a down home chirpiness. In Utah Ben felt like he was meeting and greeting faded cardboard cutouts at a stranger's family reunion.

He sensed his spit polish and prominent features might appear intimidating by comparison. Having passed the FBI height requirement by only an eighth of an inch, Ben felt ill at ease with Jack towering over him. Fortunately, his girlfriend Sylvia swore she liked a man closer to her size, a change from her gangly brothers.

She'd clung to him in a tearful sendoff. He was determined to make her proud, as well as his grandparents. If they could survive the Holocaust, he could survive a polygamy assignment in the armpit of Utah.

Ben, Jack, and Julie turned toward a bull of a man who charged out of a glass-front office, a fistful of papers in hand.

"Chief Walker," Julie said, "Meet FBI Agent Ben Wolfowitz."

Ben rose to greet the chief, who was stockier and grayer than the others, but with the same pale pleasant features.

"Hello, Ben." Chief Walker clenched Ben's extended hand. "Welcome. We'll be meeting with the state attorney general in my office first thing tomorrow. You have tonight to settle into your hotel."

"Sounds good, sir. I've been cramped behind the wheel navigating those mountain roads for hours." Ben flexed his knotted shoulders.

Chief Walker glanced from Ben, to Jack. "Meet Jack Blackburn."

"We've met." Ben nodded.

The chief hitched up his pants. "I'm assigning him to work with you feds."

Ben's smaller hand disappeared into Jack's massive grip.

Chief Walker plowed on, "I'll be square. I'm dead set against stirring up trouble with people who practice plural marriage. This department needs to fight real crime. Trains carry more than troops home through here. They haul in riffraff every day, so we have plenty of criminals. The FBI should be rounding up commie pinkos these days. They'll get us, if we don't get 'em first. We don't need FBI outside agitators poking their big noses into this state's business." He flung out a dismissive hand. "'Course it isn't up to me. Is it?"

"Sir," Ben said, "I follow orders, same as you do. I'll try not to get in the way."

"Chief," Jack said, "you did mention that a fed'd be arriving, and I'd be assigned to him. I hoped you were kidding."

"I'll be clear," Walker answered. "I said you'd be working with him, not for him. I think this exercise might do you good... considering."

"Considering what?"

"This isn't the time, Jack. Brief Ben on the situation. I'll expect both of you here bright and early in the morning." Chief Walker slapped his stack of papers on Julie's desk. "I'm warning you guys. Stay mum about FBI meddling here in Operation Seagull."

He turned on his heel. "Not a word," he barked before half-slamming his office door.

Jack's eyes narrowed at the glass vibrating in the police chief's door. Ben sensed he'd wandered into a family feud.

"Ben," Jack said, "I'm afraid you won't be welcomed with open arms 'round here. I hate to tell ya, but most of us in this state don't cotton to outsiders telling us how to run things."

Ben kneaded his brush-like eyebrows with his knuckles. "I could use a drink."

"Folks 'round here don't usually do much drinking."

"That's what I've heard." Ben held his gaze steady.

So did Jack. "I was about to go out for a break. Want to tag along?"

"Sure. Why not?"

Jack turned to Julie. "We'll be at Lil's if anyone wants to know."

"Fine," Julie said and picked up a shoe box. "Don't forget these cookies for Shortarm." She turned to Ben, giggled, and said, "Jack is quite the ladies' man with the local Mormon girls around here. They bring him homemade goodies."

Jack and Ben pushed through heavy doors into the late afternoon sun, glinting off a lily pond and the expansive concrete walkway they followed through lawns and gardens.

Stuck with an arrogant yokel for a partner, Ben gritted his teeth. He craved a smoke and fingered a roll of peppermint Life Savers in his pocket where his beloved Camel cigarettes belonged. He'd promised Sylvia he would quit. "You're so handsome, bubee," she told him. "But your smoking gets in the way of me wanting to kiss you. And I think someday they'll discover tobacco will kill you."

He offered Jack the candy roll. "Want a Life Saver?"

"No thanks." Jack's nose wrinkled. "Don't care for peppermint."

Ben popped two into his mouth. "I quit cigarettes before I left home. These seem to help, but not much."

"Smokin's one sin I've resisted."

Ben withheld comment.

Jack led him through a flock of seagulls begging for handouts.

Ben wondered at the profusion of sea birds so far inland. Audacious ones at that, he concluded, and nudged them aside with a polished toe as they immediately fluttered back to the same spot.

"Mind if I ask a question about what happened earlier?" Ben waited for Jack's nod, and said, "What's Postum?"

"It's a vile concoction." Jack grimaced as if the brew still assaulted his taste buds. They strode through the manicured grounds out to the street. "I think the Post Cereal Company conjures it up from burnt vat scrapin's. Mormons drink it because coffee's against their Word of Wisdom."

Ben was grateful to the Mormon FBI agent who had briefed him back in Denver. "The Word of Wisdom. That's the name for Mormon dietary restrictions?"

"Yeah, right. Looks like I'm stuck with filling you in on the land of Zion. How about we skip the coffee and go for a beer?"

Ben masked his distaste for Jack's reference to Utah being called Zion, a term he knew Mormons had lifted from his Jewish heritage.

"Now you're talking. But I assumed the Word of Wisdom would also prohibit alcohol." A scrappy gull with a missing leg refused to hop away from Ben's charging wing-tipped brogans. Ben graciously stepped aside.

"That's right." Jack chuckled. "Treat those characters with respect. They're the one true sainted and protected official Utah state bird."

Ben nodded. "You were about to explain your beer drinking."

"Yeah, that's why I'm assigned to you. The chief's tryin' to hammer home a lesson on teamwork. I was demoted to office black sheep the minute I traded in church on Sundays for beer and trout fishin'."

Jack brushed aside the obstinate lock of hair. Ben forced his glance away from that and from Jack's frayed shirt cuff. "Must be more to it than that."

"Yes, I'm considered a strange duck for not having a wife and kids yet."

Ben stopped short. "Come on, I'm twenty-three... about your age, and everyone tells me I'm too young to settle down."

Jack laughed. "You've got a lot to learn. Here, men my age celebrate their second or third anniversaries with the birth of their second or third child. By the way, why exactly did they send you to Ogden?"

The two waited to cross the street as Ben answered. "Because of a complaint from a Colorado Springs man. Claims his under-aged daughter was transported across state lines as a polygamy wife. With the polygamy action going on here, the powers that be decided to send me to investigate. The father's related to a state senator."

"Violation of the Mann Act?"

Ben nodded yes. "Being the newest hire and the only Jew made me a perfect target."

"And you probably resent it as much as I do. What a hoot!" Jack glanced down at him.

Ben shrugged. They turned onto 25th Street and passed Lil's Café and The Roundup Saloon.

Ben read the drab sign above a flophouse door.

ROOMS/BEDS
HOURLY, DAILY.
WEEKLY RATES.

"Are we still in Utah?" Ben eyed the set of flapping saloon doors near where they stood. "Just like Gunsmoke," he said.

Raucous laughter trailed from within the saloon after a bum who stumbled onto the sidewalk, letting the doors whack him for not stepping lively.

Too late, Ben turned his face from the boozy unwashed stench.

The drunk brightened when he saw Jack. "Hiya Jack. I got sumpin' fer ya."

"Shortarm," Jack answered. "Stayin' out of trouble, like I told you?"

One of Shortarm's sleeves was empty and fastened with a safety-pin where his elbow should be. He dug into his pants pocket with his only hand and brought out a wad of paper, which he handed to Jack on the second try.

"Thanks," Jack said. "Here's a little somethin' for your trouble." He stuffed a dollar into Shortarm's hand. "Go on over to Lil's for bacon and eggs on me. Need me to walk you there?"

"No sir, Jack. I can make it real fine." The unsavory man jammed Jack's bill into his pocket and continued weaving his way in the direction of Lil's.

Ben whispered, "Isn't that box for him?"

"Yeah, yeah. Wait up, Shortarm!"

Shortarm turned back and took the box.

"I think they're oatmeal raisin this time."

"Them Mormon girls never give up wantin' you to come to their meetin's, Jack."

"That's not all they want." Jack laughed.

Shortarm shuffled away again.

"He doesn't mind that name?" Ben asked.

"Heck no. Fits, don't it?" Jack asked, with the smirk Ben was finding annoying. "It drives the chief crazy how I come up with these tips like magic." He patted the pocket where he'd put Shortarm's note. "I know who does what crimes almost before they pull 'em. It pays to have friends in low places." He chortled.

"This isn't how I pictured Utah," Ben said. Bars, pawn shops, and cheap hotels lined the street in both directions. "Looks more like a back street in D. C. or Chicago."

"Hi there, Jack." A young woman in spike heels clicked up behind them.

"Hiya, Mitzy." Jack gave her a practiced wink as she passed.

Her peg skirt, stretched over her ample behind, wiggled farewell.

Ben cleared his throat and looked in a second-hand shop window at music boxes Sylvia might like.

"I'll show you around." Jack picked up the pace, passing more swinging doors, then, stopped. He pointed out a square, two-story brick building on the corner across the street. "Over there's Candy's Place, one of the busiest whorehouses between St. Louis and San Francisco. They have an actual pet black panther up there. I've seen it and heard it snarl. It's meant to discourage customers from starting trouble. Mostly, it works, and they don't."

"Hard to believe." Ben looked up into Jack's face for signs he might be joking.

"Swear to God." Jack raised one hand, as if on a witness stand. "On the roof is a log as big as a telephone pole for it to scratch its claws on."

The ground pulsed. Jack tilted his head. "Hear that?"

Ben turned toward the mounting rumble of a train. The lonesome sound made Ben think of home.

"Look down there." Jack pointed.

Ben could see that 25th Street ended with an imposing clock tower in front of the brick station.

"This town," Jack explained, "owes its existence to the Golden Spike. That's Ogden's bane and its glory. Twenty-Fifth Street starts and ends with that station. Everybody who comes or leaves by train must face the assorted sin along this street."

Three piercing train whistles muffled Jack's words.

"Travelers from everywhere," Jack continued, "cross paths right here. Some of 'em run out of money or luck and they're stuck stayin.' And we're stuck dealin' with 'em. That tends to stir up the self-important Mormons 'round town. People like the chief and his friends."

Desperate for a smoke, Ben chewed his mints and dug out two more. "So you have your differences with the Mormons?"

"You might be right." Jack cast a sideways glance.

"Do any of them fall prey to temptation here?"

"Yeah. On occasion. Course, that's why repentin' was invented. Here we are." Ben stopped at a glass door. Neon letters across the front blazed.

KO KO MO CLUB

"Looks good," Ben said. "Is Ko Ko Mo Utah's version of a tropical island?"

"Hardly." Jack stepped under a green awning and reached for the door.

Squawking and fluttering from above drew Ben's attention. A gooey splat hit his temple. "Oy Vay! What's this shmutz? Bird droppings?! From a gull!" The mess oozed down his cheek. His stomach writhed.

"'Fraid so." Jack edged deeper under the awning.

"Utah has a state bird from hell?" Ben sputtered. He pulled out a monogrammed handkerchief.

Jack's brow curled in staged concern, but a snort escaped his lips. "Don't waste that fancy piece of linen on bird shit. I'll get you a towel inside. Consider yourself baptized."

CHAPTER 4

GIVE AWAY

Karen hacked wild onions as if they were father's hurtful words, then she turned her hoe on pigweed and the bossy old Brother LeGrande and his four complacent teen brides. Chop, chop, chop, she slashed the hapless weeds row after row, unmindful of the heat or the blister swelling on her palm. The prophet says his girls give themselves of their own free will. Had they wanted to marry him? She would never say yes to that. Someday, she might have to explain this to Father. Could she make him listen?

The blister throbbed. She licked it and blew on cool air. She knotted her ugly flour-sack shirttails, careful not to jostle her newly emerging tender breasts. With a red bandana, she mopped sweat from her bare midriff and returned to the last row of chard.

"Karen!"

She ignored her sister, Rosemary, screaming from the porch.

"Kaaar-en!"

Rosemary could wait. One minute and she'd be done.

"Hurry up. Mother wants you. Get in here!"

"Coming." Karen flexed her aching limbs. She propped the hoe against a fence post.

"Right now or I'm telling."

What had Rosemary and Mother cooked up this time? "Hold your horses. I'm coming."

Spud, the family's butterscotch tinged border collie, barked and joined her at the clotheslines. She doubled over to pant along with him.

Footsteps approached from a trailer house parked in a grove of box elder trees. Karen stiffened and Spud's ears pricked at the sound of crunching dry weeds. The coal shed hid a sagging electric wire, which led to the trailer Brother LeGrande had built for his fourth wife, Rhonda.

The prophet had moved her and sister-wife, Millie, to the Hardy farm because father said it would be safe, secluded and inexpensive. It provided the blessings of the Prophet's wisdom and saved the Hardy's from paying out cash money for his tithes.

Karen sometimes noticed Rhonda there with a basket of laundry on her hip at this time of day. Instead, Brother LeGrande, the prophet himself, stood blocking the path. Until today Karen had idolized him as a comforting and holy presence. Seeing him now, she shivered.

"My child, you appear winded and hot." Brother LeGrande pressed a gentle hand on her brow. Momentary anxiety stunned her. Did the prophet think she had a stitch in her side? Was he about to confer a laying-on-of-hands blessing to cure it?

She glanced into his glittering pale blue eyes and tried to scrutinize him in a grownup way. Followers worshipped him for his ramrod assurance one minute and his infectious warmth, the next. Like magic, he could reach into the souls of others and draw out loyalty and love. Karen doubted he deserved such honor.

Without the heels of his boots, he'd be only a smidge taller than she was, and his belly jiggled over his belt. He made up for being short by strutting, soldier-like, chest out, head angled one way to boss, another way to cajole.

He eyed her up and down with concern until she wished she had washed up. She should have untied the shirttails and covered herself.

"You're almost a grownup young lady."

"Eh, yeah. Guess so."

"You're pretty, Karen, dear. I like your blond hair. I usually favor it for girls. I'd say you're a little too outspoken for a female, but quite lovely."

She shied back. "Mother wants me. I have to go."

Spud hung against her leg. She felt, more than heard, a tentative rumble in his throat.

She dashed off and stumbled up the stairs onto the screened back porch of the Hardy family's once-stately farmhouse. Her little brother and sister stood over a wooden block creation. They yelled, "Bombs over Tokyo!"

They each threw down a double sized block and it clattered into ruins on the speckled linoleum. "Karen," Davy said. "Come and help."

"Be right back," Karen said. "I have to check what Mother wants."

She hesitated to watch them start to rebuild.

Rosemary shoved the kitchen door wide. "What is taking so long? Hurry up!"

Karen recoiled from her older sister framed in the doorway. Father had called Rosemary the prettiest. The favored daughter posed, like a sour version of the Breck shampoo magazine ads Rosemary liked to collect and emulate. Her hazel eyes narrowed at Karen's disheveled hair as she caressed her own chocolate pageboy. It fell from glistening bangs across a high forehead and bounced in a roll at her shoulders. Karen compared her own straighter nose to Rosemary's tilted one. Her sister's lips pursed like a girlish kiss drawn with a pointy new carnation pink Crayola. And next to Rosemary's mouth, that dark blob she liked to call a beauty mark. "It's real," she'd brag, "not painted on like Marilyn Monroe's."

Karen had on her most despised faded homemade shirt and pedal pushers, both smeared with garden grime. Rosemary had worn them thin before passing them down to Karen. The castoff pants were bunched and pinned at the waist to keep them from slipping to her knees and hung like a rag bag on Karen's pole like frame. She sidled around her sister, feeling all the more frumpy by comparison. "I'm coming. Can't you see me?"

"Yes, I see you, and you look filthy." Rosemary huffed. "Don't you ever wash those feet of yours?"

"Leave me alone," Karen snapped. "I've been out in the hot sun hoeing garden. You've been in here all morning sewing your stupid Pep Club uniform. I'm not talking to you."

"At least you can take this cup of tea to Mother."

"Oh dear. She must be feeling pretty bad to want that. Nobody drinks that stuff unless they're sick as a dog."

Karen took the tea and tightened her eyes to squeeze back tears. In an attempt at dignity, she squared her shoulders and glided down the high windowless hallway toward Mother's room.

"Tough luck," Rosemary called to Karen's back. "You have to baby-sit tonight. Ralph's coming to drive me to school for Pep Club practice."

Karen resisted looking back. "Who's Ralph? Aren't you going with Matt?"

"Ralph is just the cutest boy in General Science, that's all. Matt doesn't have to know."

Karen leaned against the worn, carved scrollwork on the bedroom door. Her finger traced a dent in the ornate keyhole plate while she prepared to face Mother. She re-buttoned her shirt and smoothed it over her middle to ward off a lecture on modesty. She tucked straight hair behind her ears and took a sustaining breath before turning the wobbly knob.

Easing into the stuffy bedroom, she was tempted to throw open the windows, to let sunshine and the outdoor breeze purge the stale air.

"Mother, here's your oat straw tea," Karen whispered.

A wet cloth hid Mother's eyes and dampened the brown hair around her narrow face. She had suffered during her five previous pregnancies, each one worse than the one before. This one was the most wretched by far. For her mother's sake, Karen wanted the last six weeks to be over, but she worried about the expense and extra work of a new baby.

Sick headaches often sent Mother back to bed mid-day. She lifted the cloth to reveal bloodshot eyes buried in swollen lids and sockets. The blotched face pleaded for pity.

"Rosemary said you wanted me." Karen's blister was throbbing. She should have worn gloves.

Mother groaned as she propped herself on a heap of pillows and took the tea. She gagged, reaching her free hand for a towel to hold beneath her chin. Karen averted her gaze and waited for Mother to heave into the towel, but she only winced and held herself intact.

Karen tensed. "What did you want?"

Mother crumpled into her pillows. "I need you to baby-sit Davy and Judy tonight. Father and I have this year's worthiness interviews scheduled with the bishop at the ward house. Your father forgot to let me know."

"But Mother, I told you—I promised to tend Sister Viva's kids tonight. I can't just back out. I need the money. She pays twenty-five cents an hour."

Karen realized bishop worthiness was more important than any plans she had made. To be acceptable in the community, parents needed the church document called a "Temple Recommend." Karen knew of one shamefaced family without a recommend and they weren't worthy of friendship in this life or heaven in the next. Still, Karen hated feeling cornered.

Mother sipped and folded back the covers. "I know that. I didn't expect all of this would come up when I told you to go ahead and take that baby-sitting job."

Conversations with Mother, sick as she was, were fraught with booby traps. Karen pressed her thumb near the blister in an attempt to numb the pain.

Mother shuddered. She tidied her hair with her fingertips, sighed, and spoke in silkier tones.

"Karen, you are so good with Davy and Judy. Just think. You're getting good practice for when you're a mother. Girls out in the world don't have the opportunities you do."

Karen struggled with the here and now. She was in no mood to practice for later life. "But, Mother. Why do I always have to be the one?"

Mother put the tea cup down. "Davy and Judy like you to tend them. Rosemary has Pep Club practice. Her accomplishments are a credit to this family. Most girls who try out don't make the cut. This 1953 team is probably the best one in the history of Weber High. She's popular and is paving the way for you and the younger kids."

"Well, what about Richard?" She knew the answer before Mother opened her mouth.

"He's a male, a priesthood holder. His chores are feeding the stock and doing the milking. And besides, Richard has to keep evenings open in case he has a chance to play his saxophone for cash money with the Church teen dance band. He's your brother. You should be proud of his accomplishments, too. Do you want this family to miss out? If you'd practice your piano more, you might get to play in public too."

Karen's stomach lurched. She struggled for composure.

"But, Mother, what can I tell Sister Viva? She won't call again if I back out. And I need to buy school clothes."

"Rosemary's clothes have plenty of good wear left in them. If you can't buy new ones, you'll need to buck up. Father and I can't miss these temple interviews or the bishop might not let you be baptized for the dead. Besides, if we don't get recommends, someone might think we're in a polygamy group."

Karen couldn't stop herself. Her arms flew out, then, slapped her sides.

"But we are in a polygamy group! We have a prophet. He has meetings here all the time." The words rushed out even though she knew she should swallow them.

Mother raised her hand in warning. Still, Karen kept on.

"The prophet's trailers are right outside." She was sorry before the sentence ended, but couldn't stop from stepping closer to finish her tirade. "Two sister wives, Rhonda and Millie, live right here on our farm!"

Mother clutched and twisted the covers. A vicious whisper with drops of spit escaped her lips. "Don't you ever, ever say such things. We could be arrested. We might be excommunicated and shunned. The paper's been telling about polygamy grand juries. They're saying feds are invading the state. They're planning raids and persecutions against families like ours."

"I know," Karen said. "I'm just so tired of all the lying."

Mother's hand was quick. The blow struck Karen's mouth before she could duck back.

"No!" Karen cried with a violent jerk. Her face burned, and she tasted a drop of blood from a tooth-punctured lip. Outrage and humiliation tore at her. "I don't tell secrets. I finished hoeing the stupid garden. Now I have to make up some excuse for not baby-sitting like I promised." The words spewed out with a life of their own.

"Stop your bellyaching. You're just a snot-nosed kid. You want clothes? That's nothing. Not compared to this family's standing in the ward. You can shut up and do as you're told. Do you hear me?"

"Yes, Mother." Karen was choking on tears and had trouble forming the words.

"Watch your mouth and pray for forgiveness. You're lucky I'm too weak to give you a good beating. If you were nicer to Rosemary, she might call Sister Viva for you."

Too late to hold back now, once more Karen let loose her anger. "I can't help it if I don't like always being the one stuck at home doing chores. And I'm sick of never having my own clothes to wear. Rosemary's dumb clothes aren't in style when I get them. And they don't fit right." Her hand went to the makeshift tuck pinned at her waist.

"Enough! Shame on you. Fads are vain and worldly. Your sister has wonderful taste in clothes. She sews better than any girl in the ward. Her clothes are better than store-bought, and you're lucky to have them. Wasting anything with wear left in it is a sin."

Mother sighed and pulled the covers around her chin.

Karen rubbed her fists across dripping eyes and wished she could shut off Mother's words.

"You shouldn't provoke me so," Mother said. "I'm sick. I don't know why the Lord tests me this way. Life is harsh. Faith is the only way any of us can manage. Don't forget that." She pressed the warm cloth into Karen's hand.

Karen might think about faith some other time, but not now. She went in her mother's corner bathroom and squeezed cool water though the wash rag.

"Okay," Karen whispered when she returned. Longing to flee the oppressive room, she slipped the freshened cloth into Mother's hand.

"Put Davy and Judy down for naps," Mother said, "It's your job to tend them and that's my last word." She dismissed Karen by raising the back of a hand.

Karen slunk into the living room where sixteen-year-old Richard was practicing his saxophone. His lanky body, over six feet tall, sprawled across the gray and maroon flowered sofa in a mess of sheet music. He was playing "Good Night, Ladies," but stopped when he saw Karen. "Holy cow. What a crybaby." He flashed the clownish face he'd perfected and saved for these occasions.

She rushed by him, heading for the bathroom to splash water over her face. She took breaths to calm herself as she dried off on a sour-smelling towel.

Davy and Judy waited for her on the porch. The sax trilled "Glow, Little Glow Worm," blending with their giggles. The two little ones made a game of picking up the blocks to show off for Karen. Davy gathered an armload. "I am the thunder," he boomed, stomping across the floor. He bellowed and crashed them every which way at the bin. He fell on the floor giggling.

Judy was like a fairy floating on a breeze behind his lead. She flew about, picking up the leftovers, unaware of the stubborn wisps of ponytails poking out left and right whichever way her pixie face turned. Her rubbery three year old body bent over double for a block at her feet. The gesture exposed pink rows of panty ruffles decorating her bottom. Unlike Karen, at least little Judy wasn't forced to fret over modesty, not yet.

Davy and Judy finished their work and surveyed the clean floor, then looked to Karen. She gathered them to her and hustled them into the bedroom for naps.

Humming to them, Karen boosted Davy to the top bunk, then, tucked Judy in the lower one. Karen wondered why she could only get along with her small siblings and not her other family members. Her humming became a song as their eyelids drooped.

> Give, said the little stream,
> Give, oh, give. Give, oh, give.
> Give, said the little stream,
> As he hurried down the hill.
> I'm small I know
> But wherever I go,
> The grass grows greener still.
> Singing, singing all the way.
> Give away, oh, give away.
> Singing, singing all the day.
> Give, oh, give away.

She stroked Judy's face, buried in a cloudy pillow until the freckled stub of a nose breathed deeply in and out, the slow rhythm of sleep. Judy gave up, worn out from her life's work of chasing after Davy. Karen kissed her head.

Davy's eyes sparkled as Karen turned her attention on him. She smoothed his dark hair, feeling proud of his quick four year old mind and his knack for charming others to do his bidding. His almost navy eyes shut and fluttered open for a peep before his robust body finally lost the tag game he played with sleep.

She wished she could wipe this day off the calendar like a boogie man chalk drawing from a sidewalk. Tears dripped on the covers and she didn't bother to wipe them away. She slipped out of the bedroom, through the kitchen and out the back door.

She tore off toward the barn and, panting, scrambled up the hayloft ladder. Her frustration burst in a shriek, exploding the barn's quiet. Headlong, she shoved into an upended bale of hay. It budged, then, tumbled over the loft ledge. The bulk thudded below on the hard-packed floor. Two baling wires sprung off, releasing a flurry of hay in a puff of dust. Karen forced painful gasps through her lungs as the cloud settled.

She balled her body like a fist, and burrowed into the haystack. Remembering her dirty feet, Karen buried them under the hay, closing her eyes against the shame. She commanded herself to cry and not stop, to go on sobbing forever, with never an end in sight.

CHAPTER 5

GRASPING THE MIST

K aren curled in the hayloft until her tears ran dry. Aromas of the hay, of leather, and cow manure lulled her into a peaceful place, safe for now. She felt for her bandana. It was missing from its pocket. Glad of that, she blew her nose on the ugly floursack shirttail. It was one small justice in an unjust world.

The rotted-away rooftop sheathing boards revealed the brilliant summer day. She tightened her eyelids and let them flutter open in gradual steps, to savor the jewel-blue sky in stages, then tested phrases to describe the sight, but gave up. Better to surrender to beauty without fussing over words.

She drifted into a daydream of cuddling a cloud and floating off, to where the sky met the ragged teeth of the snow-capped Rocky Mountains. Her mind wandered back to a happy time, the week she spent with Grandma Hardy. It had been only a few months after Grandpa's death, and Grandma took pleasure in Karen's company at the lonely farm. She lived less than two hours away but to Karen it seemed like a million miles.

*   *   *

"Grandma, what's this?" Karen had crouched on the dusty attic floor beside a beat-up, open trunk. She handed over a cracked and yellowed photo.

Perched on a crate, her sturdy granny held the picture to the light of the circular attic window. Karen noticed a brown spider repairing a web that laced the small windowpane.

"This is your great-great-grandfather, the one here in the middle, front row." Grandma tapped a bearded face among many.

Being old excused Grandma Hardy's hairdo, a braided gray knot pinned behind her head. Nor did Karen mind Grandma's faded house dress, buttoned across sofa-pillow breasts bunched together over a tight waistband. Grandma sat with knees wide, wearing anklets over elastic support leggings, and high-laced shoes.

Karen took the picture back and inspected the rows of somber men in striped prison garb. "My great-great-grandfather was a crook in jail?"

Grandma's sagging face showed no impatience with Karen's curiosity. The old woman tapped one stout shoe heel, then the other in turn. Thump, thump, and thump, thump—a thinking rhythm that sent the spider scurrying into a crevice.

Karen sighed, content to be away from her own agitated family, who always seemed impatient with her.

"Your great-great-grandfather was a righteous bishop, a hero. The feds locked him up in the penitentiary for living the principle of plural marriage. They invaded Utah and threw all of those men you see, and many more, in jail for living their religion."

"But regular Mormons only have one wife, now."

"Yes, the prophet finally put a stop to celestial marriage in this mortal life. He had to if Utah was to win statehood. But in the olden days, those brave men lived the covenant faithfully anyways. They suffered terrible persecutions for it. The day Great-great-grandfather Hardy finished his one-year sentence, two hundred Mormon saints turned out from far and wide. They toted lemonade and sandwiches to welcome him. They brought out the best of their stored fruits, all cooked up into jellies and desserts."

"You're making me hungry, Grandma."

"It'll be lunchtime soon as I finish up this story." Grandma patted her stomach and continued. "Great-great-grandpa served as their faithful bishop for ten more years. He had to keep his plural marriages, all excepting the first one, secret from the feds. After awhile, they gave up on watching him."

Karen slid the prison photo back into its brown envelope. She held the forbidden subject of polygamy in her hands. Did she dare say more?

"Grandma, do you know we have trailers on our farm? To hide out polygamy wives from feds if they come back?"

"I know, Karen. I'm a regular Mormon Church lady, but I do know there are those out there still keeping the principle of plural marriage alive. You mustn't speak of it." Grandma locked a finger to her lips. "We can't be sure feds won't try to overrun Utah again."

Karen wound the string back and forth between two buttons on the envelope flap. "But—"

"Hush now, Karen. I'll hear no more talk of this."

Karen clapped the trunk lid shut and snapped the latches.

"Before we make lunch, can I ask another question about something else?" She turned the key in the hasp.

"And what would that be, honey?"

"I've been wondering. I heard somebody talking about 'The One Mighty and Strong.' What does that mean?"

"Hmmm. Well, I've heard tell of that, too. People these days don't talk about it at church anymore. They used to. Brigham Young revealed a prophecy about it. He said that a righteous leader will be called of God to usher in the last days. He'll lead the most favored of the Lord's servants back to Him before the great destruction of the gentile world. All the way back to the real Garden of Eden. You know it's in Missouri, don't you?"

"Yes, but great destruction?" Karen's face and arms quivered. The heebie-jeebies became worse when she noticed a bull fly flutter into the spider's web. It twitched and ended its life as a meal for the hungry predator. "That gives me the creepy-crawlies, Grandma."

"No need to worry. You're a good girl. Pray and have faith that the Lord will protect you from the devastation. What will come, will come."

"Okay, I guess. But I've been wondering about something else. Why do all boys and men have priesthood power, but no girls or women? My big brother has it. And just because of that, he bosses me around and I have to take it."

Grandma laughed until her breasts jiggled. "Karen. We both know Richard has priesthood power. But he can't use it in unrighteous dominion over you. Not unless you let him. He's still a youngster too, not so much older than you."

Karen pictured Richard, five years older and a foot taller. This time Grandma was wrong.

"But Grandma, I've tried everything to stop him. He's bigger and stronger and hits me so hard I cry. And no one will listen." Karen sniffed, thinking about it.

"There, there." Grandma patted Karen's thigh. "You pray and the Lord'll provide the answer."

Karen blinked away tears. "I do need answers. There's one more answer I've never dared think about. Okay?"

"Yes. I know how you are. Richard's teasing is driving you batty and tormenting you with questions. You're just a youngun, not practiced in shoving these things onto a back shelf. What is it?"

"Grandma, what's a Danite? My big priesthood brother says they'll get me if I'm not good. He said they slit people's throats and drain all their blood out into the dirt."

"Oh, pshaw." The old lady waggled an exasperated finger. "That Richard needs his mouth washed out with lye soap."

"But what are they?"

"Land O' Goshen, there's no such thing anymore. Back in the olden days, Brigham Young had police, secret ones. He had to allow for blood atonement. Not for sweet little girls like you. But he had enemies who hated the Lord. Their sins had to be atoned through death. It was for their own sakes. He wanted to curb their wicked ways. Don't you let that brother of yours fill your head full of Danite tales. That has nothing to do with you or me. You hear?"

"Yes, but Grandma, Danites scare me. I have bad dreams about them chasing me and cutting my throat open."

"Stop it, Karen. They were real once, but not anymore. You trust me, don't you?"

"Yes." Karen sat on the hard floor with her head on the old lady's ample lap. Grandma stroked her hair.

*   *   *

A wild gray striped barn cat interrupted Karen's daydream about Grandma's attic. The tomcat with a chewed-up ear pranced along a barn support beam with a mouse clamped in its jaws. Karen recoiled into the hay. She found her missing bandana hanging from a back pocket, and used it to mop sweat from her chin to her shirt collar. The feel of the coarse fabric triggered a flinch and a fit of trembling. Her neck had turned forever ticklish from Richard's first Danite story, the time he had scratched his fingernail across her throat.

Pop! Pop! Pop, clatter-rattle! The un-barn-like noises sent her springing to a knothole on the garden side of the barn loft. She peeped at Richard aiming his 22 rifle at a tin can on a post. He missed, hesitated, and slanted the barrel upward at a swooping magpie. Pop! "Got it." The black and white bird thumped, dead among the radishes. He leaped. "Yippee!"

"Richard! Shame on you!" Karen screamed. "That poor bird didn't hurt you!"

Her brother turned, and squinted up in her direction. He glanced left and right. No one else was there. He put on his grinning clown-gone-mad face and raised a middle finger at her.

"Double, double shame!" Karen screamed. "You big bully!"

The finger of his other hand snapped up. Like water pump pistons, his offending fingers, jerked up and down before Richard turned away to retrieve his kill.

Karen stamped her feet. She squeezed her eyes tight and her body shuddered.

Disgusting, she thought, and he'll rip the murdered magpie apart for fish bait. She tried to imagine Richard as a little boy, full of fun, like Davy. No, he was born with a rotten soul, she concluded, like a Danite. She turned her back and hurried to the cozier side of the loft.

To take her mind off her horrid brother, Karen glanced through the gaping window outside the loft down at a Holstein calf in the barnyard. She watched it dip its black and white face and suck in water from the bathtub trough. Her eyes rose to a cucumber-tomato plot, and beyond the pasture, to where Millie trudged toward her silver-bullet Airstream trailer. The baggy housedress draping her didn't hide the chubbiness beneath. Millie must be canning pickles because her shoulders were humped from twin milk buckets, crammed with cucumbers. Soon she'd be working over the prickly things, measuring pungent vinegar and smelly dill weed. The pressure cooker would boil and spew steam into the stifling tin-can trailer.

If the prophet had his way, Karen would be his sixth wife, living like Millie, smelling cows outside the door and pickles inside.

She choked on the thought of pickles, eating them, but also seeing them in canning jars with brine. They reminded her of a science project Richard had done when he'd preserved developing chicks in smelly liquid using the same Kerr-type canning jars. Karen gagged back the taste of acid in her mouth.

Millie wasn't much older than Rosemary, but looked more worn out than Grandma. Being young made her frumpy dress and wan face, appear all the more dreary. Karen wondered if Millie knew she was in a pickle. She didn't just can them.

In the next field, she made out their neighbor, Bishop Taylor marching the fence line. She hoped he hadn't noticed Millie.

Doves cooed in the barn rafters. Bees hummed in a wild hive under the eaves. A rusty wind vane creaked a lazy rhythm. The soothing music ushered in a dull sense of hope.

Karen heard another sound.

From a hayloft corner, five just-born kittens mewed for their mother behind a rotting harness. Three gray tabbies squirmed in a bed of straw with two black and whites. Karen resisted reaching out to them. Their half-wild mother would return in a moment from her feeding dish beside the milking stanchions. Better not frighten her into hauling the newborns to another nest, where the jealous tom might detect and kill his offspring.

Karen was proud of finding the kittens. Her insides ached for other discoveries in her future.

She curled back into her nest in the hay and again searched for a word as brilliant as the sky. A cloud took shape from a ribbon of mist. As it formed, the wisp of hope grew, and she knew the word she wanted. Escape.

CHAPTER 6

THE KO KO MO CLUB

Ben felt bird mess ooze down his cheek. He cocked his head to keep it from dripping on his jacket. Inside the dark Ko Ko Mo entry, he met a stuffed elk head impaled on a tree trunk.

"Wet towel, Eddie." Jack chortled. "On the double! It's a defecation situation here." He snorted out the request before he broke into guffaws.

"Sure thing," a voice answered from the back.

Ben tried to pull himself together by concentrating on a wall mural of snow-capped Rocky Mountains. Rough log construction and the elk head gave the place the feel of a rustic lodge, unexpected in a watering hole called Ko Ko Mo.

The bartender bustled out. His fresh school boy face broke into a smirk. "Hiya, Jack. I see your friend tangled with a seagull."

"Thanks." Ben took the towel and wiped his face. "Be right back." He escaped to the men's room.

A pinup of Betty Grable's derriere mocked him from the wall. He grimaced at his reflection. What am I doing in this pit? Damn!"

He soaped his mucked up black eyebrow. Sylvia had teased him with tweezers, "Bubee, let me fix those twin bird nests over your gorgeous black eyes."

He rinsed and cranked out a loop of waffle weave toweling. It felt like sandpaper scraping gunk from body and soul. "Okay Ben, buck up."

A fresh life saver in his mouth, he rejoined Jack and Eddie.

"Was that your normal Utah welcome?" Ben asked.

"No." Eddie winked at Jack. "I'd say you got a splashier than usual how-dee-doo."

"A beer might help," Ben said. "But I don't suppose you'd have a brandy?"

"Nope, this is strictly a beer joint. It'll do the job, though, comin' right up." Eddie released a lever and sloshed the brew into hefty mugs and let foam slide down the sides.

Ben scanned the layout. A young man in a plaid shirt waved his pool cue, indicating his intention to drop the five ball into the side pocket. He scratched.

His buddy smirked. "Humph, you never had a ice cube's chance in hell of makin' that."

A redhead on a bar stool snickered. She flicked ash from her cigarette and turned back to her beer and boyfriend.

Ben noticed Jack's surveillance eyes also dart around the room which suggested the guy wasn't a total jerkoff.

"Wondering," Ben said, "about the name, Ko Ko Mo. Why not call it something like... ah... 'The Pioneer?'"

"Just wouldn't fit," Jack scoffed.

"Here you go, boys." Eddie delivered the mugs with one hand and, with a fresh towel in the other, swatted a crumb.

"No offense," Ben said, "but are you a real bartender?"

"Sure enough. What should I be callin' you?"

"Ben," Jack said, "meet Eddie Simone. He's the real owner, proprietor, bartender, and bouncer. He's buying this place from his parents. Took it over on his twenty-first birthday. When was that, Eddie?"

"Long enough to have the hang of it."

Jack laughed and looked at his watch, then at the bikini-clad blonde on the calendar above the bar. "Guess it's been a coupla weeks."

"Actually, it's been three whole months. Dad and Mom kept the other two family bars. I like this one." Eddie's slicked-back hair, shiny round face and soldier posture radiated pride.

"That there's my mom." He pointed out an award plaque with a picture of the smiling woman who obviously had given Eddie his boyish good looks. The caption read "Most Lucky Lager kegs sold nationwide, 1948."

"Impressive," Ben said.

"You're in a mite early," Eddie said. "You guys off duty already?"

"Close enough." Jack's oversized hand cradled his mug. We're puttin' our heads together on a case."

"Yeah, sure. I'll never tell." Eddie's self-conscious posture relaxed.

"Thanks, buddy." Jack raised his mug. "Ben, you'll need to make friends with Eddie if you hope to survive in these parts."

"Thanks, it's a pleasure." Ben returned Eddie's grin.

"Same here," Eddie said. He dried water-wrinkled hands before they shook. "You're not from around here?"

"No, Denver. We have mountains like those, but not murals of them in the bars."

Eddie shrugged. "Bars all along here have those paintings. A drifter name of Tex Dunn jumped off a train a couple years ago. He traded painting for food and Jack Daniel's. The guy bunked in basement rooms for months. He did pictures like that all around town."

Jack folded his arms on the table. "Ben might be stayin' awhile."

"Something hot brewing?" Eddie took a conspiratorial pose. "Wouldn't be polygamy, would it?"

"Yeah," Jack said. "Keep yer ear to the ground." He and Ben sipped their beer.

The cool trickle wasn't as soothing as a cigarette, but it helped.

"Fact is," Eddie said, "one of my customers is a Mormon bishop, even though he don't admit it in here. Shortarm tells me he's heard reports of a polyg compound right across the road from the guy's farm."

Jack grabbed the table edge. "I'll be damned. Could ya' let us know where he lives? And maybe what his name is?"

"Shortarm knows. Ask him."

The beer washed away the peppermint in Ben's mouth. "Bishops? They're the ones who rule over Mormon congregations. Right?"

"Right," Jack answered, "Just like a rabbi. Each one bosses what's called a ward. They work for the church for free and also hold down paying jobs."

Eddie nodded. "The bish comes in about once a month. I think he lives somewhere out by Cloverdale or Plain City. He has some church meeting or other in town on those nights and he stops for an orange soda pop."

"Orange pop?" At first Ben thought it was a joke.

"He acts like he's doing something shameful just settin' foot in this place." Eddie waved an arm at the pool players and the row of bar stools. "Like as if anyone cares. My guess is he has to screw up his courage. After downin' his Nehi, he heads over to visit a working girl at Candy's. Won't order beer, but he screws whores!"

"What a jerk," Ben said. "My girlfriend would kill me!"

"Don't know everybody's name and business yet, but I'll keep my feelers out."

Shortarm shuffled in and dodged the post with the elk head. "Speak of the Devil," Jack said.

Shortarm's gait was steadier than before. Eating must have fortified him. He smiled at them and showed a missing tooth.

Jack motioned him over.

"Thanks fer the grub and the cookies, Jack."

Jack inclined his head. "Meet my friend, Ben."

"Howdy." Shortarm pointed to a spot on Ben's shoulder. "Yur Buddy meet up with a bird?" he asked.

"Yeah, not everyone is as dapper as you and me." Jack laughed. "Shortarm, Eddie was saying there's a bishop who comes in here and drinks orange soda pop. You know anything about him? His name? What he's up to?"

Concentrating, Shortarm's thin face twisted. "Yeah. I seen him. Might of heard someone call him Taylor. 'Course most-a-the Mormons 'round these parts is named Taylor, or Hardy, or Christensen, so that don't mean nothing."

"That's right." Eddie laughed and turned to Jack. "Don't you have a couple of girlfriends by that name?"

"Maybe, maybe, not." Jack tilted his head, devil may care.

Ben didn't bother to hide his scowl.

Eddie punched Jack's shoulder. "Anyhow, you can count on me and Shortarm to keep our eyes peeled."

"Shore enough," Shortarm said, "And at Lil's I got wind of a hot tip. They say there's a FBI guy fresh in town." He went silent and eyed Ben before going on. "That fed's here to run sumpthin' called the Operation Seagull polygamy bust." He grinned proudly and stuffed the dollar bills Jack offered into his pocket, he turned and disappeared down a back stairway.

"Thanks," Jack called after him. "And Eddie, we might need another round… or two. Ben seems to have a lot to learn."

"One thing I have learned is that your chief knows shit. Shortarm and everyone is aware of me and what I'm doing here."

After serving the beers, Eddie scurried off. Whistling "Take Me Out to the Ball Game," he set to work polishing a beat-up brass spittoon, now used to collect tips.

A grateful gulp and Jack said, "Thought I'd heard of every polygamy pervert in these parts. It's news to me there're some in Cloverdale."

"I'll be frank," Ben said. "This is my first out of town assignment. I plan to wrap it up fast."

"Hmm. Well, polygamy isn't likely to go away anytime soon. But the quicker you're gone, the better, for everybody."

"What's with people here resenting outsiders? And what about the chief? He's obstructing an investigation."

Jack's eyes held steady. "First off, you admitted it. You are an outsider, and you're meddling in something you don't understand."

"Here's what I do understand." Ben tapped the table. "The feds, as you call us, are trying to curb an illegal practice that your chief wants brushed under the carpet. I'm here to find a girl who's caught up in it. You want me out of your hair. So for starters, do you think Eddie's bishop customer might help us infiltrate?"

"Heck if I know. The chief, like most Mormons, is embarrassed by polygamy. It's the ugly underbelly of this state and always has been. He thinks it's best to let sleeping dogs lie. I have my own reasons for poking them when I can."

Ben sensed Jack was hiding something and contemplated how to proceed. It was disconcerting to be using interrogation techniques on his own partner. He sipped his beer as he compared the rocky purple cliffs painted on the wall to a favorite vista in Colorado. "I don't understand. So normal citizens around here don't want to stamp out polygamy?"

"No way! As I said, we wish it would fade off into thin air. But no one has the guts to openly confront it. Besides, most folks here aren't what *you'd* consider normal citizens."

"So," Ben said, glancing at his watch, suddenly fatigued, "where do we start?"

"Beats the hell out of me. You're the FBI hotshot."

"Okay. I'm assuming tomorrow's meeting will be a windbag session. Right?"

Jack nodded.

"I'm beat. Let's call it a night. We can hammer this out here tomorrow, after some shut eye."

"Suits me. This is one fine watering hole." Jack motioned goodbye with a left-handed salute.

Ben stood up. "Eddie, bring the tab. Tonight's on me."

CHAPTER 7

FENCED IN

Karen traipsed up and down the irrigation furrows between waist-high raspberry thickets. The brambles snagged her pants and clawed her bare arms as she searched out an occasional ripe berry in a profusion of white blossoms and green fruits, as hard as shelled hazelnuts. By the time she went into the kitchen, Bishop Taylor's roosters had given up crowing, which meant it was about eight o'clock.

Karen clattered the nearly empty pail onto the green linoleum counter.

"That's all you found?" Mother poured milk into a dishpan.

"Just enough for morning mush if no one hogs them," Karen said. "Feel better today?"

"Yes, thank the Lord!"

Mother swished circles in the freshly-strained, scalded morning milk, dissolving yeast, salt and honey.

"Karen, sift in about ten cups of whole wheat flour for me." Mother's fingertips dripped over the mixture.

Karen heaped flour into the sifter and cranked the red knob until her wrist ached, and powdery brown mountains floated on the milk. Mother stirred the flour and milk into a sticky mess.

"I know." The scowl line deepened between Mother's eyes. "Run down to the basement. Bring back a couple of jars of cherries from our two-years-food-supply. I'm of a mind to use that for cobbler, instead of raspberries. We'll bake plenty for family home evening tonight and for the Prophet's meeting tomorrow night."

The Hardys kept a hoard of goods as the church leaders directed, so they would be prepared for the impending doomsday.

Karen returned from the basement empty-handed. "All out," she said.

"Dear me." Mother's eyebrows tightened into the familiar crease over her nose. She bit her lip. "I wanted you to clean the bathroom and wash woodwork. Instead, you'll need to go out collecting rhubarb for the cobblers."

"Mmm, rhubarb tastes better anyway. I thought Bishop Taylor's wife told you not to use it?"

"Yes. The very idea! Just because she inherited this place as a bride! She planted the rhubarb and asparagus, but that doesn't mean they're hers. We own this land now."

"She wants to steal it?"

"Humph! She doesn't see it that way. She and the bishop are sorry they sold us this place and that's just too bad."

Karen sifted in more flour. Mother's hands formed a heavy brown pillow of dough. "Give it a little slap," Mom said. "Dough's ready when it's like a baby's bottom. Remember that for when you're a housewife."

Karen floured her fingers, and then tapped the springy bulge.

"While you're out in the pasture," Mother said, as she covered the pan with a towel, "get some asparagus if it hasn't gone to seed. We'll cook it up with stewed shredded beef for dinner tonight."

Karen gathered clean flour sacks and a heavy paring knife and tossed them on a gunnysack spread in the bottom of the rickety Radio Flyer wagon. What luck, she'd spend hours walking the perimeter of the twelve-acre pasture in peace, and afterward sneak off to the hayloft, while someone else cleaned the bathroom.

Partway to the field, she heard Spud cheerfully panting. His dust-mop tail brushed her leg as they walked along the heavy weathered fence posts and rails encircling the barnyard. She ducked between the bottom wood slats in the fence near her loft and pulled the wagon under.

Fencing was the skeleton of a farm, marking its boundaries from other farms and separating whatever shouldn't mix, cows from pigs, pigs from sheep, and all of the animals from the cultivated plots. Neighbors freely crossed other farms as needed but hunters and city slickers weren't welcome.

Karen heard a shout above the creaking and bumping of the red wagon.

"Karen, wait up! Want to play?" It was Lucinda, her angular ten-year-old friend from across the highway. Lucinda's Dutch-boy hair, eyes, and skin were all the same golden shade of thin clover honey. The darker brown freckles dotting her arms and face ran together in muddy puddles under a summer tan.

"Can't," Karen said. "Want to help me collect rhubarb?"

"Seems like you can't never play. Yesterday, you were a-hoein' garden."

"I know," Karen said. She gave Lucinda a shrug and half-smile. "Let's go this way."

Karen veered onto the far path over a hill in hopes of distracting Lucinda from Rhonda's and Millie's trailers. At the top of the ridge, Karen glanced toward Millie's Silver Bullet, parked below and against the tractor shed at the corner edge of the pasture. Karen couldn't prevent Lucinda from turning to look at Millie, placid and pudgy, sitting on a wooden folding chair doing hand sewing, her dark blond ponytail looping her shoulder. She didn't notice them from her spot in a shady circle of three pear trees.

"You have some other lady living here?" Lucinda's wide eyes were incredulous.

"Yes, it's one of Father's cousins. Her husband's in the Navy." It was the lie she'd been instructed to tell.

"It must be hard keeping track of everybody's comings and goings 'round here."

Karen and Lucinda tromped with Spud along the rutty property line in front of the bumping wagon. The fence, with a ditch on each side of it, divided the family's cow pasture from Bishop Taylor's sugar beet and watermelon fields. Irrigation ditches and barbed-wire fences lined every farm in Cloverdale. Clumps of rhubarb and asparagus flourished in the thin strip along the Hardy side of the fence rimming the pasture.

Farm fences were important, Karen knew, but fences between truth and secrets were indispensable. They didn't mend as easily as wire and wood. Karen cringed knowing she'd lied to her friend.

"Listen up!" Lucinda said. "You didn't hear me. I said I found a treasure." She picked caked dirt from a long-lost crystal button and polished it on her shirt.

"Wow-wee." Karen held it to the sun. "That's a good one. We'll put it in our treasure chest." The girls kept a secret cigar box hidden in the hayloft rafters.

"I bet some of them jewels is real valuable treasures," Lucinda said.

"I wish."

"I wonder…" Lucinda pulled a feathered weed stem. She chewed the tender end and continued. "I wuz wondering if whatever person that lost the button was a pioneer. Maybe that's who planted the rhubarb and asparagus along here."

"No. Mother told me Neena Taylor planted it."

"How come she planted along here?"

"Because it stays damp along the ditch bank. No one has to water it."

"Heck, everybody knows *that*. I mean, why'd she plant it on your farm?" Lucinda's tanned face crinkled, perplexed.

"Sister Taylor and the bishop used to own it. They sold it to us. That's how they paid for the fancy house they have now."

"I never knew that."

The two set to work yanking out thick rhubarb stems, like stalks of red celery with scoop shaped root ends filled with dirt. The girls brushed away the soil and took turns hacking off glossy leaves the size of elephant ears. They moved from one clump of rhubarb or asparagus to the next around the pasture edge, being careful to choose only tender asparagus still not going to seed, but tall enough to please Mother. They cut the spears at an angle below ground level, then, layered them into bags, rhubarb in one, and asparagus in another.

"Hotter than you know what, ain't it?" Lucinda wiped her forehead, mussing her straight bangs.

Karen laughed. Neither she nor Lucinda dared say Hell. It might conjure up an evil presence.

"Guess what!" Lucinda said. "Remember, I told you we wuz getting a television set? Well, we went into Ogden shopping, and we're gonna get one for sure." She swaggered.

Spud's tail flapped at Lucinda's announcement. She scratched between his ears. Karen untangled a burr from his side.

"How can you afford it?" Karen asked.

"We'll pay payments," Lucinda bragged.

Three brown Guernseys chewed cud and whacked at flies with their tails.

"Can I come over and watch your set?" Karen asked. "I want to see what I can about the outside world."

"Yeah. There's Sky King, and The Lone Ranger, and really good advertisements."

"I've heard Lone Ranger on the radio and kids at school tell me about seeing those things on their TVs." Karen swatted flies from her face.

"And guess what else we might get? Bishop Taylor says he might get us a water heater an'a indoor toilet. He said it is 1953, and time to get them modern things, even if we are just the farm hand family."

"Want to pull the wagon awhile?" Karen asked. She offered Lucinda the handle.

"Sure." Lucinda hooked her fingers through it.

"You can use our bathroom when you're over at our house."

"I know, but some of your family feels funny about me being inside your house. We ain't trash like people think.

Having a television and a bathroom'll prove it. The bishop's the richest farmer in Cloverdale. You'd think he'd be ashamed of that rundown outhouse we got to use."

"Lucinda, do you ever think about getting away from here?"

"What do ya mean? Where would we go?"

"I mean, would you be afraid to try it? Living out in the world?"

"Here's a secret." Lucinda lowered her voice. "My mom makes coffee whenever we go camping out in the world. She says, in the woods, there ain't no bishop or no ward teacher snoops or Relief Society busy bodies to smell it. Nothing bad ever happens when we drink it, neither."

"You don't drink it, do you?"

"Sure do."

"I won't tell anyone," Karen said. "Cross my heart."

"You're my best friend," Lucinda said. "Cross my heart, too. I say you'll get out in the world someday if you wanna. Heck, I hope ya even get to taste coffee out there."

Karen felt like hugging Lucinda. Instead, she gave her friend's broad shoulder a nudge. "Let's see if the creek's dried up. If it's running, we can cool off and pick watercress."

"Listen," Lucinda said. "Stop the wagon. Can't ya hear the water? The crick *is* running."

"You have better ears than Spud," Karen said. "I'll race you!"

Lucinda dropped the wagon tongue and darted off toward the creek. Karen caught up, laughing.

The friends flattened onto their bellies and dunked their sweaty faces into the cold trickle. They bit off moist, round leaves from the coiled tangle of watercress stems floating in the water. The leaves turned to pepper in their teeth. Spud bounded into the stream, yelping and splashing. The girls stood and shook their heads like Spud did, and giggled.

Lucinda used the burlap bag from the bottom of the wagon to dry Spud. "I like you, boy, even more than Topsy."

She shook out the wet bag. "Did I tell you about the Taylors getting a new dog? Topsy's her name."

Karen took the bag and laughed. "I betcha' Spud'll soon be over to check her out."

Karen folded the bag to dry over the side of the wagon before she pulled out a fresh flour-sack. "Mother will be glad for free watercress," Karen said. "Let's fill a sack. Want some for your mom?"

"Naw, we mostly eat corn and head lettuce for vegetables."

Karen picked bunches of cress from the creek bed. She shook off the water and tossed out the muddiest sprigs before stuffing the rest by handfuls into the sack. "Guess what? I discovered kittens in the barn. Let's go see if their mother will let us hold them. Okay?"

The two raced the stretch back to the barnyard. The wagon bucked like a bronco over clods and furrows and around fresh manure pies. They caught their breaths under a black walnut tree before they went on to the barn.

Karen showed off how she could climb the hayloft ladder standing upright.

"See? No hands!"

Lucinda tried it, but lost her balance on the third step. She grabbed for a rung and laughed. "Guess I need practice," she said when they were both in the loft.

They stood back from the kitten nest, not wanting to startle the mother. "Oh, Lucinda!" Karen said. "There were five babies yesterday. One of the tabbies is missing."

Lucinda's face fell. "Alls I know is, I just hate those toms always killing their babies. Don't you?"

"It's sad and creepy." Karen's throat caught. "Now the mom will have to move to another nest."

The two thumbed their noses at the meanness and spit over their shoulders for punctuation.

"Sometimes," Karen said. "I pretend this loft is my own secret place. A happy one. Now that a bad thing happened here, it makes me want to cry."

"Sometimes," Lucinda said, "you seem old. Not just a year older than me. I mean real old."

"Do you ever wish we weren't growing up? That we could stay kids like Peter Pan?"

"I think I get what you're saying," Lucinda said, "but it's giving me the heebie-jeebies."

"I know," Karen said, "Let's remember the tabby in heaven."

They clasped hands and bowed their heads in silence, then blew kisses into the sky through the fallen-away roof boards.

Lucinda reached into the secret shelf under the eaves for the treasure box. "Ain't these jewels pretty?" She added the button to the collection, and picked out a purple glass nugget to hold to the sun.

"Yes," Karen said, "but they're just old buttons and bits of colored glass, aren't they?"

"Yeah, probably, but I like to pretend."

"Watch this," Karen said. "I can back down the ladder with no hands."

She stepped off the loft floor, arms spread like wings. Each foot reached back and downward, step by step, feeling for the next rung. Halfway down, she stopped, teetered, slipped, and then caught herself. She turned to face front and pranced to the bottom. Lucinda whooped and applauded as Karen's toes touched the barn floor.

"Let me try," she said.

Lucinda began well, but lost concentration. Her body reacted with a daring leap from halfway down. She laughed and flourished a bow. Both girls squealed.

"Pretty good, huh?" Lucinda said. "I don't get to practice ever' day like you, and won't be turning twelve soon, like you."

"You're brave to jump like that," Karen said. "I'd be too scared."

"Naw, you're brave in your kind of way. But, Karen, about you being older, ya know? After your birthday, the Church'll be graduating you out of primary."

"Yes, I know."

"You'll be goin' to mutual meetings with the teenagers, and probably even be going off to the Temple to get baptized for the dead."

"Yes, that might be scary." Karen's voice was whisper soft. "Being dunked for a bunch of old dead ladies from a hundred years ago gives me cooties."

"I heard," Lucinda said, "you have to get nekkid in the Temple. You'll tell me if that's true, won't you?"

"They'll say it's sacred in the Temple and everything is secret. But don't worry, I'll tell you. Cross my heart. But I do know what I'll tell you now." Karen could barely hear her own whisper. "My mom sewed a white sheet she'll wear in the temple with only a hole in the middle to poke your head through. I think everybody in the temple has to take off all of their clothes and wear things like that."

"Yep! That proves temple people get all buck nekkid!"

"My mom has a whole suitcase of temple stuff. One thing is a green fig leaf apron. What if they wear those and nothing else? Like Adam and Eve?" She stared, open mouthed, into Lucinda's wide eyes, brimmed with shock.

"Kaaaren!" It was Rosemary screaming from behind the house.

"Uh-oh, I have to get these vegetables in before I'm in trouble."

"Maybe," Lucinda said, as they headed toward the house, "we can play tomorrow. I can't wait to see when Dad'll show up with the television." She helped Karen carry the harvest as far as the porch.

Once inside, Karen heaved the bags of vegetables onto the kitchen counter. The aroma of baking bread made her mouth water.

From the other side of the kitchen window, her friend signaled to her. Lucinda joined her elbows together in front of her chest and curved the fingers of each hand like the top and bottom teeth in an alligator's mouth. She opened and closed her arms like jaws and called through the glass. "See you later, alligator."

"After a while, crocodile," Karen mouthed and signaled back by opening and shutting her arms, like snapping jaws.

It was their secret code, which meant goodbye, or in emergencies, danger.

Rosemary was shoving the flour canister into place and washing the counter. "So you decided to stay out playing half the day, and I had to call you in. I made the pastry dough, but I have a date with Todd, and I'm not doing the filling."

Karen jerked her fists to her waist and snorted.

"I need time this afternoon to fix my hair," Rosemary snapped. "I still have to polish my shoes. And I have to hem and iron a dress, and do makeup. I had to clean the bathroom for you and make the living room nice for Todd when he picks me up. All the while, what were you doing? Playing in the stupid barn with Lucinda. Don't think I didn't see you two acting like fools just now." Rosemary finished her tirade.

"This is Monday," Karen said. "In this family we stay home on Mondays. Why don't you have to be here for family home evening?"

"Because. I told you, I have a date. Which is more than you'll ever have when you waste all of your time playing with a farm hand girl. Besides, I'm obeying the family first commandment. Todd's family home evening is Monday, too. I'll be at his house."

"How many boyfriends do you need anyway? Ralph, Matt and now Todd. Just shut up."

"You can't get away with talking to me that way. I'm telling on you."

"Oh, go primp for your precious date," Karen retorted. She washed her hands, pretending not to care about being in trouble for talking back and saying a bad word to her sister.

She stuffed the cress and asparagus into the fridge. Then she washed the rhubarb and diced chunks of it into long baking pans. "Mom," she called. "How much sugar for each rhubarb cobbler?"

She went to the living room where Mother hunched over her Singer electric, sewing her sacred Temple clothes.

"Karen, get over here. I have to talk to you." Mother's too-patient voice didn't hide her frustration.

Karen edged closer, but not too close. Mom grasped Karen's arm.

"I don't know what gets into you," Mother said. "I've told you hundreds of times. You are either listening to Satan or the Holy Ghost every minute of every day. Everything you do and say goes down in a book in the Celestial Kingdom. That's because you're past eight and are baptized. Karen, did you say 'shut up' to your sister?"

Mom's grip tightened and twisted. Karen whimpered.

"Well, did you?"

"Yes but Mother, she was mean to me."

"Your elder sister is a wonderful Latter-day Saint girl. You need to listen to her like Davy and Judy listen to you. Did she tell you not to play in the barn so much?"

"Yes."

"Well, Karen, that's what the Holy Ghost would be telling you if you were listening to Him."

"Okay." Karen wouldn't allow herself to cry.

"I don't know what's wrong with you that you can't get along with Rosemary. Sisters are blessings. I never had one sharp word with any of mine." Mother gritted her teeth.

"I'll try to get along, if she does."

"Try? No!" Mother's eyes were slits and her nose flared. "Just get along. I'm sick and tired of your backtalk!"

"Okay. Sorry. I have to finish the baking." Karen squirmed out of Mother's grip.

She didn't have her answer about sugar, but didn't dare ask again. About two or three cups for each pan might do it, with spoons of flour, butter, and cinnamon. She pinched the crusts into place and slashed steam vents with a knife before sliding them into the hot oven. To let off her own steam she shut the door with a swift kick.

CHAPTER 8

FAMILY FIRST

"Mmm, yummy," Judy said through a rhubarb-filled mouth. She licked at morsels tumbling to her chin.

"Yessir," Davy said. "It isn't even sour like most times. Karen makes better desserts than Rosemary or anybody."

"Karen," Mother said, "next time, ask me if you don't know how much sugar to add. We can't waste store-bought things. Besides, too much sugar desecrates our bodies which are tabernacles of the Lord. Millie overeats sweets, and just look at her." She pushed away her plate.

Mother acted like every little mistake was a sin. Karen decided to tell Davy later that she agreed with him about the cobbler. She thought Mother might never approve of anything she did.

Family home evening began when dinner dishes were done.

Father, as family Patriarch, started with prayer. Karen kneeled against the gray overstuffed chair. Davy and Judy squirmed in beside her. Richard bent down on a knee next to his upturned saxophone case. Mother and Father bowed their heads over the flowered sofa. Father combed his fingers through his straight-back dark hair and pushed his rimless glasses onto his forehead.

"Heavenly Father, we come before Thee." His low earnest voice paused for emphasis. "Tonight, at family home evening, we give thanks for our blessings of food, clothing, shelter, and the fullness of Thy restored Gospel. We're especially thankful for Thy Holy Prophet, Brother LeGrande, in our midst."

The hardwood floor tortured Karen's knobby knees. She opened one eye to see Davy grinning at red plastic cowboys, one in each pudgy fist. He slipped one over to Judy's out-stretched hand. She smiled gratefully. Karen was thankful Rosemary was on a date and couldn't tattle.

Father droned on. "Dear Lord, bless us as we are worthy. Give us strength to endure. Give us faith to obey Thy com-mandments, including plural marriage, when and if it is Thy will."

Mother shifted her body. Was her discomfort from the pregnancy or from mixed feelings about plural marriage?

"Bless the poor," Father said, "the sick, the afflicted, and all who are in need in these troubled latter days on earth. I say these things in TheNameaJesusChrist, Amen."

The family rose, each repeating, "Amen."

It was time for Richard's saxophone solo, *Put Your Shoulder to the Wheel.* The words marched through Karen's mind.

> Then, don't stand id-ly look-ing on:
> The fight with sin is real.
> It will be long but must go on:
> Put your shoulder to the wheel.

Put your shoulder to the wheel. Push a-lo-ong.
Do your duty with a heart full of so-o-ong.
We all have work.
Let no one shirk.
Put your shoulder to the wheel.

"You make us proud," Father said. "Your mother will speak to you all now, listen up. Go ahead, Hosannah."

"Wasting," Mother said, "is breaking this family. Daddy makes pretty good wages at his government job in town. But we're barely making ends meet. Understand?"

Everyone nodded, even little Judy. This was an unwelcome diatribe Mother regularly repeated.

"The problem is the bills," Mother said. "We must keep up our normal ten-percent tithes to the regular Mormon Church. And we must help out Brother LeGrande, the true chosen prophet."

"Do we have to pay him ten percent, too?" Karen asked.

"We're lucky, because we can give him trailer parking privileges, electricity, and water for two of his wives," Mother answered. "So we don't need to give him a full ten percent."

"Why," Karen asked, "can't we just choose one kind of Mormon or the other?"

Richard snorted. "You always have dumb questions, never answers."

"Richard," Father replied, "has a point." He adjusted his glasses and scowled at Karen. "I think you should know the answer to that, Karen. Everyone in Utah must get along with the mainstream Church. We don't mind because the Church makes this a decent place, unlike the wicked outside world.

Besides, the Church controls the Holy Temples. Being Temple worthy is what every decent family strives for. But we still have to help the fundamentalists because they are staying true to the fullness of the Mormon Gospel. Do you get it, Karen? Does everyone understand?" He glared over his glasses.

They mumbled agreement.

"So," Mother said, "let's get back to the subject. Don't waste. Turn off lights until after dark. Then, be sparing. Eat what you're given and clean up your plates. Don't expect so many store-bought things. Make it yourself or make do with what you have. And someone is wasting toilet paper. I put in a roll yesterday, and Rosemary told me she put in a roll Thursday. Four squares are enough. Everybody has to watch that Davy and Judy don't waste. They're too little to count squares."

"Nuh uh," Davy said. "I can count up to thirty-nine, and Judy counts up to eleven."

"Well, good," Mother said.

The diversion was momentary.

"Growing up," Mother continued, "I had to use Sears Roebuck catalog pages in the outhouse. In Grandma and Grandpa's day, they used corncobs. In this day and age, you're lucky to have luxuries. Don't anybody waste anything. That's my final word. Father, do you have words to add?"

He cleared his throat. "I agree. And don't expect to be driven places you can walk. Not to church or a friend's house. Gasoline costs cash money."

"One more thing," Mother said, spreading her arms to take in the living room, "this front room must stay spotless. Richard, keep your sheet music put away. And all of you, keep toys off this floor. Rosemary can't invite respectable boys into an unattractive home. And what if the ward teachers or the visiting teacher ladies show up? If they see a mess, the gossip would be all over town by nightfall. Having sick spells with this baby"— she patted her abdomen—"means Relief Society busybodies might be nosing around to help out and meddling in our business. Any questions?"

Karen looked at the spools of thread and heaps of fabric around the Singer.

"What about the sewing machine mess?"

"Karen, please shut off the questions for once. You know it's a plus for ward teachers to see me sewing Temple clothes. But if nonbelievers show up, like the Fuller Brush man or the veterinarian, we must protect the sacred clothing from gentile eyes. It's the same as hanging sheets in front of the long temple garments. People in the outside world must never have a chance to ridicule temple clothes or garments."

The little ones stretched and yawned.

"Karen, take them off to bed," Father said. "Then come right back. I have a very serious subject to bring up."

Karen didn't like Father's tone. She wasn't sure she wanted to return to the living room, but she knew she had no choice.

After she settled back onto the gray chair, Father held up an *Ogden Standard Examiner.* "There's more bad news in the paper," he said. "This may prove that the 1950's are the true latter days for the people of this earth. We knew that a grand jury had convened to investigate fundamentalist polygamy groups in this state.

"But now we also know that feds from the FBI are involved with local police in Ogden and Salt Lake. Their purpose is to persecute decent law-abiding polygamists. It's a free country. I can't understand why someone's religion is anyone else's business. The *Examiner* predicts raids and arrests."

"I'm worried sick about this." Mother's face was drawn.

"I know, Hosannah. For fifty years, nothing like this has happened in this state. We couldn't have seen this coming when we felt Heavenly Father urging us to follow Brother Le Grande. We've come this far. We must see it through."

Mother sat straighter and seemed to pull herself together. "I want you kids to pray morning and night that the Lord will protect us from the feds, that He'll protect all of us in the Prophet's group and any other well-meaning polygamists in this state. Will you do that?"

The Hardy children nodded. Karen folded her arms against her belly to ward off a chill in her bones.

Father clenched his jaw. He smacked the back of his hand against each offending paragraph. "So, I'm warning you kids, again, to keep quiet about the meetings we have here with Brother LeGrande and his followers, and also about who lives out back. Got it?"

His voice menaced like the growl of a cornered animal.

"Lucinda was asking about the trailers," Karen said.

"Don't tell her a thing," Father barked.

"She's not a good influence on you anyway," Mother said. "And you're too big to be out playing so much. You need to be reading your *Book of Mormon* and learning womanly duties. So don't waste so much time with her. You'll be better off and she won't have a chance to see what goes on here."

"Just because her father is a farm hand?" Karen asked. "I won't talk to her about the trailers."

Sudden banging on the kitchen door startled them. No one came to the back door at night and no one pounded like that without good reason.

"Hello, hello!" Rhonda, Brother LeGrande's fourth wife yelled from the porch.

"Good holy heck!" Father said, scrambling for the door.

He met Rhonda barging in. She wore her nighttime hair net over blond curls, a flapping robe, and untied shoes. Her blue eyes were frightened.

"Rhonda, what is it?" Mother's voice trembled. She twisted her apron.

"Someone is out back. Maybe spying. I heard voices across the side fence. From the Bishop's cornfield."

"Good gosh!" Father clenched his fists. "It's those feds. I'll go see."

Richard puffed out his chest and said, "I'll go too."

"No, you stay and protect the women and children. Rhonda, we need Brother LeGrande. Is he in your trailer?"

"No, his week with me ended today."

"Then, he's with Millie? Isn't her week after yours?"

"No, she's the week before me."

"Well, which one of you—"

"First, Miriam." She held up a thumb. "Then, Millie, me, Elvira, and Anna." She raised a finger to count them off as she recited their names. "He left for Kaysville this afternoon to be with Elvira. He wanted to get there before dark. Next week he goes to—"

"Okay, okay! Then you come with me, Richard," Father said. "Those gentile feds have no call to persecute us. We have the true power of the priesthood. With help from the Lord we'll take care of it. Those feds need to be run out of this state."

"You be careful, Edward," Mother said. "Don't do anything foolish."

"I won't. Let's go, Richard. Karen, run to Millie's trailer and get her over here."

"But…" Karen hesitated.

"No buts." Father snarled. "Get going."

Karen's legs wobbled as she rushed down the back porch steps into the darkness. Her eyes strained but she could make out only a shadow gyrating in the night. The creaking of far off crickets and the sound of her breathing rippled over silence. She caught her breath and held it, but the shadows went on breathing.

She was not alone.

"Spud?"

He pattered to her side.

"Spud!" His furry body against her leg offered support.

Karen's practiced feet knew the path to the barn, even at night. A slice of moon helped her see to pass by her ladder. She yearned to curl up safely in the hayloft and forget about the feds. Instead, she climbed through fences and willed the faint light from the trailer window to lead her over the rough pasture lane.

She heard voices from across the fence. Karen gasped and Spud bristled.

The voices grew louder.

"Stay, Spud," Karen whispered.

They heard a loud thud. Her firm, comforting hand halted the low growl in the dog's throat.

"You dropped one, you ignernt moron. And look, it ain't even ripe."

"Shut up, Enoch. Leave 'em. I heard a dog. Let's get outta here."

Karen recognized the voices of two boys her age from church. Not feds, they were only kids swiping watermelons! She inhaled deeply and noticed she had again been holding her breath. Spud yelped, also relieved, and nuzzled into her caress.

Karen tapped the trailer door. Millie cracked it open, wearing pink sponge hair curlers over her round face and clutching a faded robe. It didn't quite cover her sacred undergarments, which showed at the sleeves and neck.

"Karen, what are you doing out at this hour?"

"Father wants you to come up to the house. He thinks there are feds spying."

Millie's eyes registered confusion, then, fear. Her mouth opened in shock.

"Feds? Where?"

"Don't worry. It's just kids stealing melons. But you still have to come to the house."

"I was just about to turn in. If it's just kids, why bother?"

"Father will be real mad if I don't bring you back. He'll yell and might smack me around. He's the patriarch. We have to do what he says, even if we know better."

"Sure, I'll come if he's about to blow his top." Millie pulled a sweater over her shoulders.

Back in the living room, Karen, Mother, and the trailer-wives laughed.

"What a joke," Mother said. "But I'm shocked at good LDS boys acting like hooligans."

Millie patted her stomach. "I noticed some delicious rhubarb cobblers in the kitchen. Anyone need to satisfy a sweet tooth? Eating seems to settle my nerves."

"Sure," Mother said. "Karen can get you and Rhonda some. We've had ours."

"No thanks." Rhonda waved a dismissive hand. "I don't care for rhubarb. And my nerves are turning my stomach upside down." She massaged her belly.

Karen brought a plate to Millie. Father and Richard stomped into the house and found the women laughing.

After Karen told the story, Father said, "This certainly is not a joke. It could have been a real emergency. Anyone who thinks it's funny, needs to think again. Those feds would like nothing better than to drag us into court. They would throw the Prophet of the Lord, and me into the pen. Maybe you women, too. They'd likely as not place you kids into gentile foster homes. Don't forget. These are the latter days, the end of life as we know it on this temporal earth."

Father threw up his hands as he paced.

"The Lord works in mysterious ways. Tonight may be His way of preparing us for coming evil."

CHAPTER 9

COME TO MEETING

Mother sat gluing S&H Green stamps into a booklet. "Karen, did you sweep the porch and empty the waste baskets?"

"Yes, Mother. We're ready for the meeting. I think I dropped a barrette out in the barn. I'll run and get it."

Mother finished gluing and slid the stamp book into a stack of books bound by rubber bands. The trading stamps from participating local businesses were like cash at the S&H distribution center where the Hardys hoped to buy a stainless steel pop up toaster as soon as they collected another half book of stickers.

"Hurry right in the minute we call you." Mother arranged the books in a kitchen drawer between cookbooks and her recipe box.

Hallelujah, Karen thought as she sprinted straight toward the loft ladder.

Halfway down the lane to the barn, she heard a voice.

"Wait, Karen. Come back."

Her heart sank as she realized it was Brother LeGrande. Too late, she knew she should have made a wide circle around Rhonda's trailer and the driveway where the prophet parked his pickup.

"Yes?" Karen moped nearer.

LeGrande brightened. You're are quite the athlete. But I'd like to see you develop more quiet ladylike characteristics, Karen. You're old enough to learn about the meaning of demure."

"That word was on a weekly vocabulary quiz months ago. I got it right."

Brother LeGrande giggled which made the jellyroll of flesh jiggle over his belt. "Glad to hear it. I wanted you to ask your mother if my girls need to bring anything for the meeting tonight."

"No, I collected rhubarb for cobblers. We've got cream ready to whip for topping."

"Good. I've been thinking. You play piano, don't you?"

"Just learning. I take lessons."

"I'd like you to accompany us at meeting tonight."

"Huh? I'm not ready. I haven't practiced anything."

"Sometimes young girls are more ready for life than they think, Karen."

"I get all mixed up if people sing along when I play. I only practice the lessons in my piano book. Not hymns."

"I think you underestimate yourself. I hear you playing every afternoon when it's my turn in Rhonda's trailer."

"Just let Sister Nora do it like always." Karen turned with a jerk. "I have to hurry in the house now."

She wasn't sure why, but didn't care to have the Prophet watch her go up into her loft.

From the kitchen window, Karen watched the sunset layering the mountains. A battered station wagon pulled up behind the house with the Billingses. At the kitchen door, Mother hugged Sister Billings, who handed Mom a package. "Just a few things for your baby. I keep thinking I won't need them, but you never know." She blushed.

"Thanks, Lenore," Mother said. "I'll save them for you just in case. Where are all the kids?"

"I left the little ones home with Mary and La Mar. Most of them are getting over the chicken pox or waiting to come down with it."

"Let's visit before the others come." Mother drew Sister Lenore to the sofa.

"I've been canning pickles all afternoon," Sister Lenore said.

Karen blanched at the thought of pickles, a word that re-minded her of her sour feelings toward Brother LeGrande. She fiddled with her skirt hem and listened to the women.

Lenore was Mother's age and, like her, had six children. She wore a simple skirt and blouse and her chin-length hair was parted in the center and pulled back with barrettes. "What a job. I did twenty quarts of dills."

"I get queasy hearing the word, dill." Mother winced and patted her belly.

Lenore squeezed her friend's hand. "You suffer more with babies than most, Hosannah,. I'll pray for you."

"Bless your sweet heart. I appreciate you, Lenore. While you're at it, please pray that I'll be able to accept the principle if and when the Lord calls us. Edward's been hinting that the Lord is touching his heart, preparing him to accept another wife." Mother's face trembled like she might cry.

"Don't worry. The Lord never tests us beyond what we can endure.

"I have that same worry, myself. But really, another wife might mean more help with the drudgery. And it would be sure proof the Lord wants us with him in the highest degree of glory in heaven."

"I know. It's just that the idea is so…"

"Don't say it, Hosannah." Lenore raised her hand to cut off Mother. "The Prince of Darkness and his minions hear our every word, even our unspoken thoughts. Don't invite the adversary to this meeting tonight. We're all troubled and need the help of the spirit speaking through the prophet." Her work-reddened hand pressed her throat.

"It's so good to talk to you. Sometimes, I don't appreciate my blessings as I should."

Karen left to answer the door for the Thompsons. "Come in. Mother and Sister Billings are in the living room."

"Thank you, Karen. Being here is such a blessing." Brother Thompson spoke for all three of his wives and for his five sons, ages seven to fourteen. The first wife and the kids peered timidly through thick glasses that slid down their noses. They sidled into the next room, like mice shy of a cat.

Each of the two new Thompson wives was a blond mirror image of the other. Aged sixteen and eighteen, they became brides on a day in May when Karen was away visiting Grandma Hardy. They followed the family through the kitchen, as more knocking erupted.

It was Brother Sanders and his brood. His first wife and their six, eight, and ten-year-old daughters followed him. The second wife, Nora, carried her knitting satchel onto the porch, chatting with two of Prophet LeGrande's wives, Elvira and Anna. Nora had been an old maid of twenty-six, glad to settle for being Brother Sanders' second wife. The women wore faded dresses and hairdos that captured their tresses in pinned-up braids and buns.

Karen was relieved to see Nora, the pianist for the group. She invited the women in and left the door ajar for other arrivals streaming up the path.

The living room seats and the crammed-in kitchen chairs and folding chairs filled fast. Richard rolled the piano stool over and went for Mother's vanity seat. Voices hushed as Brother LeGrande made his entry between his youngest wives, Rhonda and Millie. He slid an arm around two of his older wives, Anna and Elvira, and pecked their cheeks. "Lovely to see my precious girls when it isn't even in the schedule."

They giggled and each leaned in to kiss a cheek.

As usual Miriam wasn't present.

Karen knew Miriam and Brother LeGrande's other wives would likely resent her if she married into their family. She was fond of Millie and especially, Rhonda, but didn't like the idea that they might boss her as a new young bride. She wondered how the wives, especially the two young ones on the Hardy farm, managed in their cramped quarters and why they could smile about sharing a man. She recoiled, thinking of them cuddling against the overpowering prophet who was as old as he was pompous.

The prophet had greeted and flirted with his wives. Next, he set to work engaging his other chattering admirers.

"Brother Thompson, there's a special glow about your countenance." The prophet stood a hair closer than others normally would whenever he talked to a follower. "I've seen it since the day you entered the covenant of plural marriage with your second and third wives." He smiled into their faces directly and squeezed their hands tighter and longer than usual.

"The Lord has blessed you, dear ladies." He held a hand from each of the young Thompson brides. "Such treasures, and so recognized of God. The Kingdom of the Lord rests on women of faith, who uphold their male priesthood holders." The brides beamed under the praise.

Karen knew that Mormons and fundamentalist group members avoided using powerful words like God or Devil. Brother LeGrande and high priesthood leaders of the mainstream church seemed exempt from such rules. They gloried in their strength by booming out the fearful words.

Brother LeGrande pumped each hand with both of his. His warmth oozed from every pore like a hypnotizing aroma. Perhaps these people didn't have confidence in themselves and needed to borrow it from a mesmerizing messenger of god.

"Jake Thompson. You are turning into a little man," he said to the seven-year-old, who grinned at the floor and blushed.

"Judy Hardy! Honey, you're such a little lady with your hair all curled up so pretty for meeting." He left out no one. The room was jammed with worshippers. Children perched on laps or on the floor with young men who gave up their chairs to ladies.

"Welcome. Welcome." Brother LeGrande's voice rang out. "The spirit of the Lord is here with all of us on this occasion. I feel it as surely as I feel my own skin." He pressed hands to his cheeks and paused for full attention.

"We'll start this meeting with prayer." Heads bowed in concert. Arms were folded.

"Our divine and loving Father in the exalted kingdom of Kolob, we are humble in our adoration and mighty in our faith. Let Thy power be with us on this occasion. Impress upon each of us Thy plan for us in these last days. We embrace Thy commandments. We seek righteousness. We waver not from tribulation. Each and every one of us seeks perfection in both thought and deed. We will not surrender to weakness or iniquity. We embrace Thy secrets. We submit to the power of living Thy sacred plan of celestial marriage. We embrace its trials and accept its joys in the sure knowledge it will lead us back unto Thee, and our eventual exaltation. InthenameofJe-susChrist we say these things. Amen."

The crowd stirred and repeated, "Amen."

"We'll sing 'Hie to Kolob.' Karen, will you favor us at the piano?"

Karen's stomach felt like an elevator going down. "But I didn't know. I haven't practiced. I'm not used to playing hymns."

"There's no time like the present to start using your God-given talents for the Lord. Don't be shy."

Rosemary, who had been sitting on the piano stool, stood and rolled it to the keyboard. Karen thumbed through the Mormon hymn book to page 284. She would have to bluff her way through with the right hand only. Her fingers turned icy. She massaged them but couldn't make them relax. Nothing to do but her best, she scanned the music and tried to absorb the first few measures in preparation. She hoped her cold fingers could keep up a reasonably accurate beat.

After the musical introduction, enough of the crowd jumped in on cue to limp along through the first few verses.

Finally, by the fifth and final verse, the congregation and her playing were synchronized.

> There is no end to glory:
> There is no end to love:
> There is no end to being:
> There is no death above.

They finished with gusto. Karen's anger and embarrassment burned her cheeks. No one else seemed to notice.

"Brothers and Sisters." The prophet paused to focus on the faces. "You are truly called of God. This room is bursting, but we are few. The Lord has gathered us together as His most chosen children of Zion. The earth is old, almost 6,000 years. Humanity is numbered like unto the sands along the oceans, yet here we are. We alone are the chosen saints, here in this very room. Only we know the greatest secrets of the universe, beyond even those in the Mormon Church. We here will return to God and be exalted as He is. This life is a trial, but is only a twinkling in time and space."

It was as if he cradled the crowd in his cupped hands. His words controlled and caressed, soon casting a spell. Every face reflected and they drew together and breathed as one body. The youngest children sucked their thumbs and some fingered their parent's collars or cuffs. No one spoke.

"I've been impressed of the spirit to tell you that the Lord is powerful. He reigns over the forces of heaven and earth. The last days are upon us. His kingdom is nigh. God rules every little thing on this planet. Ponder this. You must have noticed with me how time, itself, has accelerated. That is the power of the

Lord bringing his plan to fruition. There's much for Him to do through us. Time must rush toward its end. We know from the Pearl of Great Price in the Book of Abraham that the time difference between earth and His Realm is a thousand of our days to one of His. And I, as the Prophet, now communicate directly with God, just as Joseph Smith did in his day. It's truly revealed to me that time has actually been speeded up in the final days of this dispensation. Think about it. You've noticed it yourselves, haven't you? How much faster time moves now than when you were the size of these youngsters sitting at my feet?"

Davy cupped his hands and spoke into Judy's ear. "Time is faster than when I was little like you."

The prophet's hand reached over and ruffled Davy's hair as the congregation snickered behind their hands and hankies, relieved for a chance to take a breath.

"As you know, the Salt Lake City Mormon Church has forsaken the key to exaltation. I quote from the Doctrine and Covenants, Section 132, revealed by our first Prophet, Joseph Smith. 'Celestial marriage enables men to become gods.' That is clear to us, but not to the apostate mainstream Mormons." He paused to roll his eyes. Listeners did the same.

He continued, "'Verily, thus saith the Lord that in as much as you have inquired to know and understand wherein I, the Lord, justified my servants Abraham, Isaac, and Jacob, as also Moses, David and Solomon, my servants, as teaching the principle and doctrine of their having many wives and concubines…'"

Karen was impressed but bored when anyone quoted dry scripture from memory.

"And in verse seven…" The prophet pressed his fingertips to his temples, as if to draw the exact words from his head. "…and there is never but one on the earth at a time on whom this power and the keys of this priesthood are conferred."

A unified spirit of secret community gripped them as they shared the mysteries of God from the mouth of His only spokesman on earth.

"Is anyone so foolish as to think the Lord would confer His keys of power on the leader of a Church that has forsaken the essential commandment for salvation?"

There were derisive throat clearings and clucking as every head shook with a resounding no.

"The Lord has blessed me as leader of this group of pure and choice souls. I am humble as I speak His words to you."

Brother LaGrande's throat caught on the words as he blotted a tear.

"I have no choice but to bear this daunting burden. There is always only one on earth to hear the direct words of God. In these final earthly days, we all know that the chosen servant is called the One Mighty and Strong, as foretold in scripture. I stand up to the task because of my deep and abiding love for our Father in Heaven and for each of you."

He peered at the upturned faces as tears gathered and splashed onto his cheeks. Sisters Nora and Lenore wept with him, as did Brother Thompson. Many others sniffed back tears with difficulty.

Brother LeGrande blew his nose before he continued.

"In Joseph Smith's day, he was that one and only leader, called to speak for God. Brigham Young then picked up the yoke as did other Church presidents. But, alas, in the Church's darkest hour, Wilford Woodruff tore the Church asunder! He was the church president who ravished the sanctity of the Lord's true church. He allowed the feds of that time to pansy whip him."

Karen noticed gasps and averted eyes. Those reactions and his tone told her that Brother LeGrande must have said something shocking.

"Indeed, he did! He drove the plan of salvation underground when he denied members their God-given right to openly practice celestial marriage.

"But behold, my Brothers and Sisters, the feds can not pansy whip the Lord and Savior! He continues to call his favored children to live plural marriage. Some do it with pure hearts, as we do. It makes or breaks all who attempt it. My girls and I live it as Moses, Joseph, and Brigham did. But it is a principle that crumbles the weak and faithless. My all-abiding hope is that someday soon, my first delightsome wife, Miriam, will listen to the Lord's will and find love in her heart for her sister wives."

His face was a study of anguished love for the absent Miriam, of little faith.

"As you know, there are apostates even among the abounding scattered polygamy groups. They have multiple wives, but many of them follow false prophets.

"Our rightful choice is to trust the Lord, to embrace His every calling. You must stay true to Him through *me*, His servant. Brothers, take unto you those wives you are given in righteousness. Sisters, give yourself to a worthy husband as the Lord calls you. Wives, be generous to sister wives who join your family. Parents, don't stand in the way of your young girls who ask to partake of the Lord's principle of polygamy. For I say behold, all those who fail to harken unto the word shall be damned!"

Karen felt her skin prickle.

"We grow in God with each minute that rushes us toward the end of time. We accomplish for Him day by day. Minutes have turned to seconds. A day is like an hour. These little children learn faster than we did. These young women—" he pointed out Karen, Rosemary, and the oldest Sanders girl—"are ready at younger and younger ages to marry into the principle."

Amens rumbled through the room. Mother nodded at Richard to carry the sleeping Judy to her bed.

Brother LeGrande wiped his handkerchief across his forehead. "We so seldom get to enjoy the spirit that blesses us when we meet. Are there questions tonight?"

A few hands rose.

"Yes, Sister Lenore?"

"You talked about the roles we must follow in the plan of polygamy. I'm praying to be strong when the time comes. But my question is about the very young girls called as wives. My daughter, Mary, is only ten. I fear she'll still be more of a child than a woman, even in four or five years. Yet girls are now marrying into polygamy at fourteen and fifteen."

"Yes." Brother LeGrande answered. "We were still children at their ages. But as I said, the press of time in the last days has hastened their maturity. I would never force a girl, of course. But they deserve to give themselves into the holy sacrament of plural marriage of their own free will. They deserve exaltation. Wouldn't we all agree?"

Karen's stomach twisted. In spite of the comment about not forcing girls, she had heard Father and Brother LeGrande making heavy-handed plans for her.

"Brother Thompson. Did I see a question cross your face?"

"Yes, Prophet. I was wondering about modest dress and hairstyles for the sisters. The women of the world are wearing more scandalous clothes every day. They paint up their faces like clowns and chop off their womanly locks. Are they sinning against nature? Shouldn't we condemn these practices among our womenfolk?"

"Thank you for that. I've been meaning to address this. You might have noticed that some of my girls have short hair. The Lord has blessed Rhonda with lovely curls. She looks pretty with clipped hair and a little lipstick. I enjoy attractiveness and don't condemn it. I've seen Rosemary and Karen with lipstick and rosy cheeks. Very pretty on young girls. They don't paint themselves up like harlots. They dress with dignity. I think modern styles are fine in moderation, unlike what some of the other polygamy leaders like to preach."

Karen loved dressing up in pretty clothes, but hated lipstick. Half the time, she had to wipe off her crooked painted lips to try again. Tonight she had cried out in frustration after three failed attempts to draw a red even lip-line. She used lipstick because Rosemary, Mother, Amy and other friends demanded it. It bothered her that Brother LeGrande and her father were bargaining over the attractiveness of his daughters. She wanted to feel her looks belonged to her alone.

Brother Thompson's mousey nose twitched. He looked as if he had hoped for more backing from the prophet to keep his women in line. His wives lowered their eyes toward folded hands resting in their laps.

"Anyone," Brother LeGrande said, "can talk to me in private after the meeting for more specific guidance."

The prophet nodded at Father's raised hand.

"You mentioned the feds of old. I think a lot of us are worried about present day feds. The paper says they're here to wipe out polygamy and maybe put the children into foster homes."

"Yes, Brother Edward. Feds have blighted Utah history before and they are nosing around again. It appears they're after the Short Creek group this time, and maybe the Allreds and Kingstons. We're a small group and we blend in with the mainstream. Who could possibly know or care about our little group? We should take precautions. But we must not give in to fear, like those saints who followed Wilford Woodruff into apostasy."

The men murmured agreement.

"We'll sing 'God Be With You 'Til We Meet Again,'" the prophet said. "After that, we'll enjoy delicious refreshments and even more delectable fellowship."

Karen dashed to the kitchen to help Rosemary cut and serve cobbler. She seethed as she spooned a dollop of cream on each dessert to the tune of Nora's accompaniment in the next room. How dare Brother LeGrande force her to play piano. She hated having her house overrun with sniveling polygamists. And she despised the prophet, Hyrum LeGrande!

CHAPTER 10

WIVES AND SISTERS

Ben and Jack approached a legless figure propped against a brick store front, one arm flopped over a gunnysack of provisions. An upended squashed hat nearby showcased glossy pencils, one of which speared a corrugated sign, *"Five Cents Each."* The detectives tossed coins into the hat, but didn't bother to bend down for pencils.

At the Ko Ko Mo door, Jack's eyes riveted on a truck. "Look. Coming this way."

The bed of a rattletrap pickup writhed with skinny bodies, all bobbing and slapping hands. "One potato, two potato."

Two hawk-faced women with babies flung on their shoulders stared straight ahead. Clutching the wheel, a wild-haired scarecrow man glowered, trancelike. Worse than screwballs, Ben thought, they look like certified lunatics.

"Polygamists?" Ben whispered. He winced at an image of Sylvia's outrage over the perverse sight, thinking her tirade might qualify for a disturbing-the-peace citation.

Jack's voice seethed. "Right. Plygs!" Fury flooded his face.

Ben jotted down the license number in his pocket note-book. To him, Jack looked like coiled fury ready to spring. "You need a beer." Ben steered Jack from the parched afternoon into the boozy dark coolness of the Ko Ko Mo.

"Hi boys. Two beers comin' up." Eddie straightened from mopping the linoleum around the barstools. Ben nodded.

The ammonia wafting from the mop pail sharpened his senses. He needed to find out why Jack had turned from carefree to seething.

The two slid into their booth as Eddie delivered the beers. "Thanks buddy." Jack's eyebrows drew a harsh line across steely blue eyes. Ben waited in vain for Jack to speak, then said, "That plyg family has you steamed for some reason."

Jack rubbed his temples and gulped from his mug. "Good and cold. Just what I needed." He turned toward the amputee outside the window.

Ben followed his gaze. "Must have lost his legs in the war. Is that what happened to Shortarm?"

"Since you asked..." Jack loosened his tie. Ben thought Jack was relieved to dodge the polygamy topic. "Shortarm lost his arm here on this street. It was a few years back. He mostly stayed sober in those days, except for occasional binges. He stopped into the Candy House one night." Jack nodded toward the whore house across the street. "It was a night when he was falling down, snockered."

Ben nodded for Jack to continue as he sipped.

"Name was Buster in those days. Buster staggered in, still with two good arms. Got pretty rambunctious. Overly so, they say."

"Then what?"

"He happened to bumble into a glass-topped table and sent it crashing down the staircase, along with the crystal lamp on it. 'Course a ruckus ensued. They didn't always keep that panther chained up back then. You have to understand. It was a pet, real calm and friendly."

"You're not saying the animal attacked Shortarm!"

"'Fraid so. Gnawed him up pretty good."

The hairs on Ben's neck stiffened. "Then what?"

"The ambulance hauled him off to the McKay-Dee Mormon Hospital. Big mistake!"

"Why's that?"

"He was drunk and disorderly. The tight-assed Mormons didn't take kindly to that. They want only patients who wear Mormon skivvies. Besides that, it was clear he didn't have money for the bill. Shortarm thinks they could've saved his arm, but didn't want to bother, him being an unworthy sinner."

"That's the story?"

"Yep. That panther ripped him a new one."

"Let me guess. Were you a young police recruit, the officer called to the scene of the tragic accident?"

"You got it."

"I figured you played a part in the Shortarm drama."

"It was damned awful. I rode to the hospital with him and paced the floor that night. I hoped for the best for Buster in spite of the odds. Blamed myself for not insisting on Saint Benedict's, the Catholic hospital. But there you go."

Ben had to admit he was warming up to Jack in spite of his unkempt ways. Still, he couldn't help noticing an annoying ink blot on Jack's shirtfront as it played peek-a-boo with his flapping tie.

"To Shortarm, I'd say, you're quite the hero."

Jack nodded.

"You mentioned Mormon underwear." Ben changed the subject. "I've heard of it, and you can stop me if I'm impertinent, but do polygamists wear them as well as the regular Mormons?"

"Some do, but they wear the long kind. It covers them to their ankles and wrists. Regular LDS only wear that extreme version inside their holy temples. Wearing either kind of Mormon garments is a privilege only afforded to those who've submitted to special secret temple ceremonies. The undergarments show they earned what's called a temple recommend."

"You mean a recommendation?" Ben asked.

"Yes, but they call it recommend. At age twelve, every Mormon must submit to regular bishop interrogations. I guess you need to know these things if you're going to understand this place."

"Yes, go on."

"Whenever members meet with the bishop," Jack continued, "they have to prove they've paid their tithing, done their religious duties, and haven't sinned. If so, he proclaims them as officially 'worthy.' Whoever cuts the mustard can relax for the time being. Church standing is secure and they're allowed to access the temples. Of course the polygamists no longer get recommends after they're found out. The church now officially discourages plural marriage, but the plygs have already earned their magic underwear, and they just keep wearing it."

"Magic?"

"Yes, for those with enough faith, it wards off injury and evil."

"No kidding, and what if a bishop judges someone as not worthy?"

"Unworthy saints don't get recommends. Without 'em, members are banned from attending Mormon weddings. Women get snubbed at quilting bees. And no one shows up to the kids' birthday parties. In bad cases, a bishop puts out the word for everybody to stop buying at your store. Or to treat you like crap at work when promotion time rolls around."

Ben emitted a choking sound.

While pondering how to proceed, he watched a couple of farmhands, clad in overalls and sweat-streaked denim shirts amble into the bar and settle on stools. Next, a string of businessmen trickled in, their jackets draped on their shoulders. Raucous bantering blared above Peggy Lee, who crooned from the bubbling jukebox.

Ben raised his drink and rubbed with a paper napkin at the wet ring left by his mug. He hoped Jack's beer would loosen his tongue. "Now for the sixty four dollar question. How do polygamists fit in? I mean personally, with you in particular? Your secret's safe."

Jack searched the drops of beer at the bottom of his mug and soon Eddie delivered another round. Two sailors wearing dress whites entered and took the last stools. Coming into town Ben had seen other sailors at the Naval Supply Depot.

"It's rough." Jack's gaze was lost in the depths of beer, possibly in a search for words, or the courage to speak them. "My kid sister is stuck somewhere in one of those compounds, hooked up with some sleaze, like the one in that filthy pickup truck."

"Your sister?" Ben leaned in. "No wonder you're torn."

Jack's shoulders slumped. His glance shifted from the swirling brew to Ben's face. "She was only fifteen. My parents introduced her to an old guy they thought was the one true prophet of the Lord, The One Mighty and Strong, they called him. There are dozens of 'mighty and strong true prophets' blithering about Utah. The mainstream church has one, but most splinter groups have their own. There's also riff-raff who single-mindedly hear the call of the Lord and set out to collect wives and followers from scratch. Creeps are able to rustle up new sizable cults. Most fall by the wayside."

"About your sister?" Ben modulated his words, low, reassuring, and the tone he'd reserve for interrogations when he hoped to put suspects at ease. "Did your parents approve of her going away with this man?"

"It happened gradually." Jack said it into his beer, expecting Ben to overhear. "His silver tongue beguiled the family. He had charisma, something like Clark Gable or Jesus Christ."

"Did she go with him willingly?"

"He convinced her that marryin' him would lead to eternal exaltation."

"Incredible."

"Yeah, and that's not all. He sold her the whole ball of wax. Had her believing marryin' him would buy the glories of heaven for the whole damn family, includin' me."

"What a tragedy."

"You're telling me!" Jack's lips and jaw tightened, drawing gashes of anger along his cheeks. "She high tailed it off with that pervert. The old fart must be at least fifty years old by now."

The anguish in Jack's eyes stabbed Ben with pity. "How old would she be now?"

"She's only seventeen." Jack's face jutted.

"Pathetic. I have a girlfriend and a sister. I might want to beat that bastard to a bloody pulp if this happened to any female I cared about."

"That's exactly what I plan to do as soon as I get my hands on the friggin' pervert."

Ben massaged his brow. "Makes me want to hug my own sister. But do you think it's ethical for you to be on this case with your family being involved?"

Jack sucked in air for a sigh that turned into a shudder. "*Anybody* in these parts could have family in a plyg cult. That's partly why nothing much gets done to stamp it out."

Ben waited for him to continue.

"Polygamy is covert. No one dares admit to it, even though Mormons are proud of it in their ancestry. And they all plan to live it up in heaven."

Ben propped a snapshot from his pocket against the ash-tray. "Another photo came in the mail today. This poor girl is just like your sister. Her father says she's in the Ogden area. Help me find her, and it might lead to your sister."

Jack pulled out a wadded handkerchief and wiped his forehead. He stuffed it back into his pocket, then slipped out a picture encased in plastic. "My sister," he said and handed it over.

"See those curls? They bounced when she laughed. She laughed all the time."

"Bright as sunshine." Ben noticed the girl had Jack's hair and eyes, but a smaller turned-up nose.

"I don't know how she looks now." Jack held the photo like a fragile treasure and leaned it next to the other photo. She might be washed out and threadbare like those biddies in the truck."

"Your parents have lost touch with her?"

"Oh, yes. They eventually saw through the old guy's act. So he bolted with Sis and cut them off. I bet he's lying to her, saying none of us want her in the family anymore. Or he's telling her we're unworthy and don't deserve to see her. Who knows? For all I know that old pervert prophet is trying to knock her up this very minute."

Ben noted a shudder in Jack's voice, saw it in his shoulders.

Jack gave the table a rap. "I'm getting out of here. I'll give you a break, so you can stop pretending not to notice this piddly speck of ink under my necktie." He stood and barged through the crowd and smoke to the cash register, where he left a wad of dollar bills, and was gone.

CHAPTER 11

BEYOND THE FENCE

C urled beneath her quilt, still groggy-eyed, Karen squinted against the sun bursting through the bedroom roof-peak window. The roosters sounded like trumpets heralding a major announcement.

Hurray! Thrilling news! It was August second, her twelfth birthday! She and Mother planned to drive into the city of Ogden for a shopping spree where she could buy school clothes to start Junior High.

She sprang out of the bed she shared with Rosemary and grabbed a cocoa can and a Clabber Girl baking powder can from her underwear drawer, hugged them to her chest. She kissed the cocoa can with her babysitting earnings, then the baking powder tin with money from hoeing the bishop's sugar beets. The sum total was her life savings. She dumped wadded dollar bills, change and a dusting of brown and white power on her pillow. She smoothed and caressed each bill and coin as she nervously counted them in hopes of buying a dream load of store bought school clothes just like the other kids her age.

"Karen," Mother called up the stairwell, "the pump's broken down. Get down here and help start it. Hurry up."

Family emergencies always spoiled her fun. She stomped down the stairs to the kitchen.

Rhonda fidgeted in the doorway. "What are we going to do?"

She wrung her hands. "I can't make Postum or even wash my face." She looked like a fretful hedgehog with net on her head and bobby pins poking out in every direction.

"Can't Richard prime the pump?" Karen let herself bristle. "Isn't that a job for a male priesthood holder?"

"He's earning cash money harvesting peas for Bishop Taylor today. You'll have to do it. Now get going. And while you're there, bring back a chunk of cheese, about like this." Mother shaped her fingers into a triangle.

Please, not today, Karen thought. She detested going to the pump house.

"Turn that frown upside down, Karen," Mother said. "I could cancel this trip to town if you don't pitch in."

Karen gagged down annoyance. On the porch with Rhonda, she grabbed a half bucket of water intended for pump-priming, and hauled it out into the blinding morning. "That broken down old pump is spoiling everything," she said.

"For me, too." Rhonda caught a bobby pin slipping down her forehead. "I wanted a quiet day alone, cleaning the trailer, maybe, finishing a library book. And I have plenty of hand stitching to do. Millie and I are pooling our sewing money."

"Doesn't it bother you to be in that cramped trailer all alone?"

"No, not at all." Rhonda looked sideways at Karen. "I like feeling called of the Lord to be married to the prophet. But you know, Karen? Sometimes I admire him as the prophet more than I care for his company as a man."

Rhonda stepped off toward her trailer, fussing with bobby pins as she veered around an ant hill.

A gentle dirt and brush mound hinted at the dugout pump house buried beneath pigweed and burr bushes. Karen's fingers grubbed in the dirt for the rusted trapdoor ring. She yanked up the wooden slab, and heaved, letting it slam backwards to the ground to reveal a dark throat into the earth.

She breathed in the musty dank air and gingerly stepped down the stairwell, mottled with grime. Crumbling concrete chunks on the steps made the going treacherous. Standing on the wet clay floor, she twisted a dingy bulb strung on a ceiling timber to illuminate the cavity. Her shadow bobbed on the concrete walls, crusted here and there with orange minerals and smeared with moss. A wooden pallet across from the ailing pump held nearly empty gunny sacks for carrots, potatoes and apples. The family replenished empty sacks each fall.

She tried to ignore the roots dangling between roof timbers and the spiders twiddling in cobwebs. The moldy air raised gooseflesh over her body and she shivered not because of the underground chill, but from thinking about the crawly creatures that spiders hunted in the crevices. A wave of panic hit her. She felt trapped in buried space, easily cut off from the outside world.

A sensible person in a scrap metal yard would have stepped over the pump without a glance. What looked like a pile of junk was actually the heart of ongoing life for the family and trailer wives on the Hardy farm. Without pumping water there could be no cooking, washing, drinking, cleaning or flushing. Karen did what she had to do. She knelt on a wet board at the pump as if in prayer. Her fingers searched for the restart button. She strained to remember how to push and pull the levers as she trickled water through the system to reteach the pump its sacred duty. Would prayer and the hand of Heavenly Father nudge the gears and levers?

She chose grit and willpower instead. Close examination of the workings jogged her memory. She doggedly tried the system once, then twice. The pump lurched along only while she tinkered, then it quit, silent and dead. Determined, she crossed her fingers and offered up a birthday wish. On the third attempt, the junk heap groaned into action, grumbling and complaining, but pumping water.

Life went on, and relief washed over her.

She eased the lid off a pot-bellied gray crock in the back corner. A half wheel of orange cheddar cheese wrapped in waxed cloth rested at the bottom. She lifted a butcher knife from a hook on the wall and sliced off a pungent wedge the size of both her fists.

*   *   *

Later, Mother and Karen pulled out of their driveway. Bishop Taylor's spacious farmhouse across the highway nestled amid manicured shrubs and willow trees, his Hudson Hornet gleaming in the driveway. Karen waved to Lucinda and her mother, who sat on the steps of their squat, white frame crackerbox in the corner of the Bishop's yard. The mother and daughter were laughing at a younger sister and brother who were playing catch-me-if-you-can with the bishop's swirling lawn sprinklers.

"Karen, you'll need to shop for serviceable fabrics and sensible patterns to sew for school. That's the way to stretch your clothing dollars."

"But Mother, I can't even sew a straight seam. I'm twelve now, and I'm dying to have store-bought clothes to start junior high."

"Offer to do Rosemary's chores. I think she'd help you with your sewing. It's past time you learned. You'll need to be a good seamstress if you want to catch a worthy LDS husband."

Karen unfolded an ad she'd cut from the *Standard Examiner.* "Look here, Samuel's is going out of business. Let's try to buy some ready-mades. I've outgrown almost everything. And I want something I can wear tonight. It's my first night at mutual, and I have a Temple recommend interview with Bishop Taylor."

"That's right. I almost forgot."

Karen watched pear and apple orchards through the car window and secretly crossed her fingers for store bought clothes, not fabric.

"We'll see what's available," Mother said. "But about your worthiness interview. I'm warning you. Your downfall is asking questions when you should keep your mouth shut. Don't question the bishop. You'll make the family look foolish." Mother bit her lip and aimed a warning finger at Karen. "You're too big to keep asking those things and not listening to the answers."

"I know." Karen said in a harsh whisper. "Seems like I can't help it." Mother's accusation wounded her.

The car passed four farmhouses with gardens and fields of corn and sugar beets. At the Mormon Ward House, Mother continued.

"Here's my advice for tonight. Say, 'Yes' to every question about church commandments. Say 'No' to questions about sins. Whatever you do, answer 'No' when he asks you if we associate with apostates or polygamists. It's not a lie because we don't consider polygamists to be apostates. They are the truest of Mormons. Do you understand?"

"Yes," Karen said. "I'll try hard. And maybe if I can buy some store-rack clothes, I'll feel braver at the interview. I don't mean to embarrass the family, Mother."

"I know," Mother said. "But if the Church finds out about the fundamentalists, Daddy could go to prison. And we could be excommunicated and shunned. So you watch every word that comes out of that mouth of yours."

Karen wanted to change the subject. She looked out at the Five Points business area as they neared downtown Ogden. "Look, Mother. There's a Negro lady and her little kids."

"Yes, they look strange, but don't stare."

Karen wanted to crane her neck. Instead, her eyes strained to scrutinize the mother carrying a baby with a toddler clinging to her skirt.

"Did you learn in Sunday School or Primary why they have black skins?" Mother asked.

"They were cursed," Karen said, "with the mark of Cain in the preexistence."

"Good," Mother said. "I'm glad you listen to your gospel lessons. And why were they cursed?"

"Because," Karen answered, "they chose not to follow Jesus in the pre-life war of good and evil in heaven."

"That's right," Mother said. "And why were we born white and delightsome here in Zion?"

"Well," Karen said, "because we were valiant in the war in heaven?"

"Yes, right again. We're lucky to be God's chosen people here on earth in the last days."

"I heard that in Sacrament Meeting," Karen said. "If I ever get to meet a Negro person, maybe I can find out what they're really like."

"There you go questioning again, Karen." Mother's voice trembled. "Sometimes I worry that you did something in the preexistence to make you think the way you do. I've tried hard as a mother." Her shoulders sagged. "You have a way of making me feel like a failure."

Mother often broke down in tears when she discussed disappointment in any of her children. Karen hoped Mother wouldn't cry today. She fenced off the guilt she felt for hurting her mother, but allowed herself a quick peek at a long-buried worry about pre-life curses. Was she cursed for being less valiant than other Mormons? Is that why she had different ways of seeing things? This was the first time she had heard her vague fears spoken aloud. She blinked away her own threatening tears and took a breath. Her birthday needed to stay hopeful.

They drove down Main Street, passing the Paramount Theater where Karen had seen Shirley Temple films and one with Donald O'Conner about Francis the Talking Mule. These movies were a glimpse of the outside world. Except for gangsters in a scary James Cagney movie, the non-Mormons seemed nice, not rude and unworthy as she'd been taught.

They passed Baker Shoes, Kress five-and-dime, and J. C. Penneys. That's where Mother bought sacred Mormon undergarments after the layaway clerk checked her Temple recommend.

Karen's favorite landmark was the Egyptian Theater. She was in awe of its exotic statues of the Sphinx and rows of stiff gold painted cutouts like paperdoll bodies facing front, heads aimed to the side. She had seen two or three moving picture shows there with the silly but likable Abbott and Costello and a musical with Fred Astaire.

"Look, Mother." Karen pointed. "See that car pulling out? They might have money still left on the meter." Anything free cheered Mother's mood.

"Yes," Karen sang out. "The red flag isn't up. There's at least fifteen cents left."

"What's wrong with people?" Mother asked. "Wasting pennies in the meter that way? It's a sin to waste, even for the wealthy. But we'll take what we can get."

Karen felt for the envelope of money in her pocket before she stepped out of the car.

Mother hesitated at the two deep steps up from street level to the high sidewalk. "Give me a hand. This baby makes climbing a chore."

Karen took Mother's elbow. "Where first?" Karen asked.

"I have a list here somewhere for Woolworth's." Mother stirred in her handbag and unfolded a scribbled envelope. "I need thread and bias tape to mend Judy's clothes for the new baby. And let's see… my two-cup measuring cup is broken."

"I love Woolworth's," Karen said, "and it's next door to Samuel's."

The two paused to window shop through the plate glass on each side of Woolworth's swinging doors. Treasures were tucked in the folds of white sheeting spread over stacked orange crates. There were painted tin whistles and doll dishes, rubber balls and plastic boats and cars. Karen imagined them in Davy and Judy's little hands. Karen recognized most of the kitchen doodads, but these were shinier and more modern than the ones at home.

As she held a door open for Mother, she caught a whiff of the store from the entryway. Once inside, her nose sorted the worldly smells floating above the clean scent of floor wax and wood polish. She took in the ladies' talc and cologne counter, leather belts and handbags. Roasting nuts, chocolate, and popcorn led her by the glass candy cases that formed a pen around a white uniformed candy clerk.

While Mother fretted over measuring cups, Karen watched and envied shoppers resting on stools at the lunch counter. They sipped ice cream sodas and floats or ate slices of white cake with coconut frosting. One non-Mormon man dribbled spilled coffee from a saucer back into his cup while reading a newspaper. He sat on the stool where Karen had once sat with her best twelve-year-old friend, Amy. That lucky day they had shared a strawberry milkshake from a heavy footed glass taller than a Kerr canning jar.

During summer break, Karen missed her best chum, Amy. The two shared homework, friends, secrets, and hopes for the future more often than they shared sodas. Now that Karen was twelve, she'd be in Amy's church activity group again, and of course they'd be in classes and have lunch together after the fall school term began.

Mother was chewing her lip and agonizing over sewing notions, carefully comparing the cost of bias tape to seam binding to rickrack. Her face reflected her inner battle with shopping. Wants and needs waged war with stubborn reluctance to spend money. She estimated yards of thread per penny on large and small spools. She selected button cards and several rolled bundles of fabric ends from a sale bin and stepped to the register with her purchases. At the last minute, she handed a roll of fabric to Karen.

"Run back to the remnant bin with this. I've changed my mind."

Karen wondered if money was not in actuality the root of evil, but perhaps having enough of it would be a savior from worry and harsh scrimping.

"I need to rest," Mother said sinking onto a bench. "You run back to the car with these packages. Stay on this side of the street and don't stare if you see that amputee selling pencils. Stay away from Twenty-Fifth Street." Her voice lowered to a whisper. "You know, that's where hobos and Negroes hang around in the saloons. They commit unspeakable sins there. Don't you even think about evil things like that."

Scurrying to the car, Karen was free to imagine what she'd like to buy in each store if she had the money, a Nancy Drew book, an overnight case, a box of bubble bath packets, dusting powder in a jar with a poodle dog decoration on the lid. She turned away from a sad man with no legs propped against a storefront. Father said these men had lost limbs in the war and had nowhere to go so they stayed wherever their train ticket took them. She felt uncomfortable knowing there were sinners drinking whisky and other bad things in the saloons down the street from the car. She quickly locked the packages in the trunk and headed back to meet Mother.

A train whistle blew and triggered a yearning to one day travel to faraway places she'd seen in movies. As she approached, she saw someone slumping against Mother on the bench. Uneasiness tore at her when she saw her mother's arm slip around the convulsing figure of Sister DeLanna, Heber Jessup's fourth wife.

"Karen?" Sister DeLanna looked up and blotted her tears with a sopping handkerchief. Crying had made her face as puffed and blotched as an over ripe tomato.

"What's wrong?" Karen asked.

"You didn't know," DeLanna answered. "We were raided and Heber is being held for investigation." Fresh tears streamed from DeLanna's swollen eyes.

Karen felt her face drain. "But no one said anything about this at Brother LeGrande's meeting."

"No. This calamity struck later that night." Mother pointed to Samuel's and gave Karen a nudge. "You go on and start your shopping while we talk."

"Sorry, Sister DeLanna," Karen whispered, glad for an excuse to leave.

She pushed the revolving door into Samuel's. Stepping across lush carpeting and past the expensive fragrance counter made Karen feel as if she were in a lavish Fred Astaire movie world. She stood tall and pretended she belonged there, and not climbing farm fences with Lucinda.

She sorted through racks of lovely, worldly clothes. She sneaked a glimpse of Mother and DeLanna huddled together on the bus bench like a tragic painting in a gilded frame. Karen remembered the predictions of the end of the latter days of earth. If world destruction was near, she wanted to spend her final days wearing store-bought clothes. Hopefully, Mother would be too occupied to stop her.

Every tag was scribbled with markdowns, and Karen was delighted to see prices smaller than her savings. An attractive saleslady showed her to the fitting room where she tried on a smart navy-and-white dress and admired herself in the mirror. She preened wearing a polished print blouse and skirt and then the same skirt with a white blouse. They were pretty and cheap, with modest sleeves and necklines to appease Mother. Karen spread her precious finds on the counter in front of the cash register. Excitement beat through her as she caught the saleslady's smiling eyes.

The clerk wore a sleeveless, orange-striped dress. The bare shoulders meant she couldn't be wearing sacred undergarments. "Looks like you've found some wonderful buys."

"Yes," Karen said. "I need everything new to start junior high. She pulled out the ragged envelope with her earnings and counted out dollar bills and coins.

"Then you must be about twelve?"

"Yes, twelve today," Karen answered.

"Today? How nice. Happy birthday!" Her smile was painted red, and her cheeks were almost as bright.

"Thank you." Karen noticed the name tag pinned to the dress.

"Is your name Karen Hardy?" Karen asked.

"Yes, that's me."

"But that's me too," Karen said.

"Same exact name, and you look just like me at your age." The older Karen sparkled at the coincidence.

Karen laughed. "My father says Hardy must be a hardy name. There are so many Mormon Hardy pioneer families around Utah."

"Is that your mom out there with the fundamentalist lady?" The clerk lowered her voice to a whisper.

Karen nodded. She felt a surge of courage from being alone in Samuel's with money to spend. Curiosity, with a life of its own, stirred and bubbled to the surface.

"You're not LDS, are you?" Karen asked.

"No, not any more. I'm helping my uncle close out the store before I finish my last year of college in Arizona."

Karen stopped counting out her cash.

"You used to be Mormon, and now you're not?" Karen knew this was impertinent but was unrepentant.

The clerk didn't seem to mind. She laughed. "That sums it up, honey."

Karen glanced outside at Mom and DeLanna and plunged ahead. "Are there nice people in Arizona, or are they all evil and mean like some people say?"

The clerk laughed again and reached out to give Karen a reassuring tap on the shoulder. "I'll tell you something. There's a big mixed-up world of all kinds of people wherever you go."

"Gee whiz, thanks," Karen said. "I don't usually get to meet people from other places and never, non-Mormons."

The clerk's face lit up. She glanced around. "Wait here. I'm going to ask my uncle about a bright idea I have." She disappeared through a door at the rear of the shop.

Karen waited and wondered what was happening. The clerk opened the door and motioned her into the back room.

"I have a few things to show you." From a bottom shelf, she pulled out a carton of clothes. "These are damaged items. I was planning to donate them to Deseret Industries, but Uncle said I can let you have them for twenty-five cents each if you want. I told him it's your birthday and all."

"Yes." Karen grinned. "Thank you. But… but… I don't know what to say…"

"Good. Let's see what's in here," the older Karen said.

The two rummaged through and found a dress, two skirts and a blouse in the right size. "And I have the missing buttons you can sew on."

The clerk picked the buttons out of a flat nylon stocking box and put them in Karen's envelope.

"I thought I used up my birthday wish this morning, but I guess I'm getting extra wishes this year."

The saleslady laughed and dug to the bottom of the box. "Do you think your mom would let you have a couple of bras?"

Karen gulped. She wasn't sure what mother would say but was in no mood to worry about it now. "Yes, I do."

"Well, let's see, here's one with the little bow between the cups torn off. Oh, and here's another one. These look like your size."

"I don't know what to say… I heard you have to have bras in the shower room at school and all."

"Yes," the clerk said. "That's okay. Good luck in junior high and happy birthday. We Karen Hardys have to stick together."

"Goodbye, and thank you again." As she turned to leave, she saw Mother about to enter the store. Sister DeLanna was gone.

Karen held up her shopping bags as she pushed through the door out to the sidewalk. "Look, Mother, I bought two dresses and three skirts with blouses. They were cheaper than cloth and patterns. And even brassieres." She whispered the last word near Mother's ear.

Mother's mouth drew a deep frown. She seemed too distracted to take her usual interest in Karen's purchases. "I guess it's okay if the blouses and dresses have necks and sleeves that cover you up," is all she said after Karen told her about her luck with the saleslady.

"What about the raid?" Karen whispered as they turned toward the car.

"It's terrible news," Mother answered. "The feds arrested Brother Heber right in front of DeLanna and two other sister-wives. Some of the kids saw it happen. She's leaving fundamentalism to get a job to feed her children. Brother Heber is in jail and his followers are bolting. They've said they won't be paying him tithing from now on. There's barely money for his first wife, none for the others. I'm afraid the latter days are numbered, Karen."

Karen shifted the packages in her arms. "But Brother Heber's group is smaller than Brother LeGrande's."

"I know that, Karen."

"Mother, Brother LeGrande prophesied that the feds would only go after the big groups."

"Karen!" Mother's voice was exasperated. "On the way home, could you just let me concentrate on my driving? I'm wrung dry."

"Yes."

Karen wouldn't think about raids. She hoped days could go on forever. Mormon doctrine about world destruction, combined with talk about World War III and atom bombs, frightened Karen and her friends. She hated the word "latter." She had new clothes and wanted a future of school days to wear them.

"We're not driving home yet. So can I ask something else? What kind of job can DeLanna get? She can't type or anything, can she?"

"No, but I told her the Lord would provide if she fasted and prayed hard enough."

"Couldn't we go back to Woolworth's?" Karen asked. "I have money left for a purse and some neck scarves."

"I know you need a purse this year for school. But don't worry. You'll have it. You'll get presents tonight. That's enough for now. I'm worn to a frazzle. And we need to get home right away. I want to warn Rhonda and Millie about raids." Mother gnawed on her lip.

That's fear on Mother's face, Karen thought, as she slammed the car door. Karen was also frightened. Not all of Brother LeGrande's followers had plural wives. Karen was relieved Father still had only one. But he and Mother had said people could go to jail just for protecting polygamists. Karen hugged the packages in her lap. She and Mother barely spoke on the drive home. The world was teetering. She could use another birthday wish, a revelation of her future.

CHAPTER 12

THE JEWISH GENTILE

Oblivious to the office din, Ben thought about smoking a Camel. Peppermint Life Savers flavored his coffee, his beer, and every conversation. He tried not to think about how his hotshot FBI coworkers back in Denver would be undercutting him. Thinking about not thinking, never worked.

"Ben," Julie called. The secretary held the phone out to him.

Her voice barely pierced his reverie. He'd gladly exchange three square meals today for one cigarette. The image of Sylvia's sweet pout restrained him.

Ben put the phone to his ear and shielded the mouthpiece. Seeking a modicum of privacy, he turned his back to Jack, who sat beside him buried in file folders.

"Hello, Sylvia?"

"Ben, you told me not to call you at work, but I can't help it. Have you thought about our conversation?"

"Yes, but this isn't the time."

"Ben, I miss you. You promised you'd always be with me."

"And I am with you in spirit. You knew what I meant when I said that."

"Yes, bubee, but…"

"Sylvia, this kvetching is tiresome. The situation is no picnic for me either. Be brave, honey."

"I know I'm a silly goose. I'll let you do your work. I can stand it a little longer. Just remember, you swore to me you wouldn't touch cigarettes while you're away."

In the end, they finished the call as usual. He said, "Sylvia, you're my girl, and I love you."

"Love you more, my bubee." She giggled goodbye.

He stared out the window at the craggy mountains, beautiful, but not as stunning or as hospitable as the ones back home.

A soldier strutted by the window in his crisp dress uniform. He halted beside a stone sundial atop a knoll, where he ogled passing women. A secretary clicked by in high heels, returning to the building from an afternoon break. He whistled. She sped by, but blushed in acknowledgement.

"Ben!" Jack nudged his elbow. "Thinking about your ball and chain back home?"

Ben pursed his lips. "We've been through every file of every known plyg group in Utah. He slid a folder over to Jack. "This file on the Kingstons looks interesting. They're a huge cult for this part of the state."

"Yes, but they're ingrown. They marry off daughters to half-brothers and double-uncles. The Kingston group would consider my sis or the girl you're tracking to be untouchables. Gentiles."

"What are you talking about? Gentiles?"

"To Mormons, that's a slur word. It means any non-Mormon. All of them are officially termed unworthy."

"You're telling me the Mormons think they're Jews?"

"Not exactly, they think they're Israelites and Jews are only from the tribe of Judah."

Ben scratched his head. "So, do they consider me to be a Jew or a gentile?"

"Hmm, according to Mormons, probably a little of both."

"Oy! I need a new roll of Life Savers." He wadded the empty wrapper and tossed it dead center into the waste basket.

"Not bad. Net only." Jack stretched in his chair and folded his hands behind his head. "Of course each plyg cult considers the mainstream Mormons to be apostate outsiders. Some of those cults classify every person on earth, except the handful in their little circle, to be in that detestable class."

Ben covered his mouth and rasped to clear his throat of excess peppermint.

"Hold it." Jack peered out the window. "Shortarm's on 25th Street, headed this way."

"Shortarm?" Chief Walker turned from a nearby filing cabinet. "That bum? Stay away from the lowlifes." He slammed the drawer shut.

Jack tossed down the Kingston file. "Just checking out leads." He shrugged.

"I have a lead for you." The chief fluttered a sheet of paper between them on the desk. "Looks like the FBI and local police team in Salt Lake could use help. They're feeling the pinch from stirring up a hornet's nest down at Short Creek. Give 'em a call. Offer your services. I'll do the paperwork to make you part of their taskforce. And remember what I told you. Don't let this polygamy stuff tarnish our department up here. Our jurisdiction is clean."

"You're ordering us to stand down?" Jack asked.

"You heard me. Keep your noses clean." Chief Walker hurried off toward Julie, who motioned him to the phone.

Jack stuffed the Chief's paper in his shirt pocket, glanced at Ben and pointed to the door. Ben stacked their folders. Before leaving, he said, "Remember that Mormon girl brought you brownies. You said you'd give them to Shortarm?"

He grabbed the box. "Yeah, yeah, yeah."

In the hall Ben bristled. "Call Salt Lake if you must, but I have no intention of staying in this state a minute longer than necessary."

"Can't blame you for that." Jack held the door and led Ben to where Shortarm waited.

"What's cookin'?" Jack asked. He put the brownies on the bench.

"I seen that bishop, Jack. That one from Cloverdale."

Ben realized Shortarm reeked of mothballs. The odor wafted off a donor's shiny suit jacket, two sizes too large for Shortarm's thin frame.

"This time he wasn't in the bar. I seen him over by that Mormon stake building. And, this is the good part. He was bending your police chief's ear." Shortarm grimaced at the police office windows.

Shortarm's stance and speech were steady. He had cut back on his booze.

"Did you hear what they said?"

"No, 'fraid not. But I could tell they was well acquainted."

"So they were friendly?" Jack asked.

"No, more like they knew each other enough so's neither guy trusted the other one."

"No kidding?" Jack pulled a few bucks from his pocket and held them out to Shortarm.

"What were you doing on that end of town?" Jack asked.

"Eddie's got me hooked up with the Catholic Church. You know the one where he used to go to school back when his mom was workin' the Ko Ko Mo?"

Jack nodded.

"The priest helps people like me. He's givin' me a place to stay. And he's signed me up with a bunch of other guys down on their luck. We have meetings in the church basement. The priest says they might help me out."

Jack patted Shortarm's shoulder. "Good for Eddie."

"One more thing." Shortarm waved a crumpled scrap torn from a brown paper bag. Ben glimpsed pencil scrawls as Jack reached for it.

"I done real good." Shortarm beamed. "Gotcha the bishop's license number."

CHAPTER 13

A QUESTION OF WORTHINESS

Between bites of meatloaf and buttered beets Karen eyed her birthday gifts stacked in the rocking chair. The family knew to watch their Ps and Qs at birthday dinners. Karen counted on their full attention. She described each purchase at Samuel's, leaving out the part about the clerk being an ex-Mormon from Arizona.

"Not fair," Rosemary said. "I can't go to the sale with Carol and Belma until Thursday. By then everything will be picked over. Eat faster," she said to Judy and Davy. "Don't be such slow pokes. I don't have all day. You want some of that chocolate cake I baked, don't you?"

They finally patted their full tummies and then each other's. Rosemary was already hurrying to the table with the lighted layer cake. The family sang quickly before the candles melted into the frosting.

"Mmm," Judy said. "Yummy cake."

"Yumbly, crumbly," Davy said. He and Judy giggled at his poetry.

Father agreed. "It's excellent. You'll make a fine housewife for some lucky fellow, Rosemary. Be certain he's worthy."

Karen took a bite. "This chocolate cake is better than the coconut one I saw at Woolworth's this morning."

"I spent half the afternoon baking it," Rosemary said. "So I didn't have time to dress up for my date with Todd."

"Todd, again?" Richard put down his fork.

"Yes, but the point is I'm really rushed." Rosemary whisked plates off the table and removed the candle stubs from the cake to save for the next birthday. "Karen, hurry up. Open the presents. Let's see what you got."

"Yes, go ahead," Father said.

Karen ripped paper off a shoe box with navy flats from Mother and Father. She slipped them on.

"I'll wear these with my new navy dress tonight," she said. "I can't wait."

Rosemary handed her a tidy square package with a neat bow. Karen squealed at a boxy little handbag, also navy. "No more old envelopes for my money." She compared the shades of navy. "I'm glad I didn't buy a purse today."

Richard's gift was obviously a book, still in a store bag.

"Hardy Boys?" she asked him. "Is this a girl book?"

"It's a classy book for anyone. You always talk about the outside world. This book tells about it. Besides, they might be relatives of ours."

Davy and Judy gave her a red neck scarf and hand-colored pictures. Karen laughed at Davy's picture of the family. He had drawn himself bigger than everyone. Judy explained her colorful scribbles, saying she was following Davy over a rainbow.

After the celebration, Rosemary dashed upstairs, then yelled back at Karen. "You'll be late for your Bishop interview and your first Mutual meeting. Ya better get a move on."

*   *   *

All of Cloverdale's twelve and thirteen-year-olds chattered and milled in the jammed basement hallway at the Mormon ward house. Karen saw Amy wedged against the door to Bishop Taylor's office. Her best friend stood out from the others because instead of pale skin and hair, she had an olive glow and maple brown hair. Thick glasses concealed dark expressive eyes and lashes.

"Excuse me," Karen said to Enoch and his friend, Dwayne. She edged her way toward Amy. Those boys would always remind her of the scary night when she heard them stealing the Bishop's watermelons.

Enoch's answer was a swift elbow to her left breast. She gasped, wondering if he knew how sore and tender twelve-year-old chests could be.

"Karen," a boy said, "has asked to be excused, not elbowed, Enoch."

"Well, la-dee-da, Brian. Who died and made you boss?"

Karen gave Brian a crooked smile and made her way over to him. "Thank you." She said it so only he could hear. She meant it sincerely. Until this gallant gesture she had considered Brian's nose too large, and his eyes too small, but no more.

Brian blushed. "Eh, you look really swell, Karen," he whispered.

Enoch, Dwayne, and the other boys whistled at the two. "Who cares what roughnecks think," Karen whispered. "I just hope his warts aren't catchin."

Brian frowned. "They might be but I haven't caught them from being forced to shake his hand. At least we know the freckles aren't catchin." They laughed.

The teenaged boys held the Aaronic Priesthood. This designated them at the entry level on the path toward becoming Mormon Gods of their own planets after life on earth. Older male teens and men held the Melchizedek Priesthood. They could speak for God in conferring blessings, do high-level church duties, and sometimes receive messages from God.

Girls had no such designations. Their duty was to uphold the male Priesthood and to become helpmeets on earth and in heaven.

Amy waved. She edged along the wall and past the crowd to greet Karen. "Did he hurt you?"

"Yes, but I tried not to let him know it, or he'd do it again."

"I know," Amy said and squeezed Karen's arm. "Look at these guys jabbing people, burping, and… ugh…," she whispered, "doing even worse than burping." Her cheeks reddened as she turned her back on a loud fart and follow up hoots and jeers. "They were always rude," she went on, "but they're twice as bad now that they have the Aaronic Priesthood."

"Yeah, just think how bad they'll be when they get the Melchizedek Priesthood. They'll think they're halfway to the Celestial Kingdom and being Gods already." Karen whispered the word "God," hoping she wasn't taking a Holy Name in vain.

"Are you scared about the interview?" Amy asked.

"Yeah. My mom told me to say 'Yes' to commandments, 'No' to sins, and don't ask questions."

"That's what my mom told me," Amy answered. "Except not the part about questions." She laughed. "You're the one who thinks questions are the same as breathing."

"Not this time," Karen said. "Cross my heart."

The girls sat against the wall to chit-chat. Karen told Amy about the shopping trip and her new clothes. She described the presents and cake. She was careful not to talk about the news of the polygamy raid.

"Amy, do you worry about the end of the latter days?"

"Yes, sometimes, now that I know what 'latter' means." She laughed. "I used to think the word was 'ladder' and meant we had to climb step by righteous step."

"I remember we used to talk about why ladders were important at church. But, Amy, I sometimes worry about latter days until I can't breathe and my stomach hurts."

"Don't," Amy answered. "Remember, the end can't come until the moon turns red. It's a revelation. Just look at the moon and feel safe when it's still yellow."

"Wow, that's good to know. The best thing about turning twelve is seeing you in mutual. I missed you back in primary after your birthday and they graduated you out."

"Me too," Amy said.

The interviews took only two or three minutes. Each person came out waving a small paper and leaving the door ajar for the next to enter. Nancy, the girl in front of Amy emerged from the office.

"Well, I'm up." Amy groaned. "Wish me luck."

Every possible question and answer meandered through Karen's brain as she waited. Her eight year old baptism interview with the bishop had been a cinch. But this was different. She dreaded the possibility of exposing her family to raids and prosecution if she made a mistake.

A grinning Amy reappeared with her recommend. Karen read, *"Limited-Use Recommend for Members ages 12 and Older to Baptize for the Dead. Good for one year."*

"Go on in," Amy said. "It's a piece of cake, birthday cake." She laughed.

Karen's heart fluttered like hummingbird wings. She inched open the door and stepped into an office lined with shelves and filing cabinets. The only decoration was a painting of the current Mormon Prophet, Seer, and Revelator, President David O. McKay, framed in ornate gold. The president's pale wrinkled face, much like Brother LeGrande's, wore a sweet smile and was topped with mounds of white, billowing hair, like whipped cream on a bowl of vanilla ice cream. Karen averted her eyes.

Bishop Taylor lounged in his chair with his feet propped on his desk. He peered over his oxblood-and-white dress shoes and said, "Hi, neighbor."

Karen had watched Lucinda's mother polish those two-toned shoes for him in her little house with no hot water or toilet.

"Hello, Bishop Taylor." Karen sat on a slick cold folding chair across from his desk.

The bishop was the only middle-aged man Karen knew who sported the new crew-cut hair. With his brown suit he wore a swirly yellow tie, loosened at the collar of his white shirt. The sacred garment neckline barely showed. Karen usually saw him with a shovel propped on his shoulder when he crossed her yard to go to and from his fields. His workaday uniform was overalls and rubber hip-boots which he needed to wade into irrigation ditches and flooded fields. He seemed out of place in a suit and behind a desk.

"How's it going, Karen?" he asked, sitting straight. His callused hands with dirt-caked fingernails and cuticles shuffled through paper. "Remind your father to let me know when he's ready to sell the farm back to me. Small family farms like his can't make it in this day and age, especially when the… a… farmer has a town job."

"Eh… I don't know about that. I'm sorry."

"Yeah, that's okay. Here's a clean form for your replies." The bishop read from a book. "I represent the Lord in determining worthiness to enter His Holy Temple. Recommend holders must live up to Church standards, even those who will only be doing proxy baptisms for the dead." He sniffed and met her eye.

"Yes, I know," Karen answered.

"You see, Karen, I'm a farmer, but the Lord has called me to cultivate souls for Him. So, if you are in need of counsel, you can count on me. Parents sometimes need help with teenagers. That's my job. It's like when your father calls in the cows for milking. He might need Spud to chase down an errant heifer now and again. I do Spud's job for this ward."

"Uh… uh…" Karen paused, trying to think of what to say but came up short. "Thank you," she finally answered.

"Do you believe in God?" The bishop was all business, reading again from his list of questions.

"Yes." Trying to conceal her nervousness, Karen sat primly in her new navy dress and shoes.

"Do you sustain the president of the Church?" He nodded at the portrait.

"Yes."

"Do you live the Word of Wisdom?"

"Yes."

"So no one you know uses alcohol, tobacco, tea, or coffee?"

Karen remembered Lucinda's mom making coffee on camping trips. She hesitated and said, "No."

The bishop pulled back at Karen's hesitation. "Tell the whole truth, young lady. Does your family live the Word of Wisdom?"

"Yes."

"Do you pay your full ten percent tithe?"

"Yes."

"Do you affiliate with any group or individual whose teachings or practices are contrary to, or oppose, those accepted by the Church, or do you sympathize with any apostates or polygamists?"

"No." Karen kept her voice steady. She refused to think about polygamy raids, court cases, or excommunication.

"Are you honest?"

"Yes."

"Do you attend all required church meetings unless you are too sick?"

"Yes." Karen kept her mind on the regular Mormon meetings, not the ones with the fundamentalists.

"Do you live the law of chastity?"

She knew chastity was somehow related to purity, but wasn't exactly certain what either word meant.

"Yes, if it's a commandment, I do it."

"You don't sound so sure of that. Remember, Karen, the Lord has given me the power of discernment. He'll reveal to me if you lie. Are you chaste?"

"Uh- huh."

"I see." The Bishop's brow furrowed. He deviated from his printed questions. "Do you masturbate, Karen?"

She hesitated, not knowing what to say. Masturbating must be somehow related to chastity, but what could it mean? She couldn't ask questions. Not here, not now.

The bishop squinted at her and pushed his papers away. He tapped his fingers. His eyes widened. He seemed determined to pry something out of her. She hoped he'd blink. Instead his eyes bulged.

"Well, Karen?"

"Bishop, I keep all of the commandments as best I can, especially the ones I understand. This is my first day of being twelve and out of primary. The other kids here at mutual may know more commandments than I do. But I'll be learning."

Bishop Taylor rubbed his eyes. He looked confused and tired.

"Let's put it this way, do you treat your body as a Holy Tabernacle of the Almighty Lord?" He aimed a shaking finger at her.

"Well, yes, I do as best I can. I don't use coffee or tobacco, but my mother says sometimes I use too much sugar when I bake. I won't do that anymore if it's a sin. I know the Church says bodies are Tabernacles."

"Are you being square with me, Karen?"

She searched for something, anything to appease him.

"I know my body is a Tabernacle, but sometimes I forget to wash my feet, and I know cleanliness is next to Godliness. But I don't think getting a little dirty is always a sin because some-times you and your family forget to wash up too." She caught herself glancing at the grime ground into the cracks of the bishop's hands.

Bishop Taylor's mouth moved but didn't speak. His throat emitted a growly sound like Spud when he was threatened.

Karen felt herself squirm and blush. "Uh, I mean when you have dirty chores like irrigating or plowing, or shoveling out the cow stalls."

Bishop Taylor's face reddened and twitched.

"...but of course bishops know best," Karen finished.

Karen folded her hands and sat in silence. Quiet humbleness might work on him. She focused on his sloppy necktie knot to avoid staring at his dirt-caked fingernails.

Neither spoke.

Karen set her face into a placid mask. She thought about her namesake in Samuel's and the easy comfort of talking to her. Bishop Taylor was not a person to go to with problems no more than Brother LeGrande or her own mother or father.

Another minute slogged by.

The bishop caved first. "I'm checking off that you live the law of chastity and that includes no masturbating. Is that the truth, young lady?"

"Yes, Bishop Taylor."

He scribbled on his form and on a slip of paper he tossed at her. "Remember to see me if you are tempted by the flesh. No decent LDS boy will want you unless your body is pure."

His harsh tone startled her.

"And tell your father I won't wait forever to take that weed-infested farm off his hands. I can't even catch watermelon thieves with your family sitting smack dab in the middle of my holdings."

"Goodbye," Karen said, picking up her recommend. She read it as she left. It took longer to achieve, but was exactly like Amy's.

Passing by, Enoch said, "What took you so long? You been breaking commandments? Not such a goody two shoes after all, are ya?"

Karen cringed. "The bishop was talking about watermelon thieves. Sounds like he might know who the punks are. He'll get 'em and they'll be sorry." She glared into Enoch's pig-like freckle specked face. "Your turn. What are you waiting for?"

*   *   *

Mother and Father were still awake when she returned home.

"You received one more gift tonight." Mother smiled and handed her the small package.

Karen ripped off pink paper to find a fuzzy blue box. She lifted out a thin silver chain with an oval locket, decorated with a serpentine design. She opened it. Inside was engraved "MEANT TO BE."

The card was from Brother LeGrande.

Karen dropped it back into the box.

"Oh my, how nice." Mother said. "The prophet must have had a sign about you. Perhaps you were more valiant in the preexistence than anyone could have known."

"Karen, you must be growing up," Father said.

"Brother LeGrande isn't even a relative," Karen said. "I can't believe this."

Karen was confused and embarrassed. She wanted to wish away the locket and pretend it never happened. I've had enough to worry about today, she thought, and snapped the box shut.

She climbed the stairs to bed.

CHAPTER 14

SON OF ZION

The groomed lawns and flower gardens outside the police station reminded Ben of the university in Boulder. Pink roses near the window reminded him of Sylvia. They were her favorite and almost the only blooms he knew by name.

"Ben," Julie called, "pick up on line three."

"Hello?"

"Ben, honey…"

"Sylvia?" Ben cupped his hand over the telephone receiver and turned his back to the teaming office. "Listen, we just put together a team of informants who know about… you know."

"But Ben."

"I'll try to call you later. I'm at work."

"Yes, bubee, but…"

Ben noticed the chief eying him from across the room. Slow progress, a dead-end environment, no cigarettes, and Sylvia, pouting, again. Enough! He wondered briefly what he saw in her.

"I have to go. Goodbye." He hung up the receiver.

He stared out at the rose bushes and imagined lighting up.

"Ben," Julie called again. He bumped a stack of files to the floor and barely heard her. He bent down and gathered them up.

Julie's cherry-red fingernails tapped the phone on the desk. "Hello, Ben!" He snapped to attention.

"Now hear this!" She mimicked an exaggerated salute. "Eddie's on the phone from the Ko Ko Mo. I can't find Jack, you need to take it."

"Sure, sorry, Julie. Jack's... eh... indisposed at the moment."

"Hi, Eddie. What's up?"

"Hiya, Ben. I have news. Can't talk now. I'll send Shortarm out to meet you and Jack under the dragon at the Star Noodle. Can you be there in five?"

"Oh yeah, that's the Chinese restaurant across from your place. We're on our way. We owe you. Bye. Thanks, Julie. Jack and I will be out of the office for awhile."

"Okey-dokey." Julie lifted her fingers from the typewriter and waggled goodbye, still keeping her eyes on the page.

Ben met Jack outside the men's room. "Eddie called. We're meeting Shortarm at that neon dragon. He'll fill us in. I brought that box of crème puffs from one of your Mormon admirers."

"Let's go."

They hurried out of the building and waded through the seagulls to 25th Street. Ben soaked up raw energy from the sleaze and run-down glitz.

"Quick!" Jack caught his arm and focused on a sequined female who undulated ahead of them down the street. The seedy elegance tempted every kind of sinner, a natural setting for the woman flouncing about in a shimmering dress and swinging her glittering handbag in the sun.

Under his breath, Ben mimicked a wolf whistle. "This street has something for everyone."

"Away from the little woman too long?" Jack winked at him and poked a finger into Ben's chest.

"Oh, shut up!" Ben popped a peppermint into his mouth.

Jack smirked.

A minute later, they stood with necks craned at the garish dragon sign. Orange and red neon bulbs danced up and back along a wriggling dragon, which spit a minor conflagration over the noodle letters and the sidewalk. The green dragon's writhing was every bit as provocative as that of the spangled working girl. "The noodles they serve aren't half as delectable as that sexy dragon," Ben said.

Jack's answer was interrupted.

"Guys!" Shortarm motioned to them from the shadowed doorway. They stepped out of the glare. His face was wan, but held a confident gaze.

"What's up, Shortarm?" Jack's hand reached out, but today Shortarm didn't need the support.

"Eddie sent me special." Shortarm struck a self-important pose. "He says you guys want to gawk at the bishop, the one in there drinkin' sody water. Ain't no law against downing a wet one, is there? Even for the righteous? But anyhow, that's the message."

"We've been out and had a look at where he lives," Ben said, "but haven't seen him face to face. How'll we know him?"

Shortarm laughed, which started him coughing. "He'll be the over-dressed feller, acting guilty. Mormons don't need no signs on their necks, 'cuz of the pokers they got up their asses."

"Easy to spot the orange pop." Jack laughed.

He slipped a couple of dollar bills between Shortarm's fingers and the door frame he clutched. "Have you had a square meal today?"

Trying to remember, Shortarm's face twitched.

"Go on in." Jack opened the café door. "Get yourself a heaping plate of chop suey. And here's some cream puffs for dessert later. That's an order."

"Yes sir, Jack. You're the boss."

Jack put the box of sweets into Shortarm's hand and nudged him inside. He thanked them and headed for a table, all empty at that time of day. They waited until proprietor Billy Yee approached their friend with a menu. Shortarm sat tall, with dignity that only ready cash can buy.

"Let's go," Jack said. Ben followed his graceful stride as they crossed the street and into the Ko Ko Mo. How could such a social klutz move like Fred Astaire, he wondered?

The detectives ignored the men along the bar, including the overdressed one with a crew cut.

After settling in his seat across from Ben, Jack tipped his head in the direction of the brown-suited man. The bishop slumped over an orange Nehi bottle with his face so close Ben worried he would poke his nose into it. In a comical attempt to hide his identity, he shielded his face with a hand along either side of his ears. *Bump-a-thump. Sigh, bump-a-thump.* He couldn't seem to restrain the toes of his oxblood-and-white shoes from tapping a message of guilt on the wooden foot rail, like a sheepish kid, waiting for the principal.

Ben and Jack smiled up at Eddie as he approached with two mugs.

"Thanks," they said together.

"Too busy to talk now." Eddie rolled his eyes at the bishop on the barstool, and bustled back to fold towels.

Jack held up his mug. "Here's to us," he said softly. "We managed to avoid gettin' into that messy Jessup raid in Bountiful the other night. No leads there to help either one of us."

"Right," Ben said clinking his mug against Jack's. I just hope we can avoid Salt Lake entanglements as well. No way will I be caught up in dead-end surveillance work."

The bishop emptied the soda bottle into his glass and downed it. He stood and used his hand to cover a burp, then waited at the cash register to pay.

Eddie turned away from the man and wiped at a spot on the counter as if he were polishing a work of art. He stood back to admire his effort before he sauntered over to ring up the charges. He fumbled in the change drawer, seemingly unable to decide which coins to choose. Either Eddie had contracted a sudden case of aging bones or was deliberately keeping the bishop waiting.

"Here you go, sir." With plodding deliberation, Eddie counted out the change to the penny.

Under the watchful eye of the elk head, the stoic-faced customer fidgeted and waited to pocket his handful of coins and make a quick getaway.

Eddie held out his empty palm to Ben and Jack. "My tip. He never leaves one. And I'd have twice the business if tightwad bishops like him didn't punish anyone they catch coming in here."

From the window, Jack, Ben, and Eddie watched the bishop head to the whore house on the corner. He paused for a furtive glance left and right before he pulled off his swirly tie, pocketed it, then entered.

The three broke into laughter. "Good job, Eddie." Jack gave a thumbs-up. "We happened to see one of the little tarts from that establishment when we were comin' here."

"She has her first customer for today." Eddie swiveled his hip and grinned.

"Shall we have a pool on how long he takes in there?" Jack quipped.

Ben flipped open his notebook to jot a quick sentence. "Looks like Jack and I need to pay the bishop a call."

Eddie bent over, shielded his face to mimic the bishop's guilty antics. "That guy's nervous as a cat. He'll be ready to spill the beans as soon as you drop a hint or two about his extracurricular activities."

"Sure, he's nervous around here," Ben said. "That's because he's worried those gals may not get his priesthood powers up."

Eddie snickered. "Ben, consider yourself a son of Zion."

"Oh." He laughed. "So I'm no longer a gentile, but it's by adoption?"

Ben used his notebook to salute and returned it to his breast pocket. "Thank you, Eddie. What's the payoff for your efforts?"

"What do ya mean?" Jack asked. "He's well paid. The police, including me, don't check into any of the more serious sin and debauchery that goes on in the underground."

Ben raised his bushy eyebrows. "Underground?"

"Yeah. There's stuff happening every day down in secret tunnels below our very feet."

"Tunnels?" Ben perked up. "You're serious?"

"Sure am." Jack raised a finger. "It's like Swiss cheese under this bar and beneath all of 25th Street. This part of town is a regular Little Chicago. Right, Eddie?"

"Come on! Sure we have basements, and some of 'em might connect. But so what?" Eddie tapped his chest, like a schoolboy proud to be teacher's pet. "I'm helping you boys out of the goodness of my heart."

CHAPTER 15

YOUTH TEMPLE EXCURSION

Karen dressed in her new print skirt and blouse to travel to the temple with her friends. They had proudly passed their bishop's worthiness interviews and earned recommends for entry to the Lord's sanctuary where prophets walk and commune with Jesus in the world of spirits.

Down in the kitchen she sliced cheese and dark bread for a sandwich and with fumbling fingers she wrapped it in waxed paper. She knew there were ghosts waiting for her in the temple to be baptized. She wondered if she should fear them more or the living people who would scrutinize her. Her belly ached with worry.

Once the baptisms were done, the kids could gossip and giggle over picnic food in Pioneer Park. Summer would soon end and she had missed her friends, especially, Amy. With a calmer hand she packed her lunch into a brown-paper sack.

Mom's bulging abdomen bumped the counter as she sliced potatoes. "Karen, run and dump these spud peelings and slops to the pigs."

"But, Mother, I'm all dressed up. Amy and her dad will pick me up any minute."

"Remember, young lady, this is your first temple excursion. Everyone will be watching you, so mind your Ps and Qs."

"I know."

"Hurry up so you won't keep Brother Gilbert waiting."

Karen dumped the peels into the slops bucket of sour milk and dish scrapings. Spud met her outside. "Down, boy. Stay back." She patted him gingerly to keep his muddy paws off her skirt.

The rising sun streaked the mountain peaks where the last snow had finally melted from the shaded ridges. The sow and two yet unsold piglets rooted at the empty trough. Karen stood back from the grimy fence and dumped the slops and set off a frenzy of grunting and snorting. The smells aggravated her nervous stomach. With a hand pressed into her belly, she dashed off.

Scurrying toward the clotheslines, she heard someone clear his throat. Brother LeGrande appeared in cracked leather bedroom slippers with his shirt unbuttoned. The breeze batted his cloud of uncombed white hair. He had an even smile that reminded her of the magical beasts in fairytale books.

"Karen, I noticed you through the trailer window. You're growing into a lovely young woman." He sipped a heavy green mug of Postum.

"Morning, Brother LeGrande."

"Did you get the birthday locket I sent you, and are you wearing it?" His eyes dropped to her neckline.

"Uh, yes. It's pretty, but I haven't worn it yet."

His smile soured.

"You're all dressed up so bright and early. Now why don't you run in and put on that birthday locket before you leave?"

"I'm going to the Salt Lake Temple and jewelry isn't allowed."

"Then I understand. Enjoy the experience. Entering the temple is a transition, an adult awakening for young people. You're a woman or nearly so. And remember, next time I see you, I'll expect to see the locket on your neck."

Karen turned in time to dodge the fingers he extended toward her cheek. Talking to Brother LeGrande churned up familiar anxiety which added to her dread of doing dead Temple work.

As soon as Brother Gilbert pulled up, Karen hopped inside with Amy and at the church they parked behind a yellow school bus. The girls heard raucous crowing as they jumped out and walked past the circle of young show-off deacon boys. Brian Nelson smiled up and waved to Karen.

Amy nudged glasses off her nose. "I saw that look he gave you. What a dreamboat." She socked Karen's shoulder.

"And you know, he stuck up for me to Enoch at the bishop interviews."

The two girls joined Camille and Nancy near a sign, "Church of Jesus Christ of Latter-day Saints, Cloverdale Ward." Camille Hardy, a third cousin, was a stately blonde whose father was almost as rich as Bishop Taylor. She liked to brag about shopping at Samuels early every season for the best selection before markdowns.

Nancy's clothes were homemade, but always fashioned from the latest fabrics and Butterick patterns. She fluffed the plaid bows tied to long dark ponytails then flipped them off her shoulders. "I was so, so afraid," she said, "that my period wouldn't be over in time for this Temple excursion." She twiddled a curled tip of one ponytail.

"Why's that?" Karen asked.

"Come on, don't you know you're not allowed in the Temple font if it's your period?" Nancy rolled her eyes and brushed her lip with the curl of hair. "Have you heard of 'being on the rag?' That's what Anne Marie is. So she's stuck at home. Gosh, it's like she's broadcasting her time of the month. The boys might never get over it!"

"I don't have to worry," Karen said. "I haven't started yet."

"Well, it's a curse." Camille tossed her bouncy pageboy with authority. "You're the youngest girl here, but you'll find out soon enough."

Karen and Amy took front seats in the bus for the forty-mile journey. The boys bumped and pushed to nab the long bench seat in the back where their antics might go unnoticed.

Brother Dale Taylor, the Bishop's nephew, stood, a hand raised to command attention. His pinched nose and upturned chin reminded these human charges to knuckle under, the same expectation he had for his family and the young steers he bred. His unenviable church calling was to rein in the twelve to thirteen year old deacons, the ward's youngest and rowdiest beginning-level Aaronic Priesthood holders. "Bow your heads. I'll offer up a word of prayer," and his scowl deepened.

"Our dear Heavenly Father, we come before Thee as our youth depart on a special excursion to Thy holy Salt Lake Temple. We ask Thee to bless this day with Thy presence. We pray humbly that the special souls on the other side of the veil will accept Thy restored gospel as these young people are immersed in their stead. Bless us that we will maintain a spirit of reverence throughout this most especial of days. We say this InthenameofJesusChrist, Amen."

A smattering of voices chorused, "Amen."

Karen was used to hearing *especial* and *special* in church settings more often than *the,* or *and.*

The girls' mutual leader, Sister Viva stood, her hand also held high, a female taskmaster, tight in every way, from her lips and narrow shoulders, to her officious mannerisms. Karen and some of her friends secretly scoffed at these cranky well-meaning saints and how they used steely voices and evil eyes to demand compliance.

"Remember," Sister Viva said, "We're on a special mission for the Lord. Salt Lake is the capital city. Non-Mormon tourists flock there. It behooves us to set shining examples for these prospective converts. And please thank your especial mothers if they donated the special cupcakes or lemonade for our picnic."

The kids clapped and the boys pierced the stale air with shrill whistles through their teeth.

Brother Dale shouted. "Remember, no light-mindedness. In Plain City we'll load up their deacons and Beehive girls and then head out."

The bus lurched onto the highway. Karen and Amy flattened their palms to the ceiling to deflect the pitching and avoid slamming their heads.

The Plain City group soon piled in. Red-faced and exuberant, they yelled hellos and landed friendly pokes at Karen, Amy and the other kids they hadn't seen all summer. Sister Viva and Brother Dale quashed quarrels over seating as Sister Luetta and Brother Gerrick, the Plain City youth leaders, finally climbed aboard. They didn't attend Karen's church ward but she recognized them from the quarterly stake meetings held in Ogden. Already looking frazzled, the two slid into the last empty seat in front of the no-man's-land back bench.

Brother Dale's brow furled and he pointed at Karen then Amy. "You two, switch seats with the Plain City leaders. Adults shouldn't have to bounce around back there. Now let's get going."

Karen and Amy groaned and everyone else cheered as they changed seats.

"Not fair," Karen whispered.

"Sure isn't." Amy's scowl faded in a moment, and her eyes lit up, a look that meant she had juicy news to tell. "Guess what?" She lifted her arm and pointed under it. "I got my blood type tattoo."

"My gosh! It must of hurt like crazy?"

"Yes, but not now."

"My mom says we can't afford them, and I'm glad. She says we have to trust our fate to Jesus, and not to tattoos."

"They only cost three dollars, and my mom says even non-Mormon kids in the outside world will be getting them. Everybody's scared of the A-bomb."

Karen winced and gazed out the window at a woman digging in one of her garden plots.

"What's wrong?" Amy asked. "Are you still worried about destruction in the last days?"

"Well, yeah. There's the A-bomb drills at school and my family can't afford an underground shelter. And lately, the Church is saying good Mormons will have to pack their two-year supplies and flee to Missouri after everybody else is dead. Jesus will descend there, it's pretty scary. Kids getting blood type tattoos. All because so many parents and doctors will probably get killed. I hate it!"

"Yes, but we're just kids. And Jesus loves children. The bomb'll only smite the wicked. You and I are pretty righteous. We pay tithing and don't lie or even cheat on tests."

The guilt of telling lies grated on Karen's raw nerves. "I can sometimes forget about latter-day destruction during the daytime." Karen folded her arms against her belly. "I guess right now I'm just dreading being baptized for dead people in the Temple."

"Why's that?"

"For one thing, what if the spirits don't want to be Mormon?"

Amy laughed. "You're such a worrywart. We're doing them a gigantic favor. Everyone wants to be a Mormon."

"Well, maybe so." Karen ignored someone kicking the seat from behind.

"I can't wait. It'll be fun." Amy's glasses slipped and she perched them back up. "Don't you want to see the font? It's pure gold and it's sitting on twelve solid gold oxen."

"That can't be, not pure gold. The ward only has a cement font for live-people baptisms."

"Well, today we'll find out," Amy said. "And we get to have a picnic."

"Yes," Karen said. "That'll be so much fun when the dunking's over."

Amy laughed. "Just like you calling baptism 'dunking.'"

The back-seat ruffians hooted. One guy socked his fist into the next shoulder. "Pass it on!"

The pummeling dominoed from one boy to the next, gaining force as it traveled up and down the line.

"Yeeowee! Take that. Pass it on."

"No! You take it. You pass it on."

Boys slugged until they were falling on the floor to avoid the next punch.

"What'sa matter? Ya YELLA?" Enoch barked so loudly Karen flinched. She hated him for his bullying, but just as much because he grew things on his body no one wanted to see. His angular head sprouted cowlick devil horns, and on his face the freckles looked like fly specks massed on an abandoned picnic hamper. Worst though, were the grimy warts knobbing every one of his knuckles and distorting his fingernails.

A chewed glob of lunch bag flew into Karen's lap. She turned in time to see Enoch smirk at her with his finger up his nose as he chomped another paper wad.

"Enoch, cut it out," Karen snapped. "Didn't you hear Brother Dale and Sister Viva?"

He slapped his speckled cheeks in mock horror and gazed at the ceiling. Karen didn't look away fast enough to avoid gagging over the horrid wart infestation.

"Oooh, Karen is pretty tough, today, eh guys?"

"Settle down, Enoch," Amy said. "We have to be examples."

"Well then, for example, where's Anne Marie?" Enoch turned to Dwayne and used a stage whisper. "Why do girls sometimes get banned from going to the Temple?"

"I could never guess, Enoch," Dwayne answered. "Does it have anything to do with a rag?"

"None of your beeswax," Karen yelled. "Just shut up!"

Sister Viva stood. "I'm coming back there. I heard someone say 'Shut up' and we're barely started. Didn't any of you pay attention to Brother Dale's prayer?"

Enoch, with an angelic smile, raised his hand. "I know who said it, Sister Viva."

"All right, Enoch. Who was it?"

"Karen said it to me for no reason."

"Is that true, Karen?"

"Uh, yeah. But he was being mean to Anne Marie."

"She isn't even here today, Karen, dear." The word 'dear' came out sounding more like 'brat.' "Brother Dale and I were hoping you and Amy could be special examples for the boys. Instead, you're setting them off. Now everyone settle down."

"But—" Karen protested.

"No buts, Karen. Enough!" Sister Viva turned and navigated back up the aisle around kids' flailing limbs.

Enoch elbowed Dwayne and winked at Karen.

Karen and Amy fumed and watched farms and gas stations fly by outside the bus. They soon bumped shoulders and relaxed into a quiet chat for the next thirty miles, ignoring heckles and knee-kicks to the back of their seat.

Brick bungalows appeared, then businesses, busy streets, and on to taller buildings and heavier traffic. A bronze statue of Brigham Young at Main and Temple Streets welcomed them to Temple Square. Since most kids only visited Salt Lake City once or twice a year, their anticipation seemed to electrify the air and inspire chatter about the rich shoppers on sidewalks and the newest model cars humming along wide avenues. Karen wondered if she'd dare to live in a city so fine.

Through a wrought iron gate, they could glimpse the massive turtle-roofed Tabernacle in the shadow of the Temple, like a gothic fairy tale castle of gray, granite blocks. Karen counted eight steeples jutting from each of six towers and many squealing kids pointed up at the statue of Angel Moroni gracing the highest peak. He tooted a golden horn, and the orange glint played off the jeweled sky.

They had all attended church general conferences in the tabernacle, and paintings of both the temple and the tabernacle adorned many Cloverdale living rooms. But today they would finally set foot inside the temple itself. Electricity seemed to crackle as kids bounced and craned, oohed and ahhed, and the bus pulled up and parked. Karen and Amy grabbed hands to share their excitement.

CHAPTER 16

A STATE BIRD FROM GOD

In the bus Brother Dale rose. "A final word before we depart. Show everyone how special you are." His chopping hand punctuated his clipped words while the kids gritted their teeth and tensed like runners at a starting line.

"This is the holiest place on earth. Jesus Christ walks the halls. You're here to build His Kingdom. The *Doctrine and Covenants* says 'the living and the dead can commune underground in the temple'."

Karen wondered, would the brother's ranting never end?

"File out." Brother Dale finally allowed the rush to pour to the sidewalk.

Karen's stomach tensed and fluttered in turns. She massaged it with one hand and squeezed Amy's hand in the other.

"Commune with the dead underground?" she quoted Dale's scripture to Amy, who shrugged.

The barely subdued group passed under the arched entry gate and through the grounds between perfect petunia gardens, groomed into geometric patches of red and purple.

They craned up as Brother Dale led them in a ring around one of the monuments, a carved block supporting an erect stone shaft which thrust up to hold a granite ball topped with several stone seagulls.

Brother Dale cleared his throat and set off a bobbling frenzy in his Adam's apple.

"Oh no," Karen mumbled. "Not the seagull story, again."

"Early Mormon pioneer saints faced starvation," Brother Dale recited. "They prayed their first harvest would feed both them and the immigrants soon to arrive. But what did the Devil do to thwart the Lord's chosen people?" His eyes scanned the faces. He snapped a finger at Brian.

"He sent hordes of crickets." Brian must have been paying attention. Karen listened too in case Brother Dale nailed her next.

"Correct." The good leader nodded approval. "They devoured every vegetable leaf and blade of grain in their path. The saints prayed and battled the insects until the Lord answered their pleas. What happened?"

Karen focused on her shoes to avoid being called on.

"Camille?"

The girl flipped her blond hair to one side to cover her embarrassment. "Up until then, there were no seagulls in Utah. But that's when the Lord sent them, and they saved the day."

"Yeah," Enoch piped up. "It wus a miracle. Seagulls flew all the way from California beaches to get here."

"Right," Brother Dale continued. "Flocks of birds filled their gullets and flew to the Great Salt Lake where they regurgitated cricket bodies."

Dwayne elbowed Enoch. "In case you're ignernt, regurgeetate means puke."

"In short order," Brother Dale continued, "they repeatedly returned to ingest more of the evil swarms. The birds saved the Latter-day Saints in 1848, including your own pioneer ancestors.

If not for the gulls, you would all still be unborn and languishing in the preexistence. In all the forty-eight states, Utah has the only official bird sent from God."

The young people shifted in their places, then followed Brother Dale through the massive doors of the Temple into a high-ceilinged foyer with potted plants and seating.

A priesthood holder, as ancient as Melchizedek, himself, nodded at them. The codger seemed almost transparent, like a shriveled ghost stooped over a tall desk and was the smallest and ugliest man Karen had ever seen, possibly a real live goblin.

The man's eyes, behind wire glasses, were dull and dry of life. He squinted toward their temple recommends but couldn't seem to focus. The shaky hand fluttered the forms, one by one, from the bottom of the desk to the top while he pretended to examine the fine print. His gnarled hand pushed the stack back to Brother Dale's safe-keeping.

The boys split off with their leaders while Karen and the other girls followed Sisters Viva and Luetta.

A woman, nearly as ancient as the goblin man, appeared. "Girls, follow me. We'll go to the lower reaches of the Temple permitted by your youth recommends."

Karen imagined brushing against the sister and breathing in closet smells, castoff clothes and dust, lavender and mothballs.

The elderly lady led them one way then another in a maze of yellow-tiled passages and down several stark stairwells.

"It looks just like plain ordinary halls and stairs," Karen whispered. Amy squeezed Karen's hand and tightened her lips to shush her. They stopped behind the Temple matron at the end of a hall.

A painting of Church President David O. McKay reminded Karen how much Brother LeGrande's white hair and ingratiating smile resembled the mainstream Mormon prophet. She fingered her throat where Brother LeGrande's locket would fall if her excuses for not wearing it ran out.

The lady beamed an other-worldly welcome.

"I'm Sister Eliza Eldritch," she said. Her blue eyes under sagging lids at least seemed to have life left in them. Her simple white dress, cinched at the waist, had fold lines like it had come from a drawer or suitcase not a hanger. Her feet were laced with purple veins and stuffed into white slippers. Her voice lilted and teased, like spun sugar melting in her mouth.

"This is indeed an especial day." She paused for rapt eye contact. "Every day, unseen entities pace this holy hall," she crooned. "Today they wait for you."

Karen locked her knees to fight off the heebie-jeebies.

The old lady patted her bluish sausage roll hairdo. "These spirit women may have waited for eons. This is their special day and yours too as you stand in for them. Most did not enjoy the blessings you have of growing up in Zion. They knew nothing of the one true church." Sister Eldritch sniffed back tears for the deprived non-Mormon souls. Words like *holy, eons, blessings,* and *Zion* did a waltz on her tongue and over her smile before they danced out of her lips.

"Today, these departed spirits will accept the gospel and become Mormons. They'll enter the path to the Kingdom of Heaven. There, they'll be the wives of Gods. They will procreate spirit children to populate planets like Earth. What you do today will change the universe."

Sister Eldritch's face shone with the glory of God's plan for women. The message was not new to anyone, but lilting words and gestures seemed to mesmerize Karen's companions.

"Worthy girls always sense, and sometimes see or hear spirit women hovering in this temple. Ponder what I say." Sister Eldritch caressed the nearby door frame. "Open your hearts to these especial dead women."

Her head bowed to her chest and she folded her hands against one cheek. Suddenly, she sprang awake. Her eyes sought contact with her audience. "You girls are Heavenly Father's fond hope for His Church."

She led the group through the door. Beyond it, the bare floor turned to lush carpet. The walls were polished wood, not tile. "Does anyone wish to share a special feeling?"

Karen's tentative hand went up. Amy's hand darted out to pinch Karen, but too late.

"Yes, dear," Sister Eldritch said.

"I feel I'd like to ask a question."

The sister waited.

"I just wondered," Karen said, "what happens to the dead souls we miss."

"Why, what do you mean, 'miss,' young lady?"

Sister Eldritch's tone was bewildered. Had she expected Karen to mention departed spirits in their very midst? Karen felt compelled to continue.

"Well, there must have been millions of people who lived on earth before writing was invented. What if they were worthy and they are waiting for eternity to be baptized? What if our genealogy doesn't have their names?"

Sister Eldritch's countenance chilled. "God is just and all powerful. Do you always ask questions like that, girl?"

"Er, no," Karen stammered. "I mean… are questions like that bad?"

"Humph." The sister shrugged. "Pray and humble yourself. The Lord provides answers when you are worthy."

The matron beckoned them closer, then locked her small fists on her hips. "I almost forgot. We're all females here, so I'll be blunt." She blushed and gazed over their heads. Sensing her embarrassment, Karen followed her lead and averted her eyes.

"If any of you are in your menstrual flow now, you must let us know. Just whisper to me or to one of your leaders. No one will think ill of you." She raised her palms to them.

"You see, girls, cleanliness is next to Godliness. A droplet of blood would defile the holy font."

Karen remembered poor Anne Marie left behind in Cloverdale.

"Now girls, we've departed from the Temple's outer halls." Sister Eldritch hesitated. "We're about to enter a more sacred area nearer the baptismal room. Be reverent."

Her voice softened to a more awed tone, but her finger shook a stern warning. "This is your first step in the Temple toward the sacred endowments you will someday perform when you are ready for Temple marriage. On your wedding day, you'll be ushered into the higher realms of the Temple. You'll then be worthy to do adult spirit weddings and sealings for the dead."

Karen and the others stared straight ahead and moved with measured deliberation through the next door. On the other side, they found only a counter with lockers and several draped cubicles like the Samuel's ladies wear dressing rooms.

"Line up at the counter to collect special baptismal clothes from your leaders," Sister Eldritch instructed. "Take the packet to the other line. Then wait for a dressing room. Take everything off. I'll be looking in on each of you before you step into your baptismal attire. I must make certain you're wearing no panties, undershirts, or bras. So often they have days of the week stitched in colored thread, or gray in the elastic waistbands or fasteners. Any non-white thing would invalidate the baptisms. When you're in your special suit, put your street clothes in a locker." The sister was pure efficiency.

Clutching thin packages, girls entered cubicles. Karen watched Sister Eldritch pop her head in on them with a mumble or two as she moved along the stalls with perfect timing, somehow knowing when a girl would be ready for inspection.

Barefoot girls emerged, loose clothing in hand and looking bedraggled, some bending to retrieve dropped socks or underclothes.

Karen's insides groaned at the hideous outfits, skimpy white long johns cut off at the knees and held together with buttons, like utilitarian knobs on a tool chest, from chin to crotch.

She waited with her jumpsuit for Camille to emerge from behind a curtain. Once inside the cell, Karen stripped and folded her things. Sister Eldritch peeped in, signaling permission to step into the ugly costume.

Karen planned to tell Lucinda about nakedness in the Temple. Her cheeks burned at having unfamiliar old eyes view her new breasts and the hairs sprouting at her crotch and she suspected Temple-going adults had to endure more blatant bodily intrusions. She hoped being a grown-up woman would make it easier.

She left the cubicle and with regret, she stuffed her new clothes into a lunchbox-sized locker.

Karen felt awkward and ugly in the special temple suit as she and her friends waited to enter the baptistery. They mumbled and fingered their puckered seams and knobby buttons. The girls' eyes focused on the great doors and waited to see what lay beyond.

CHAPTER 17

THE SHAME OF WOMANHOOD

The grandeur of the icy palace set the scene for the worst moments of her life. In the font with everyone staring, Karen heard muffled heckles and gasps all around. The crowd watched her slip along the wet floor and stumble out behind the seething sister. They all saw the first trickle of her first period redden the crotch of her baptismal suit.

In humiliation from the Mormon sisters' displeasure, she dressed and they sent her from the temple where she obediently followed Nancy's lead. She might have preferred having Lucinda or Amy with her at a time like this, but Nancy was a comfort. They had always been friendly.

Karen climbed into the bus and sobbed while Nancy fiddled with her ponytail. Nancy left to dampen Kleenex in the lawn sprinkler for Karen's face. Seagulls outside fought over a Cracker Jack box.

The girls shared a stick of Black Jack gum, and Karen's tears waned. She blew her nose, then gathered the tissues into her purse, and finally drew a deep breath. "I have one question," she choked out. "You know how we always have to worry about modesty?"

Nancy nodded.

"Well, every day we hide our thighs, and our shoulders, even our collarbones, but in the temple, everybody has to get nekked as jaybirds. We wear see-through torture chamber suits. I just don't get it. Do you?"

Nancy fidgeted. "Karen, we have to have faith. There are reasons for everything. I think you're just really upset."

"Yes, this day stinks, all right?"

"And," Nancy said, "we mustn't talk about the Temple. It's too sacred. Maybe we'll understand someday when we go back to get married."

Karen felt like she'd slammed into a wall. Smacking the gum helped a little.

Brothers Dale and Garrick eventually returned to the bus and handed them cupcake trays to carry. Dale lugged jugs of lemonade and Garrick wrestled a cardboard box of sack lunches.

Karen's eyes had been cleansed by the tears and returning through the formal gardens back to the Temple, she now saw the stately statues as sinister and the designs of petunias as geometric prison cells.

The boys in the cafeteria groused at a long table. Karen overheard, "Not fair." "You kiddin' me?" "Karen?" "On the rag?"

She squeezed in with the girls, subdued, tainted by her shame. They mumbled about sandwiches and lemonade. The picnic attitude had been drenched like their ruined hairdos. Karen's stomach churned. She crammed her sandwich back into the lunch bag. She sipped lemonade. It tasted sour.

Back in the bus, Karen hunched in a seat beside Amy and watched the boys drag on board, their energy also wrung dry.

"Karen, it wasn't your fault," Amy whispered. "The girls understand. The boys are stupid. And guess what? Brian punched Enoch for calling you a dumb broad."

The insult and gallant gesture overwhelmed her muddled brain. She shrugged.

"When Enoch dishes out grief over this," Amy whispered, "you can throw that middle name, Zurflew, into his freckled face."

Karen nodded.

"And, everyone saw that birthmark. The purple hand grabbing his… you know… tub spelled backwards." Amy cleared her throat.

They bumped shoulders in agreement.

Amy pushed up her glasses. "I'm just going to sit and think about being a grownup someday. None of this will matter then."

Karen rested her head against the window. She couldn't sort it out now. Maybe Amy was right and none of this would matter, someday, somehow.

She closed her eyes.

CHAPTER 18

MANY ARE CALLED

Ben and Jack shifted in their car seats and cast glances at Grandma Hardy's farm house.

The chief had ordered them to do surveillance for the Salt Lake boys and they were following orders under protest.

"It'll soon be sunset." Ben juggled his wadded Life Saver wrapper from one hand to the other. "I need a cigarette."

Jack stretched in the passenger seat. "I'm bored stiff. At this rate, I might take up smoking, myself."

"I'm sick of smelling horse shit." Ben aimed the candy wrapper out of the car window and hit a rusty tin can near the stable door. "What's for dinner tonight?"

Jack patted his belly. "You like foot long hotdogs?"

"They're pork and I'm Jewish."

"Oh, sorry. That reminds me of somethin'. I bet you didn't know there're Nazis living here in Utah."

Ben leveled his gaze at Jack. "What? Did I hear you correctly? Are you saying German-Americans? Or real Nazis?"

"Honest Injun. Remember I told you about going to the hospital with Shortarm? That's when I found out. Hitler got along with Mormons. He liked the idea of polygamy and assigned coupling. He used genealogy forms like theirs to profile the German population. He allowed Mormon churches and missionaries to continue all through the war. At the end, some of his Nazi guys ran off to Canada. From there, they've been trickling into this state."

"Hold it! Is Utah trying to take down these madmen?"

"No, they ignore 'em, same way the chief wants us to ignore polygamous madmen. Listen to this. The Dee Hospital has hired Germans. Wanna know why?"

Ben gestured for him to get on with it.

"They send nurses out to schools. The nurses tattoo blood types on the kids. So young Mormons are getting little blue A's or O's under their arms. All of the Hitler troops had 'em, too."

"Come on!" Ben let out a derisive groan.

"I swear to God! Mormons think we're in the latter days. They expect an A-bomb to blow us up any day now. It'll take out medical records, but it won't destroy tattoos on worthy little Mormons. They'll survive to trek off to Missouri with the other chosen saints of Zion. Jesus will come down and be King."

Ben raised his eyebrows. "Missouri? I can't believe this!"

"According to Mormons, Jesus will descend there to rule over what's left of the world."

"I think you're serious." Ben's groans grew louder with each sentence Jack spoke. "Sorry, but I think this place is an insane asylum. Furthermore, this is the last dinner of cold beans and scooter pies I plan to choke down. Let's get back to Ogden tonight, locate your missing sister and the girl I'm tracking. I plan to jail some of those damned madmen and go home. Post haste."

*   *   *

Davy and Judy snuggled with Karen in the arms of the overstuffed gray chair. She read *Blueberries for Sal* to them, even though they could recite it from memory. The telephone jangled the signal for the Hardy family party line, two long rings, and a short.

"Hello," Karen spoke into the black receiver.

"It's Grandma Hardy. Hurry up and fetch your mother for me, Karen!"

She dashed to the kitchen. Grandma phoned only when someone was dying or dead. She fretted over wasting money on talking, something that should be free.

"Mother! Long distance! It's Grandma Hardy."

Karen's mother hugged her pregnant belly as she lumbered into the living room.

"Grandma? Are you okay?" Mother frowned. Karen listened to Mother's side of the conversation.

"What? I can't hear you. Did you say feds are watching your house?" Mother's shoulders sagged.

"What makes you think so?" She fingered the hem of her smock. Mother eased onto the sofa and twisted the telephone wire.

"You saw a car hiding out back behind the stable? Good heavens!" Mother's breaths turned to a series of noisy gasps.

"What?" She opened her mouth and eyes wide.

"Wait! Is someone on this line? Please hang up. I'll be done in one minute. This is a long distance call. An emergency."

"Grandma, try to stay calm. I know you're not a fundamentalist Mormon." Mother's eyes bulged, making her look like a fish flapping on the river bank.

"What?" Mother grabbed the *Improvement Era* magazine from the telephone table shelf and fanned her face.

"Okay." She turned a pale shade of gray.

"I'll call Edward at work." She dropped the magazine. "He'll know what to do."

Worried that Mother might faint, Karen wondered if she should throw open the doors and windows. Instead she picked the *Improvement Era* off the floor and waved it in front of Mother's face.

"Yes, I'm sorry you're a widow." Mother's voice was frog-like.

"I'll give him the message right away. Goodbye," the last word, a hoarse whisper.

Mother clunked the receiver in the cradle and for several moments battled for air.

Finally she choked out a few words. "The feds are closing in. They're watching Grandma's place."

The word "feds" triggered the heebie-jeebies in Karen, and she wondered if they had Tommy guns aimed at her grandma?

Mother picked up the receiver and recited Father's office number to the operator.

"What?" Karen asked. "Father really has fundies living at Grandma's farm? She's not a polygamist."

Mother stuffed the receiver under the couch cushion, then grabbed the *Improvement Era* magazine from Karen's hand, rolled it up and swatted Karen's head. "Shut up. The operator could have heard you!"

Karen's head wasn't hurt, but her feelings always stung when mother hit. Still, she also wanted to laugh, like she was trapped in a scary version of the Sunday color comics. Mother hadn't watched *her* tongue on the phone, and yet she blamed Karen for speaking up.

Mother fished out the receiver and spoke with caution to Father. "Edward, your mother called long distance about the… house guests. She has uninvited observers."

Mother smoothed her smock and listened, her face more stoic.

"What?"

Father asked something that set off a minor fit of panting, like before.

"How should I know?" Mother gasped. "Edward, you need to come home right now. We can talk better here."

Father obviously was not bucking up Mother's spirits. She picked up the mangled magazine.

"She's seen gentiles hanging around." Mother fanned. "That's all I know. Please hurry." Mother clunked the receiver back in place. She threw down the tattered *Improvement Era*.

"I was afraid something like this would happen. The feds have been trailing the Allreds." She wrung the hem of her smock. "Let's pray they don't think we're connected because of Grandma. May the Lord have mercy."

*   *   *

Father stormed into the house an hour later. Karen worried about the look in his eyes, the harsh line of his jaw, his balled up fists. He paced the kitchen.

"Karen," he said, "You're going with me to Middle Fork. Only first wives are safe at home with their husbands these days. Grandma's been letting Roland Allred's third wife stay holed up with her. The feds are there spying on them. You'll have to help me get her and the kids out of there. This has nothing to do with Grandma. She isn't even a fundamentalist."

Mother chewed her lip with a vengeance. Father raked his dark hair and slammed his fist into his palm. Karen didn't dare object, though she wished the task on Rosemary or Richard, anyone but her.

"There's no use dragging our feet," Father said. "Let's get outta here. We can be there before dark."

Karen grabbed a sweater and followed Father to the car.

As they left Cloverdale, Farther glared straight ahead, his grip on the steering wheel vice-like. Unintelligible mutterings escaped his lips.

Karen strained to make out the words. "Did you say something?"

"Those freakin' feds have no right to torment law-abiding, God-fearing polygamists! Why aren't those buggers out hunting down commies?"

Father's rage frightened Karen. She wished she had ignored his mumbling.

"Who do they think they are?" Father ranted on. "Utah pantywaists are caving in under the corrupt federal government."

She hated being penned up only with her imagination and her seething father during the long fifty-mile drive. What would happen to her family and to her? She wondered if the feds would lock her up if they barged into Grandma's house. She knew there was a reform school in Ogden. It was for bad kids, some as young as she was. The idea made her squirm.

Father harrumphed off and on until they reached Middle Fork and Grandma's farm came into view. At the front gate he killed the engine next to a sign on which peeling letters read "Farm Fresh Eggs." Three ancient trees stretched arms over and around the white plastered farmhouse, enfolding it in shade too dense for lawn. The vegetable gardens and orchards basked in the setting sun outside the shadows. All appeared peaceful, not a fed in sight.

Grandma had sold the farm animals or slaughtered them for meat, except for her best laying hens and Bess, her favorite Jersey cow. One neighbor exchanged chores for a share of the milk and eggs, and another bought the pasture land, growing fields, and most of the farm buildings. Since Grandpa's sudden death, Grandma had made ends meet on cash from the sales and on pasture rentals from her remaining acreage.

*   *   *

The front screen door banged open as they entered the gate. Karen's round granny bustled out drying her hands on the apron over her usual old lady housedress. She clunked down the walk in her stout black shoes, a scowl darkening her face.

"I've been a bundle of nerves waiting for you, Edward."

Grandma was affectionate, much more so than Karen's parents. She kissed everyone before they stepped onto her porch. This time she whispered as she caressed Karen.

"Take a gander at Ned and Jed's stable."

Karen stepped up the wide porch stairs and stood on tiptoes. She spotted a barely visible black sedan parked near the stable where Grandpa's work horses had once lived.

She started to raise her hand and point. "You mean over—"

Father slapped her arm down and said, "Get inside!"

* * *

Near the stable in the police car, Jack said, "Hold it."

Ben peered through binoculars. A young girl and someone who might be her father left a Rambler and hurried toward the front porch. He watched as an old farm lady bustled out and hugged them like long lost family before she whisked them inside.

"Jack, the girl saw us."

CHAPTER 19

FEW ARE CHOSEN

The aroma of cooking onions and bacon welcomed them at Grandma's threshold before the screen door clattered shut.

Karen recognized Eva, one of Roland Allred's six wives, cowering in Grandpa's leather wing chair. The young woman used no makeup on her pale, pinched face. The Allred polygamy group demanded naturalness of its women, meaning an 1800s pioneer appearance. She wore an ankle-length calico dress, more out of date than Grandma's housedress. Eva's white blond braids were crossed and pinned in a U-shape at the back of her neck.

"Thanks for helping, Brother Edward," she said.

Mormon families favored compliant women, while polygamy groups made female servitude a holy commandment. Eva avoided direct eye contact and spoke in a murmur, mindful of Father's Priesthood power. Her shy, bland ways couldn't cover her desperation.

Two little girls and a brother played on Grandma's rose-bouquet rug. They were freckled towheads and, like their mother and every other Allred, their lashes and brows were invisible except in sunshine. The six-year-old boy, Gered, ran the game. Five-year-old LaNae, and Emma, age three, gathered up clothespins for him to toss at milk bottles.

Beyond a plastered archway, Grandma's round dining table was set for dinner. In Karen's experience, the weighty table with its solid oak pedestal and bulky feet never left the circle of braided rag rug. It would take four strong men with the help of the Lord to lift it. A flowered oilcloth bore plates of sliced cucumbers, tomatoes, homemade bread and a pitcher of Bess's milk.

"Come give me a hand, Karen."

Karen listened in on Eva's and Father's conversation in the living room while she poured the milk and carried out buttered string beans and a crock of bubbling bacon and potatoes, teeming with onions. Grandma brought out a platter of steaming corn-on-the-cob and a bowl of homemade cottage cheese.

"Everyone, hurry on in here, before supper gets cold."

Ordinarily, Father chose someone else to bless the food. Emergencies warranted prayer from the ranking Priesthood holder. "I'll pray," he said before he began. "Our dear and powerful Heavenly Father. We thank Thee for this food and ask Thee to bless it that it will nourish and strengthen our bodies and do us the good we need."

That usually ended a food blessing, but today the prayer continued. "Mighty Father, protect us from those lawless federal agents from the outside world. Help us do Thy will. As Thy humble servants, keep us safe from those feds in the black car. NameofJesusChrist, Amen."

"The feds have been here off and on since yesterday." Grandma's voice was low and tense. "I like to help, but I'm old.

These worries are wearing me to a frazzle. I miss Grandpa." She squared her shoulders and fished in her bodice for a hankie to mop her face.

Karen and the adults picked at their good food. The kids plowed into their plates. Twice, Father left the table to glare out the window and grumble under his breath at the black sedan lurking outside.

"We appreciate all you've done," Eva said.

"Don't worry," Father said. "You'll be safe with us for a few days until Roland works things out."

Karen helped clear the table. In the kitchen, she washed dishes, handing them to Grandma to rinse and dry. "Do you ever get tired of so many kinds of Mormons?" Karen asked.

Grandma stirred out the fire in her old-fashioned wood stove. Karen waited for her answer. Finally, Grandma shut the door between them and the others.

"I'm just an old Mormon church lady. I grew up with polygamous parents as a girl. Everyone did in those days. When polygamy was outlawed, men kept the wives they had. The church wrote up a manifesto. It said they'd stay within the law, but even the leaders didn't follow it. As time went on, there were ever fewer plural marriages."

Grandma wiped the counter.

"But groups like Allreds splintered off and went on with the old ways. Polygamy's never been legal in this country. Most of us hoped people in these groups would have given it up long before now. The main Mormons finally did. Official Mormons only allow for plural marriage in heaven. Not for here and now. That's how it's been for more than sixty years. Oh pshaw, maybe they'll never learn." The expletive "pshaw" slipped out of Grandma's lips only under stress.

"But if it's against the law," Karen asked, "why's it bad for the feds to haul them to jail?"

Grandma dumped the greasy dishwater from the dishpan into the sink.

"Because feds are outsiders. Gentiles. People in Utah have to learn on their own. I agreed to take in this mother and her babies because I couldn't see them suffer. I just pine for a day when everyone will stop practicing all this polygamy foolishness."

"Sometimes," Karen said, "I think all kinds of Mormons are foolish."

"Karen, shush."

Grandma rested her damp hand on Karen's shoulder and glanced at the dining room door. "Let's go out to the orchard. I have peaches ripening up. Your mother will need extra food for Eva and her kids."

She and Karen each grabbed a peck-sized basket from the screened porch on their way out. The path, buckled and broken by tree roots, led to the peach trees.

"There's no one to hear us. And there are things I've been a-wanting to say all my life. Old people think about old times. Something's been gnawing at me. The feds have me in a dither. And Grandpa's gone. He can't calm me down like he used to. You may be of an age you need to hear some of it. Remember that day in the attic when we talked about Danites?"

Karen hesitated. She noticed for the first time that she had grown taller than her grandmother. She felt less of a child now that she had had her first period, almost like Grandma's companion.

"I've been thinking about a lot of things myself," Karen said. "And I don't have anyone to talk to either."

Karen climbed a ladder and handed peaches down to Grandma. The fruit was smaller and less abundant since Grandpa was no longer there to tend it.

"What things, Grandma?"

"Well, honey, this is between you and me. I don't want you being scared of Danites. Thankfully, they're gone. But in the old days before there were modern policemen church leaders had to take matters into their own hands. The trouble is their blood atoning was more evil than the sins they punished."

Karen could tell this was a scary story. She was proud to be Grandma's confidante, but frightened too. The first basket was nearly full.

"Once, a young couple, Brother and Sister Grey, moved into Utah. They had a sweet little girl about the age of Emma, Eva's youngest, and your sister, Judy. They came all the way across the ocean. Then they traveled over the plains by covered wagon. My uncle was the missionary who baptized them over in London."

"What happened?" Karen whispered. She brought a handful of peaches down the ladder with her.

"They didn't like it here, had trouble being obedient, said Mormons were pushy. They were offended that people considered them outsiders, being as they were just new converts and had only one wife in the family."

"And?"

"They asked permission to leave, but were denied. They left anyway."

"Then what?"

"The story goes; Indians ambushed them thirty miles over the Nevada border."

"Indians?"

"Yes, but after that, their tablecloth showed up on the bishop's table. And his wife claimed he sent back east for a mantel clock for her birthday. But the clock was English. I had seen it in Brother and Sister Grey's house every time I sold them butter and eggs. That was twice a week until they left. I saw other people with things the couple had, a hat, a shawl, a belt buckle."

Karen felt as if she had peach fuzz in her pores. She couldn't rub away the goosebumps on her arms. A far-off dog howled.

"The saddest thing was…" Grandma's throat caught. "The saddest part was I saw the bishop's daughter playing tea party with the Grey girl's rag doll."

"You don't mean they killed a little three-year-old?"

"Pshaw." Her chest heaved. "Oh, pshaw, I didn't want to know what happened to that baby. The church says that only baptized children over age eight have discernment. Not even Danites would kill a baby younger than eight. Some claimed that little thing got sold to the Indians. A more likely story is the Danites gave her to a Mormon family in Idaho to raise up. I think only a few knew and they stayed mum."

Karen trembled. "Do you mean the Danites could have killed or sold a little girl like Emma or Judy?"

"I've thought and thought. I figured it could be true, Karen."

"Grandma, do you think other places out of Utah are bad like people say?"

"Karen, when I was a girl, we didn't get choices. My parents were Mormon pioneers. That was that. Times are changing. You might be able to run your life in a new direction if you want to."

The two carried their baskets along the path and rested them near a rusting, six-foot-tall hand pump, a reminder of the time before modern plumbing.

"Nowadays," Grandma said, "most folks have radios, and telephones, and cars. Rich ones have televisions and travel on aeroplanes. I was still carrying buckets of water from that pump after I married."

Grandma lifted the creaky handle and let it clank.

Karen watched the sunset play over Grandma's face.

"You're luckier than me, Karen."

Karen saw regret in her grandmother's eyes, mixed with glimmers of hope. The wrinkled eyelids squeezed back brimming tears. The two hugged. Each carried a basket to the house. The blood-red sunset lit their path.

A car rumbled. They gasped.

"They're leaving." They both spoke at once.

Karen raced ahead to tell the others.

"The feds have left. Hurry! We have to go."

Eva was folding undershirts and socks into a shopping bag. Another bulging bag stood ready.

"Good," Father said, looking out the window to see for himself. "Hurry! Load up the car. Let's make tracks."

Karen hauled the packed bag to the car trunk. Grandma met her at the door with a basket of peaches. "I've got some fresh-made loaves of bread and a chunk of bacon for your mom. They're in the kitchen."

Karen's stomach lurched. She wanted to run like crazy and never stop. She scurried to the kitchen window. The fed car was still gone.

"They probably went to Middle Fork Grocery or to get a couple of those foot-longs at Jake's Hot Dog Joint for their supper," Grandma said. "Oh pshaw. Everyone hurry. Skedaddle. Now! Oh pshaw, pshaw, pshaw!"

The kids were lined up at the bathroom door.

"Gered is taking forever," LaNae said, "doing number two."

Little Emma was holding herself and dancing in front of Grandma's wood stove near the bathroom door. Finally, the flush sounded. Next, they heard something like an animal bellowing at slaughter. It was aging water pipes screaming with trapped air. The feeling of being caught in a nightmarish comic strip made Karen want to laugh and cry at the same time.

The children finished in the bathroom as Eva folded their blankets and stacked pillows. Karen felt as if they were moving in slow motion, like a film she once saw at school.

She grabbed the girls by their washed but moist hands and half dragged them to the car. Eva hustled back from car to house, once for her hairbrush, and a second time for her robe. Finally everyone settled in their seats, and Father peeled out. Karen waved to Grandma, who was silhouetted in twilight near the open gate.

The adults sat in the front seat. Karen tended the kids in the back. She started a game of Simon Says.

"Karen, you're not here to play," Father commanded. "Keep watch out that back window. Tell me the second any car seems to be following us, especially that black fed car."

Karen kneeled on the back seat and peered into the last moments of dusk, no cars in sight. The kids fought over pillows. Karen helped them play "eenie, meenie, minie, mo" for first picks on pillows as she kept watch.

"I see a car," Karen said. "I think it's brown, and way back there. It turned off toward Draper."

"I'm going to swing on over to Farm Bureau Road," Father said. "It's a straighter stretch and there are more chances to lose anyone who spots us." He didn't slow down much for the turn. The car pitched the kids first one way, then the other.

"There's a car closing in on us," Karen blurted. "Their lights are off. I couldn't see them until just now. But they saw us turn. It looks like the black fed car." Karen couldn't keep her voice steady. She noticed the two older kids flinch at the shrieking tone behind her words.

"Holy shinola," Father said. He gunned the engine. It backfired and almost died. The car rattled and swerved.

"They're closing in," Karen said. "Get down, you kids. Don't let them see how many are in this car."

The black car was near enough for Karen to see silhouettes of two men, one a tall passenger, and a shorter one behind the wheel.

"I'll turn into that filling station grocery," Father said, "and see if they follow."

The car bumped off the highway into a graveled parking area. The tailing black car pulled in on the opposite end of the lot. Father opened his door and took a few steps toward the store. The two feds rushed into the building.

Karen felt her panic exploding. What if they grabbed Father now?

That's when Father leaped back into the car and skidded away in a spray of gravel.

The taller fed burst out of the market as Father peeled off. Karen watched the man bound back into the store, waving wildly, and probably yelling for his partner. Father kept up the speed, well over the fifty-mile limit. The car shook and tipped on the narrow road. He had never pushed it so hard, Karen was certain. She admitted to herself she was scared, maybe terrified.

Father had a good head start.

"Edward," Eva said, "is there a bridge to cross that creek? I think there's a tractor lane on the other side."

"Yes, at least there used to be. Let's see... that's Jump-off Creek. I remember two or three ways across it. But I haven't used them since I was a kid. Watch out for a brown barn with Steed's Feed and Seed painted on the side."

"We got way ahead of them back at the market," Karen said. "But they must be back there somewhere."

"I see the barn coming up," Eva said.

Father slowed. "Watch for a narrow bridge. It will be hard to see, just wide planks with no railing."

"There it is!" Karen and the two adults chorused.

The car eased onto the time-worn bridge. Karen crossed her fingers and caught her breath. The bridge was seldom used and needed repair. Somehow, it supported their fully loaded car.

Once over Jump-off Creek, Father shut off the lights and rolled behind a line of poplar trees. They watched and waited. A decrepit pickup, heaped with junk, poked by, followed by two or three local cars. Then they spotted the fed car passing an old coupe.

"That pickup truck slowed them down," Father said. "It's probably a sign from Heavenly Father. We should stop and give thanks."

Karen couldn't hold herself back. "No, no, no!" she said. "Not now!" She was crying. Her words were a shrill scream. "They'll see we're not up ahead. They'll come back here looking for us any minute. Please turn around. Go back. Isn't there another road to the highway? Can't we go to Draper or Provo? We can't stay here. We just can't!"

Father jerked around to her like an animal ready to spring. His hand lashed out.

"No!" Karen said and shied back in time to dodge the blow.

"Edward," Eva said, "we're all keyed up here, but it will be okay."

Father seemed startled to see a non-family member in the car.

"Of course we defer to your priesthood power, but think about it," Eva went on. "Karen is right. Let's double back and we'll be gone before they see they've missed us up ahead." Eva's voice was low and reasonable.

"Good gosh!" Father shouted. "Women will be the death of me."

He backed up the car past the bridge. They turned onto the crossing planks for a second time. It held.

Karen caught her breath and soothed the frightened children as best she could. She watched for the Draper turnoff. Father saw it without help. Soon they were shooting onto the highway back toward Cloverdale.

"I think we shook them," Karen said.

She noticed Emma crouching on the floor with a sweater pulled over her head. Gered and LaNae looked pale. Their hands covered their eyes. "Did they get us?" Gered asked.

"No," Eva said. "We're safe for now."

"Thank the Lord." Father slowed to the speed limit.

Karen fumed in silence. She thought of what Grandma said about pining for the day when all the Mormon groups in Utah would give up polygamy. She was sick of the confusing kinds of Mormons pushing and pulling her in every direction. Karen yearned to curl up and hide in her hayloft, safe away from all of it.

At home, she carried the sleeping Emma inside. The sofa would be a good bed for the night, but she found Mother, Rosemary, and Richard sitting on it and chatting with Brother LeGrande.

"Yes, yes, dear Sister Hosannah," the prophet was saying, "you are so kind to offer shelter to the persecuted."

Karen was startled to see them where she wanted to put Emma. She turned quickly and carried the little girl into the room with Judy and Davy. There she tucked her in with Judy.

"Karen, dear," the prophet said when she came out, "join us for a prayer circle to thank the Lord for your happy day. You helped deliver some of his chosen from the clutches of evil."

She hoped LeGrande saw her mouth form the words, "shut up." Aloud, she said, "No, I'm going to bed."

She escaped upstairs. Rosemary and Richard could help unload the car and settle the fugitives. They could thank the Lord without her. She wanted to scream, but settled for rest.

CHAPTER 20

DISSENTION IN THE RANKS

Jack slopped beer down his shirt and laughed.

"Anyone ever tell you you're a slob?" Ben asked.

"And did anyone mention how you can't tail a suspect worth a damn?"

"Give me a break. I don't know these country roads. Besides, I needed Life Savers more than we needed to follow that car. And what's with that Ma and Pa Kettle store not carrying calamine lotion? This stinging nettle's killing me!" Ben pulled up his pants legs to expose festering welts above his socks.

"Nettles are nasty," Jack agreed. "That's why we avoid 'em when we have to pee."

"The Wolfowitz clan never lived in Utah. The shrubs here are almost as crazy as the citizenry. The store was out of Camel cigarettes or I might have started smoking again. That's how desperate I was." Ben gulped his beer and averted his eyes from the splashes on Jack's shirt.

"Oh yeah? I hid their last carton of Camels. It was out of the goodness of my heart. I know you. You'll soon want to cozy up to Sylvia again. You owe me."

"Gee, thanks. Damn it! We know exactly where to find those suspects when we want them. Chasing them was a worthless exercise."

"Yes, you're right."

"Finally, we agree on something!" Ben rubbed his ankle. "My legs feel like a million bee stings. And I'm chomping down the state's Life Saver inventory faster than they can truck them in." Ben vented his spleen with bitter laughter. "Furthermore, as law enforcement professionals, who are we assigned to watch? Traitors? Assassins? Mobsters? No." Ben answered his own question. "For three days straight, we observe a quiet little old Mormon widow woman. She invites a lady friend and her children for a visit. They spend their time doing subversive activities like hanging out laundry and gathering eggs."

"And who," Jack asked, "do we pursue when they make a run for it? We tried, but failed to tail a Mormon who is so dumb he can't keep his secret underwear from hanging out his shirtsleeves. Also, a woman, so scared she can't walk straight and a carload of squirrelly kids in a broken-down Rambler."

"I'm not sorry they got away," Ben said.

Jack nodded. "The only breakthrough was proving the chief is an ass for ordering us there!"

"Yes, what a yutz." Ben frowned. "That goose chase was obstruction of justice."

Jack leaned forward, his cheeks, livid. "First thing tomorrow, he's getting a piece of my mind!"

"Hold it." Ben's hand reached out to Jack. "Let's not deploy our ammo, not yet. First, we tie up our cases. Let the chief stew in his juices. Let's use this to our advantage."

"I can hold off. But, when the time comes, I'm telling him to shove it!"

Ben settled back in his seat. After a month in Ogden, the Ko Ko Mo felt almost as much like home as his own neighborhood. "Changing the subject, Jack. You're right about Sylvia. No offense, but I'd rather be looking at her instead of your mug. I think I'll give her a call."

"Oh yeah?" Jack flashed his grin at two women entering the bar, one tall and tan, the other well-padded and freckled. They would have looked like nurses in their identical white uniforms, if it weren't for the words "Farr Ice Cream" stitched across their bodices. They sidled up to a couple of bar stools.

"Well," Jack said, "I'm more than ready to wrap up the case. Right now I need to find out how sweet Farr Ice Cream is."

Ben took out his note pad and scanned it as he talked. "We've done enough work tracking Allreds for the Salt Lake boys." He flipped three pages. "Three days wasted."

"So…" Jack gave the table a rap. "Now, we let the team down there worry about 'em."

"Absolutely."

Jack brushed the errant curl off his forehead. "Now we're back, let's pay a call on Bishop Taylor tomorrow, assuming he isn't at the cat house. Maybe he can help us throw that prophet behind bars. And," his knuckles thumped the table top, "you never know. We'll see if my sister is on that filthy farm."

"Agreed. What do you say we make a plan of how to deal with the Chief in the morning, when we're sober?" Ben drained his drink.

"Eddie," Jack shouted at the bartender through the crowd and smoke, "how 'bout another beer? Ben, you go on ahead. I see four ice cream cones about ready to melt."

CHAPTER 21

NEW DAY DAWNING

Safe from the feds for now, Karen nestled on her side of the bed under one of the double wedding ring quilts Grandma Hardy had stitched. She hugged her pillow and slept.

Hundreds of familiar faces crowded into her dream. They were neighbors and family, but with contorted features. Some were fundamentalist group members. Others were Mormon friends and church officials. Her grandmother was there, off somewhere, droning in a harsh uncharacteristic voice about blood atonement. The voices pleaded. Hordes of people shoved and elbowed in a fight to control her. For her own good they bellowed. From nowhere, the feds plowed into the throng. Their black car careened through the mob toward Karen.

Cool night ebbed into a late summer morning. Half asleep, Karen kicked off the stifling quilt. She yawned, balking at the ache in her muscles and the sticky sweat dampening her nightgown. She felt embarrassed by her own body odor and yearned for a bath. But this wasn't a day to expect free-flowing hot water or solitude.

She slipped downstairs, sidestepping blankets, pillows, and squalling Allreds in the path to the bathroom. The instant Davy emerged, she was inside running bath water. The opportunity was a bit of luck. Visitors needing water might overburden the cantankerous pump. Once in the tub, she ran the soap up and down her body before anyone could catch her.

Bam, slam, bang. A fist assaulted the bathroom door. Karen lathered faster to the tune of the door bashing.

"Who's in there taking all day?" Rosemary's tone grated like stone honing a blade.

"Hold your horses. I only just got in here." Karen submerged and was rinsed in seconds. Heaven would be an hour-long, private bath with billowing suds and ever-flowing hot water.

The pummeling on the door thudded like a jackhammer.

"Karen," Rosemary screamed, "I told mother you're hogging the bathroom and wasting water. She said to get out of there, now. Mom's yelling for me to help her finish breakfast. You better get out and help too, or else. There's getting to be a line out here."

Karen blotted her dripping body with an already soggy towel before she pulled clothes on her damp body and hurried into the kitchen. Her stomach rumbled from the aromas of fresh biscuits and bacon in the frying pan. She peeled and sliced peaches into an amber fruit bowl.

Rosemary stacked plates and bowls and counted silverware. "We'll have to eat in shifts. We don't have enough spoons or space at the table for everyone."

Mother dribbled hot bacon grease into a drippings can on the stove. She sliced more meat into the smoking cast iron skillet, which was big enough for two stove burners. Crisp bacon strips drained on a platter.

"Father will have to miss work," Mother said. "He'll find out where Brother Roland is hiding out. We can't go on providing for so many for long. I have this baby to worry about." Mother glanced at the shelf of a baby bulge bumping the stove in front of her.

Squabbling in the living room let them know Eva's three children weren't getting along with the Hardy kids. Karen hurried off to quash the dispute.

"I have the biggest priesthood power because I'm the biggest," Gered said. "You have to do what I say, and I had that car first."

LaNae and Emma were puffed up behind him, to fight.

"Nuh, uh," Davy said, "I have better priesthood power than you because this is my house. You can't take my things first! Can he, Karen?"

"None of you kids have priesthood," Karen said. "Davy, take your car into your room. See if you can find some clothes and get dressed. I'll help you as soon as I can." She found crayons and an old school tablet to keep the visitors out of trouble.

Rosemary caught Karen in the living room dressing Davy and Judy. "Here you are sluffing off! I had to finish cooking breakfast by myself."

"So what? I'm glad you did," Karen said.

Mother's thin face was taut. "You girls cut that out. I have enough to worry about. Karen, get Eva and her kids in here. We'll eat when they're done."

The guests devoured gravy over biscuits with the bacon and bowls of peaches floating in cream. Then the Hardys took their turn. Breakfast went down in gulps, but tasted good. Both families calmed down once they were dressed and fed.

"Karen," Mother ordered, "take all the kids out to play. Rosemary can clean up today."

"What about my hands?" Rosemary asked. "All of this dishwashing will ruin them for my date with Fred tonight."

Karen grinned back at Rosemary's scowl.

The two mothers folded bedding. They sighed good riddance as the kid commotion followed Karen outdoors.

"Let's play in the sandbox," Karen told the children. "You can dig tunnels or cook pretend sand puddings."

Karen filled a watering can to dampen the sand.

"Karen!" Lucinda called out as she hurried over from the front gate. "Guess what? We got our TV set!"

"Wow, Lucinda, I can't wait to see it."

"Mom made me shut it off smack in the middle of Mid-morning Movie. The visiting teachers are over there giving their lesson. They're talking about how the Lord loves clean bathrooms or something. Ain't that funny? We don't have no bathroom."

"What? The visiting teachers are there?" Karen eyed Lucinda's house. Sure enough, Sister Brown's Studebaker was parked out front. "Lucinda, I'll ask Mom about coming to watch television. But I have to go in now. See you later, okay?"

Karen rushed into the house. "Mother, Mother, the visiting teachers are coming."

She found Mother sitting on the sofa crowded beside heaps of clothes and blankets. She was in an exchange with Eva, Rhonda, and Millie. "Edward will see that Roland finds another safe house for you, Sister Eva. Until then, you'll have to cut back on using water. Our pump can't keep up with the demands."

"Mother…" Karen repeated.

"Karen, wait your turn. This is important."

"I'd better knock real loud," said a woman's voice from the front porch. "Do you hear arguing in there, Sister Brown?"

"I've been trying to tell you," Karen said, over the knocking. "The visiting teachers are here!"

Alarmed, Mother jerked upright. "Karen, you'll have to go to the door. Tell them I'm sick… and resting because the baby is almost due. Say I can't have a lesson this month."

Karen would have preferred cleaning duty. She cracked the door to Sisters Brown and Christensen, who clutched copies of Mormon home teaching manuals to their bosoms. The ladies' faces were of similar even features with identical smiles, typical for the women of Zion. They both wore light brown Toni home-waved hair. Their shirtwaist dresses were alike, one pink, one blue. How could non-family members be such bookends?

"Karen my dear, hello. We're here with the monthly Church Relief Society message for your mother." Sister Brown's words sing-songed like a chirpy well-worn nursery rhyme.

Karen hoped her own smile appeared more sincere than the one the church sisters mirrored. "Yes, I see that. But my mother is resting. She's really worn out and sick from the baby. It's nearly time for it to be born."

"Well, we'll just come in and give a quick lesson by her bed. We must complete our assignments. One-hundred-percent. It's a requirement from the Brethren in Salt Lake." Sister Christensen pulled her words around her mouth like butter taffy. The ladies' tilted chins expressed support for the one-hundred-percent policy.

The two squinted into the dark room from the bright porch. Karen prayed they couldn't make out Mother and the polygamy wives slumped in the shadows.

Karen stepped outside, closing the door behind her. "I'm sorry. Mother didn't sleep last night. She had to go to the bathroom a dozen times, and I think her back is killing her. She can hardly walk."

The women hesitated and moved in view of the front window. Sister Brown shaded her face to glance behind the glass. Karen couldn't tell what they saw in the living room.

"Well, good-bye." Karen said. "Mother loves your Relief Society lessons and all. She'll be sad she missed you."

"Listen," Sister Brown said. "You're a big girl. You be sure to take care of your mother and help with the younger kids."

They turned. "And be sure you and your sister help with all of the visitors too, Karen."

"Imagine inviting a houseful of guests the last week or two before a baby. I declare…" Sister Brown spoke in a stage whisper loud enough for Karen to hear.

The kids were out of the sandbox, running wild. Gered was in a mad rush to escape with a silver sand shovel. LaNae and Emma raced close behind. LaNae and her brother dodged in time to miss slamming into the visiting teachers. Little Emma was slower. Sister Brown was a mere step or two from the safety of the gate when the toddler smacked with full force against the woman's fleshy thigh.

Davy and Judy tore after the Allred kids, intent on protecting the Hardy family sand tools. The unexpected sight of staunch women halted them in their tracks. They took refuge behind Karen's legs.

"That's enough, kids!" Karen said. "Sorry, ladies. Thanks for coming."

"I'm afraid your mother may need more help than you and your big sister can provide." Sister Christensen rolled her eyes heavenward.

"I'm afraid you're right." Sister Brown clucked her tongue. They bristled back into the Studebaker.

Karen shooed the kids onto the back porch to read them stories. When the youngsters grew too wiggly to listen, she pulled out the box of blocks.

"Karen, come on out a minute." Lucinda was back, calling through the screen wall of the porch. She looked worried.

Karen joined her on the back steps. "What's wrong?"

"Sister Taylor called Mom into their house to take a phone call. My Granny Twila has something called phlebitis.

"Fleas bite us?" Karen couldn't stifle a snicker.

"It sounds funny, but it ain't. It hurts Granny something awful. Dad is going to drive Mom up to Goshen tonight to bring her back. She'll stay with us 'til she's better." Lucinda twisted a lock of hair.

"That's scary, Lucinda. I'm really sorry."

"Idaho is way, way up there." Lucinda pointed north and sniffed back tears. "And Bishop Taylor's making Dad finish the irrigation and do afternoon chores before they go. They have to stay up there overnight. Only Mom and Dad and Granny can fit in the pickup cab."

"You mean you're not going?"

"I have to stay home alone tonight to baby-sit Barrymore and Fay Wray. It's way far for us to ride in the truck bed." She hunched her shoulders and fiddled with a lock of hair.

"Are you scared, Lucinda?"

"Uh, huh." Lucinda whimpered. Tears puddled in her eyes. "Couldn't you beg your mom to let ya' stay over? I wouldn't be scared if you wuz there."

"Well, she might let me. I'll try. I can run over later and let you know."

*   *   *

After lunch the children napped. Karen found Mother resting in her darkened bedroom and asked about spending the night with Lucinda.

"Karen, I don't like you being under farm-hand influence. I've told you that until I'm blue in the face." She punched a pillow with her fist and stuffed it under her knees.

"Yes. But it's an emergency. We're supposed to help our neighbors. Isn't that right?"

"Yes, but we have our hands full helping persecuted polygamists." She kneaded her forehead.

"This will help them. And it will help our family, too," Karen said. "Eva's girls could sleep better upstairs in my place tonight. That would make less mess in the living room. And it would save water."

"Well, maybe you're right." Mother chewed her lip. "With luck, Roland should be here at the crack of dawn to pick them up. Thank the Lord. I'll let you do this if you come home right after sunrise to help with breakfast and minding the kids."

Mother sighed and fluttered her eyelids shut. The matter was settled.

"Yes, I'll be back first thing. I'll go pack an overnight bag."

Karen scrambled up the stairway, and gave a leap and private yelp for joy on the landing. Waiting to leave made the afternoon of babysitting drag on forever. There would be one whole night away from the Hardy farm, overrun with polygamists and her fretful family. She was already savoring the reprieve.

CHAPTER 22

THE WORD OF WISDOM

Ben studied the ceiling and waited with Jack for Chief Walker to finish a phone call. For the moment, the chief used the same namby-pamby tone Ben had heard in local Utah luncheonettes and at the Farr Ice Cream Parlor.

"Sister Neena, I'm so proud of you and Alden and your callings in the church. You're a credit to the family."

He listened while Ben and Jack waited.

"Neena honey, it's a priesthood matter of great import. Be sure to have Alden call me right away after he gets in from plowing up things. Or whatever kind of farm-type chores he's out seeing to. All my love to the young'uns. Take care."

The Chief hung up the phone and turned his attention to Ben and Jack. His face reddened and his voice turned to a growl. "Let me get this straight, you two boys have cooked up a scheme to raid a quiet family farm in Coverdale? And you expect to dump some no-account prophet into my jail?"

His voice ground like un-oiled machinery. This was the chief Ben knew and secretly scorned.

"You got that right, boss." Jack said. "The so-called prophet has at least five wives. Some of 'em kids your daughter's age."

Walker's fist whacked his desk. On a flimsier surface, the blow would have sent papers and ink bottles jostling. "You'll leave my daughter out of this!"

"We know who the bishop of Cloverdale is," Jack said. "He must be worried about the situation, and rightly so. He lives across the street from a nest of polygamists."

"I thought you two were keeping your noses clean. When did you stop following leads on that Allred group out in Murray?"

"We lent a hand with that," Jack said. "Didn't you read my report? That group happens to be hooked up to the Ogden area ones we're discussing."

"Ogden. Now that's the rub." The chief's eyes were a double barreled shotgun aimed at Jack. "Jack knows what I'm saying if you don't, Ben, you being of the Jewish faith and from back East. Ogden is my city. I don't want it besmirched. The bishop in question answers to me. In fact, that was his wife on the phone just now. She's my wife's sister. I happen to be the stake president of these parts. That outranks bishop. If I tell Alden Taylor to back off working with you, I'll expect him to do it. You boys will too if you know what's good for you."

Jack's face turned stony. He grasped the edge of the chief's desk and met his glare.

Ben reached out to warn him back into his seat. "Jack, let me explain it to the chief. Sir, this isn't about you or the local politics. This isn't about the LDS Church or Jack. It's about under aged girls being sold into sexual servitude. I'm from the U.S. federal government, which doesn't take kindly to such things. I won't dishonor your town. I expect you won't either."

Chief Walker's face swelled and reddened. "I don't like your impudence, boy!"

Ben shrugged. He held up his hands in a placating gesture. "Looking out through your glass wall, I see Julie there chomping at the bit, trying to catch your eye. You're a busy man. We won't continue to take up your time."

"Let her wait. Here's my point. I'll hammer it home, Agent Wolfowitz. I want no arrests made here. Disobey my orders, and you'll wish you hadn't!"

Ben let his eyes bore in on the chief for a moment before he spoke. "Chief Walker, I expect to do whatever's necessary to complete my assignment, including this case in Ogden."

The chief stood, snapped his fingers, and motioned Julie inside. "Place a long distance call for me. Please get Agent Wolfowitz's supervisor on the line. That will be all, gentlemen."

∗   ∗   ∗

"Bishop Alden Taylor?" Jack called through a half-open door.

Before entering the Cloverdale Mormon ward house, Ben had agreed to let Jack start out taking the lead.

Jack swung the office door wide for a full view of the bishop behind his desk and an ornate painting above his head, a white haired gentleman with words beneath: *"President David O. McKay, Prophet, Seer, and Revelator."*

The bishop jerked and snorted. "Who are you? What are you doing here?"

"I'm Detective Blackburn." One stride brought Jack to the edge of the desk. He opened his palm near the bishop's face to show his badge. "Ogden Police Department. This is Agent Wolfowitz."

"FBI," Ben said, also flashing his badge.

"The bishop half rose and accepted cursory handshakes. "Is there a problem? This is my ward. I'm in charge."

Two-faced was Ben's first impression, so much so that Ben half suspected he'd find a second face staring out from the back of the bishop's head.

Jack grabbed two folding chairs from a stack in the corner and set them up. He and Ben sat down.

Jack jutted his jaw. "We're here to investigate reports of polygamy and under-aged cohabitation in your ward." His fists were tight at his sides.

Looking from Jack to Ben, the bishop's eyes narrowed. "You boys are wasting your time. This is not Short Creek. None of those shenanigans go on up here in Cloverdale. Not on my watch."

Jack's fists eased forward on his knees. He bent in close. "Sir, a very reliable informant gave us irrefutable information about Brother Hardy's polygamy compound."

Shortarm's image flashed through Ben's mind. He held in a smirk as Jack continued. "Our source directed us to your farm across the highway from the Hardy's plyg pit. We've been there. We talked to your hired hand within the last hour. That's how we knew where to find you. We're here as a courtesy."

"Courtesy?" Taylor's voice bellowed. "You don't know the meaning of the word. You're a belligerent city slicker, a kid, wet behind the ears!"

Ben blinked at hearing this hayseed Mormon call his slob partner a "city slicker." He turned to hear Jack's retort.

"You're speaking to the law of the land," Jack said. "The LDS Church has an article of faith commanding you to honor it and I'm here to see that you do."

Taylor was silent. Fury contorted his features.

"Agent Wolfowitz." Jack turned to Ben. "Please check your log as of last Friday. Isn't that the date we observed Bishop Taylor in town patronizing that establishment, the one called the Ko Ko Mo Club? I think it was about 4:45 in the PM?"

Ben flipped open his notebook. "Yes, that's correct, Detective Blackburn. Except it's 4:49 to be exact."

Bishop Taylor rose, fumbled to close the door and returned to his desk.

Ben noticed the man walked with a strut, not regal— like a peacock—more the swagger of a roustabout rooster.

Jack continued, "As I recall, the bishop here imbibed a cool glass of refreshment? Do your notes corroborate that, Agent Wolfowitz?"

Ben nodded a curt yes. "That's correct."

Bishop Taylor flew out of his chair, eyes ablaze. "How dare you impugn me! This is my ward and my office. Shame on you! Get out. Leave. Go!"

The two didn't move. Ben turned a notebook page. "Bishop Taylor, please sit down."

The bishop opened his mouth to protest then sat down with such force that the springs on his chair sounded assaulted.

Ben continued. "I represent the highest branch of federal law enforcement. The FBI has no interest in local rumors about law abiding Mormons, such as yourself, none at all. We are interested in the safety of under aged minors. I'm following leads at the behest of a parent in Colorado. The girl seems to have been transported across state lines to this vicinity for the purpose of illegal cohabitation. Moral turpitude of this magnitude requires a full investigation and prosecution under the Mann Act."

Jack held up a hand. "We're cooperating on that case and we're looking for a Utah girl who is also missing."

"I can't help you with that. I'm a bishop, not the sheriff."

"Understood." Jack's eyes hadn't left the bishop's face. "My associate doesn't care about what you've done in town. But I think your ward members would be concerned. I'm absolutely certain your wife would take an interest. Isn't her name Neena? And your stake president brother-in-law, a city slicker like myself, and the police chief—he would be outraged."

The bishop flailed like a windmill run amuck. "You have no right to meddle in my business. None whatsoever! I drank an orange Nehi. The Word of Wisdom doesn't prohibit soda pop. Besides which"— he seemed smitten with a sudden brain-storm—"going into that establishment is not against any law of the land."

Jack wore an unpleasant smirk. "After downing that orange soda water, you crossed the street and entered another 25th Street establishment. Is that right, Agent Wolfowitz?"

"Yes, that was at 5:17 PM, Detective Blackburn."

"Exactly."

"Hold it." Ben sat taller and accentuated his authoritative tone. "Detective Blackburn, I think Bishop Taylor can be reasonable. He's a responsible cleric and a family man, esteemed by his church congregation. I don't think there's a need to be pushy." He rested a hand on Jack's shoulder. "You do want to cooperate don't you, Bishop Taylor?" he asked, keeping his voice low, his demeanor, reassuring.

The bishop was a study in coloration. His face turned from scarlet to rosebud, to the washed-out gray of library paste.

"I can't help you." He sounded as if a trout bone had caught in is throat. "It would destroy me."

"Have a Life Saver, Bishop." Ben opened a new roll. "Go ahead. They freshen up the mouth, as well as calming the nerves."

A flurry of tics started, first with the bishop's left eye, spreading to the flare of his nose, and to his lips. His hand fumbled as he reached for and dropped the candy onto a Book of Mormon in front of him. It rolled off, and he caught it. In spite of the spasms, he pried out a candy and put it in his mouth.

Ben retrieved his peppermint roll and popped one into his own mouth. He offered it to Jack, who waved it off.

"So," Ben laid bare his strategy, "give it a little more thought. Isn't it possible you did notice something which slipped your mind at first? Tell us exactly what goes on at the Hardy farm, directly across from where you live."

The bishop's face turned a new shade, the color of cream of pea soup. "I think I did happen to see one of those new-fangled silver bullet trailers over there. I thought it might be a hideout for the culprits who've been vandalizing my watermelon crop."

Ben was sorry he happened to glance toward Jack; glad he managed to look away in time to curb his impulse to chuckle. Jack bit his lip and did the same.

"A trailer?" Jack asked. "Did it occur to you that it might house polygamist cult members?"

The bishop creaked his chair from side to side, emitting the piteous whine of a child with a toothache. Then Ben heard another noise, *Bump-a-thump, bump-a-thump,* from under the desk where he could see argyle socks in ox-blood and white shoes tapping a guilty rhythm.

"Yes," the bishop finally answered. "A member of my ward bishopric did speculate on that possibility, but I'm not the type of man who easily casts aspersions."

"When we took a look around out there," Ben said, "we actually noticed two trailer houses. Have you seen the occupants?"

"I think someone told me the Hardys have cousins living there temporarily. I figured it was none of my business."

Jack cleared his throat. "Today, your hired hand told us a name he heard from his daughter and a friend of hers. Does the name Hyrum LeGrande ring a bell?"

"No, can't say it does."

"Anything else you could tell us would be appreciated," Ben said.

"Well, let's see, they do sometimes have real big gatherings on Saturday nights. Cars pour in and fill the lot behind the house. The overflow cars usually line up along the highway in front of it."

"And?"

The bishop's mood had relaxed from furious to pensive. "And some of the guests wear frontier clothes, calico dresses, braids and such, like they're rehearsing a pioneer handcart pageant or something."

"Next time you see those crowds arriving, give us a call." Ben handed him a card.

The bishop stared at it and nodded tentative agreement. "I'll call you, but only if you promise to keep your mouths shut on certain sensitive subjects that don't relate to the case in point."

"You can count on it." Ben turned to one of the last few clean pages in his notebook. The questioning continued until he and Jack were satisfied.

"Fine," Bishop Taylor said at last, "then, that's that. The two of you can stop in for a slice of homemade chocolate cake and a glass of milk when you're out this way. I'll tell the little woman to expect you."

Ben felt a touch of writer's cramp. His notebook was full by the time they thanked their new confidante for his cooperation and bade him a pleasant good day.

CHAPTER 23

FRIEND

Grandma's castoff carpet bag swinging at her side, Karen darted across the highway toward Lucinda's house. She imagined owning an overnight case like Camille's. At the last sleepover, Camille had flounced in and showcased it on Nancy's navy blue bedspread. The eye-popping bag was a thing of beauty, sizzling pink with waxy black polka-dots, gold tone clasps and rhinestone handle grips. The girls squealed at the sight of it against the dark satin fabric. Nancy said, "It's exotic, like the neon dragon sign in town at night."

Karen hid the hand-me-down bag behind her legs where she wouldn't have to look at it as she climbed the wooden pallets which served as Lucinda's front porch.

Inside, Lucinda's mother, Ruth Crumm, was singing a duet with Rosemary Clooney on the radio.

Ruth's voice on the other side of the door was mellow and clear, like apple cider with a pungent after-bite. On the long notes, she exaggerated the twang for the sake of drama. "Tra-la-la, tweedlee dee dee it gives me a thrill. To wake up in the morning to the mockin' bird's trill."

Karen banged on the door loud enough to be heard.

The radio shut off.

Ruth Crumm pushed open the flimsy screen for Karen. "Hi there, honey. Ain't I ever glad to see you! I'm just pleased as punch you can stay over with Lucinda and the kids." The bulged-out screen had torn loose from the tacks along the bottom frame.

"Thank you, Ruth. I'm sorry about Lucinda's granny." No one in Cloverdale put on airs by calling the Crumms Mr., Mrs., or Brother, Sister. The parents were Ruth and Darrel, plain and simple.

Ruth was a stunning beauty with rich honey skin, like Lucinda's. Karen admired her full, red painted lips and short inky hair. Three children and a diet rich in grease and sugar had taken its toll on her figure. Seams suffered distress where her clothes couldn't stretch over the ample bulges of her tummy and backside while buttons down the front of her blouse barely bore the strain.

Karen stepped onto the worn black-and-white plaid linoleum of the spotless threadbare living room. She sat on the turquoise plastic sofa.

"I sent Darrel down to the filling station market," Ruth said of her husband. "He picked up some orange pop for a treat to go with your dinner tonight. He brought home a little dessert for later, too." She whispered, "I hid it out behind the breadbox." She licked her lips. "I feel almost like I'll have a grownup here now that you're staying. You're ever so reliable for your age."

Karen often heard that compliment outside her home and wished her own family would show her similar respect.

As she listened, Karen's eyes were drawn to the new television. It held the place of honor where the Crumm family displayed their Christmas tree every December. The set rested on a cloth-draped table in the west window corner of the room, in plain view for passers-by to admire from the highway. The bulky box was as wide as an outstretched arm. The blank screen was much smaller, about the size of a school penmanship tablet. Karen resisted asking if she might turn it on. Instead, she resorted to imagining an eye inside was looking out at her from the blank screen as she read and reread the word Philco under it.

Lucinda's father stomped up the back stairs in his oversized work boots. Leaning forward, Karen could see him clomp into the kitchen and noticed how his blue denim shirt and overalls accentuated his barrel-like torso. He rolled up his sleeves and soaped his face and arms using the only running water in the house, then he swished the grime down the drain.

Lucinda followed him inside carrying his work gloves and water jug, and Karen rushed into the kitchen to greet her while Darrel dried off with a clean towel from Ruth.

As usual Darrel's hefty neck gave way for a nod at Karen. His huge callused hand lifted his sweaty straw hat off the kitchen table. He brushed it across his sunburned forehead to emphasize his one word of greeting. "Howdy." In Karen's experience, the word rounded out his usual vocabulary of yes and no.

"Hooray, Karen!" Lucinda rang out. "I wuz scared your mom wouldn't let you come."

Lucinda's mother bustled after Darrel. "Everything's ready for you. Lemme help."

The parents soon emerged from the bedroom. Darrel carried a cardboard suitcase, yellow, ringed around the center with brown stripes. More attractive than her carpetbag, Karen thought, but in no way as captivating as Camille's dotted pink masterpiece. Darrel had changed into clean blue jeans and a plaid shirt. Ruth had put on colorful clip-on earrings and fresh lipstick. They stopped in the kitchen to pick up pasteboard boxes of sandwiches and Nehi sodas.

Lucinda gathered Barrymore, her seven-year-old brother, and Fay Wray, aged four, to kiss and wave to their parents by the back door. Ruth did the talking for herself and Darrel. "You kids mind yur big sister."

Ruth repeated that same directive at least four times, changing her tone and a word or two here and there. Darrel nodded agreement. He responded with patience and measured gruffness to the hugs and goodbyes. Karen stood back, feeling a little out of place during the family instructions and farewells. She did join in waving until the truck pulled out of the driveway and was rolling up the highway.

"Let's go in and make dinner," Lucinda said after the pickup faded from view.

Barrymore jumped up and down in Lucinda's face, coaxing, "We want to play tire swing."

"Naw, the sun'll be setting," Lucinda said. "The skeeters would eat you alive. I don't want you up all night with the itching."

"I haven't seen the television work yet," Karen said.

That settled things. All four of them gathered around the set. Lucinda unplugged a table fan to connect the TV cord. She clicked a knob and fiddled with the rabbit ears. The twelve-inch screen turned a lighter shade as a picture, Howdy Doody's grinning puppet face, materialized. They gaped at Clarabelle, the clown, beeping a horn and chasing two men, hidden under a donkey costume, off the stage. The TV audience went crazy. The peanut gallery in Lucinda's living room hooted along with them. This program inside a simple brown box was magic.

"Karen." Lucinda pulled at her sleeve. "You want to see my mom's movie magazines?"

"I guess so." Karen's eyes stayed on the set.

"I just love to sneak and look at them when I get the chance."

"I won't tattle." Karen dragged herself away from the TV set and followed Lucinda into the Crumm parents' bedroom. Lucinda rummaged under the bed and brought out a stack of worn tabloids. She fanned them out across the bed. "Mom's magazines are full of juicy pictures. You'll be shocked."

"Ooh, I'm getting goosebumps." Karen sat down and picked up a magazine. "Here's Clark Gable. And look, this guy's called Robert Taylor. It's funny that a movie star would have such a Mormon name."

"All us Crumm kids got our names from them magazines. We're named for real famous and important people." Lucinda pretended to polish her nails on her shirt top and blew on them with exaggerated pride.

Karen laughed. "No kidding?"

"Sure! My first and middle names are Lucinda and Ballard. She's a snazzy costume designer lady. Barrymore and Fay Wray are movie star names. Mom said we can't be rich, but leastwise we can have swanky names."

In the next room, the younger kids cheered Pinky Lee's antics. Their giggles blended with the sound of the star's bumbling over furniture and his lisping jokes and chortles.

"And see?" Lucinda laid out a magazine with the cover falling off. "Here is a whole magazine of nasty women who are half nekkid." Lucinda pointed to Jayne Russell stretched out in a stack of straw.

"See, it calls that yellow straw a haystack. Everbody knows good fresh hay is greener and leafy." She waved a dismissive hand.

"City folks must not know much." Karen laughed. "I wonder if they'd say I was dumb about town life."

"That's called cleavage when you show your boobies like that." Lucinda turned the page. "See, here's Marilyn Monroe."

Karen grabbed the picture and held it up. "Rosemary thinks that's how she looks, just because she has a mole on her cheek like this one." She touched Marilyn's beauty mark.

Lucinda tilted her nose in the air and posed with a come-hither wink like the photo. Karen laughed and egged her on by clapping.

Lucinda crossed her eyes and pointed a finger into her cheek. "Look at me. I'm Marilyn Monroe. Duh!" Karen flopped on the bed in stitches.

Karen thumbed through pages of movie stars with low-cut necklines and scanty bathing suits. "My mom would never let me see movies with sinful women like those. Would yours?"

"Probly not. But my dad takes her to see 'em sometimes on payday. I heard them laughing about 'tits' when they came home from the show late one night."

Lucinda cracked the door to look in on her siblings.

Karen took the chance to see Pinky Lee charming a bowler hat to roll up and down his arm, spin like a whirly-gig through the air, and flutter over and back across a tabletop before he smashed it back onto his head, upside down.

"I know about the word tits." Lucinda's whisper was louder than her conversational voice. "It's like teats for cows, only on ladies."

"Yeah, I've heard that word before." Karen looked down at her chest.

Lucinda looked at her own. "I'm catching up to you even if I am younger."

"Well then, you'll soon be having periods, like me. Just don't go to the temple until then. You know what happened to me there."

"Yeah. Me and everybody else in town."

"Humph! It wasn't my fault. It just happened. Now kids and grownups that used to like me look at me funny and probably hoot behind my back."

"Yeah, people in these parts is mean all right. Makes me see why you want to get away from here someday."

"I do wish I could." Karen gathered up the magazines. "Heck, I'd buy a shiny suitcase and stuff it with store-bought clothes."

The sun out the window had slid low in the sky and turned orange-crimson like a ripe Elberta peach.

Lucinda hid the magazines back in their place. Together they smoothed the bedspread.

Karen helped Lucinda open two cans of Franco-American spaghetti. They scraped the pasty mixture into a dented aluminum pan and put it on the stove to heat. Then they set the table.

Lucinda smeared slices of Wonder bread with oleomargarine. Karen folded them over and put one on each plate. They added hunks of head lettuce and drizzled them with spicy red Kraft French dressing from a tall bottle.

"My mom always melts slices of Velveeta cheese on spaghetti," Lucinda said. "Do you like that?"

"I've never tasted canned spaghetti or Velveeta cheese," Karen said. "But I'll try it."

"You're so rich. I don't know why you don't have no television or any fancy foods like on the advertisements."

"Well, we don't feel rich," Karen said. "I guess you're luckier about those two things, at least."

"We do eat good. Leastwise, for most of the month unless money runs out."

Barrymore's tanned face grinned as he stuffed it with spaghetti. "This shore is hunky dory."

Fay Wray followed his lead. "Even better'n Mama makes cuz it's drippin' with cheese." The little girl's mouth was full, but Karen could make out the words.

"This dinner is delicious," Karen agreed, "especially this soft, gooey Wonder bread and margarine. It's like eating cake. We usually have to eat heavy homemade brown bread and hand-churned butter."

Lucinda grinned, proud of her meal. "Have some more bread. And oleomargarine, too." Karen did.

"Now for a surprise!" Lucinda leaped up and reached behind the breadbox. She returned to the table with pink and white Hostess Snowballs wrapped in cellophane. "We're having a special dessert!"

The children cheered.

Lucinda tore open the packages. "I'm not a girl," Barry-more said. "Give me white."

"I am a girl. Fay Wray stretched her little hands up into Lucinda's face. "Please, please, I want a pink one."

"And Karen?"

"I've never tasted such a thing. Guess I'd like pink."

"Good. We're all happy." Lucinda handed them out and everyone bit into a gooey ball of marshmallow coated with coconut. Inside was a blob of chocolate cake with a scoop of white creamy frosting at the center.

"Mmm! The marshmallow outside is like eating gum, but better," Karen said.

Everyone smacked their lips and agreed. The younger kids delighted in pulling the topping like it was rubber, then squeezing marshmallow between their fingers before popping it on their tongues.

"It's like a party with pop and boughten cupcakes," Lucinda said.

After dinner Karen heated water on the stove for dishwash-ing. Lucinda left to take Barrymore and Fay Wray to the outhouse while twilight still lit the path.

Back inside, Lucinda dipped a wash rag into the water heating for dishes. She scrubbed the day's dirt from Barrymore's and Fay Wray's arms and faces.

She recited the warning their mother ordinarily gave. "I'm putting the slop pot right here by the bedroom door in case anyone has to pee in the night. The chipped pot was white enamel with a bulging shape like a jug, and a matching lid. Karen had used it before when she spent nights at the Crumm house.

"If you kids wet the bed," Lucinda said with her hands at her hips, "I won't wait for mom to get home to paddle your behinds."

After tucking in the kids, Lucinda led Karen into the kitchen. "Karen," she whispered," there's something funny going on outside with the Taylors."

"Funny weird or funny ha-ha?" Karen searched her face then waited for an explanation as she poured heated water over the dish pan of silverware and utensils.

Lucinda went on, "I heard the Taylors talking about your family and your farm."

"Where are they? How could you hear them?" Karen poured water into a rinse pan.

"I heard them talking when I was bringing the kids back in from the outhouse. You know my ears are so sharp I can hear a horse whinny a mile off. I can tell which horse it is and what the whinny means. The whole Taylor family's on the lawn, gaping at the sunset. They're talking about your farm. I think the bishop wants to get it away from you."

CHAPTER 24

FOE

"Holy cow!" Karen stamped a foot on Lucinda's kitchen floor. "The bishop expects to get anything he wants just because he's the bishop?"

"Yeah," Lucinda said. "He's so busy with church stuff, he ain't got time to be nice."

Karen stamped both feet. "Do you think we dare go out and try to spy on what they're saying?"

Lucinda perked up. "Yeah, let's do it! Like when we snuck up to the window and watched the bishop give his bratty boy a whippin'."

Karen's fists were at her hips. "Yes, because Norma caught him peeking in her bathroom window."

On the TV set, The Kennecott Copper Family Theater was playing *The Prince and the Pauper*. Barrymore and Fay Wray had curled up in their beds with their tattered comfort blankets left over from babyhood.

"We're going out in the yard," Lucinda told them. "The TV can keep you company until you fall off to sleep. We'll be back real soon."

"Remember," Karen warned at the back door, "My ears are just ordinary. I want to sneak in as close as we dare."

"Well, I dare. I double dare!" Lucinda crept down the stairs with Karen close behind. She grabbed Karen's arm. "Don't make a sound or we're done for!"

Karen nodded yes, a finger to her lips.

They picked their way across the gravel driveway with the barest crunch of stones under their heels. With effort they could make out the forms of the Taylor tribe lounging in folding chairs on the lawn, willow branches flowing overhead. The family gawked out toward the west, as if they hadn't noticed that the sunset had turned muddy and mosquitoes were out hunting for blood.

The two girls edged closer behind the cover of snowball bushes along the house and the shadows under darkening twilight. Mid-step, they hesitated when they heard the Taylor's three children chattering.

A mosquito buzzed into Karen's ear. Instead of slapping or giving in to the squirms, she bravely sacrificed herself to the dot-sized blood sucker.

The Bishop and Sister Taylor, like many of their neighbors, expressed creativity in naming their children. They had concocted original names by rearranging family favorites. The youngest child was seven-year-old Aleena, named for her parents, Alden and Neena Taylor. The name of the ten-year-old middle child, Donald Dene, rhymed with Ronald and Gene, two worthy uncles. The oldest son, a fourteen-year-old, was named after two grandfathers, Cliff and Pitt. His name was Clitt.

The Taylors' black Labrador yelped and leaped into the circle of chairs. The two spies froze.

"Clitt, have you fed Topsy tonight?" the bishop asked his eldest child. Karen couldn't make out the next muffled words. Clitt raced Topsy to the backyard doghouse.

Taking advantage of the commotion, the girls inched closer until Karen could hear most of the conversation. She willed her brain to fill in the words here and there that faded into the evening air. The friends were as one, sharing the same thoughts, barely daring to exhale, and facing the same fate. They stood lock-kneed, not rustling the cover bushes. Both knew that without stealth and luck, there would be fury to pay.

"But, Mom…" Aleena whined.

"You promised ice cream before bed." Donald Dene demanded his rights.

"Yes, I know. I picked up butterscotch this morning at the Farr Ice Cream Parlor. Tell Clitt he can have some too."

The kids dawdled, playing catch-me-if-you-can, and finally trotted off toward the house. Karen and Lucinda stood still, without as much as a jostle against the snowball flowers. Running her tongue over her back teeth, Karen tasted a last shred of coconut from the dessert.

Once the kids were gone, Sister Neena's voice took on a tire-skidding screech. "Alden! It's clear to me you're not yourself tonight. Out with it, what's going on? Is someone dying or something?"

He cleared his throat. "W-well," he stammered. "I'm afraid I'm up to my neck in hot water, and I hate to worry you with it."

"What! You're going to have to, Alden. Out with it!"

"W-well, this afternoon I was catching up on paperwork down at the ward house. Two detectives barged in on me.

They're hooked up with that bunch chasing after the Short Creek polygamists. One guy is FBI. And they're poking their noses around right here in Cloverdale. They said they suspect the Hardys are hiding out plygs in those strange trailers I noticed. Remember, I told you about 'em. The two cops said I have to cooperate or I'm in trouble too."

"Goodness gracious, Alden! Face it. This has been going on right under your own nose. You, the bishop! My heavens!"

"Yes," he said. "But you know that stake president brother-in-law of yours. He's dead set against messing with polygamists. Now I see exactly what he's getting at when he phones here and dances all around the subject."

"Let me get this straight, Alden Detmar Taylor! The federal government is crawling all over Utah, stirring up trouble. And you're more worried about what my sister's no account stake president-husband says than you are about being thrown into the hoosegow? How would the kids and I manage with you in the state pen? We'd be humiliated, destitute. Our lives would be ruined." Karen heard a shuddering, then, sobbing and nose blowing. She knew the good sister carried a hanky in her sleeve for emergencies.

"Calm down, Neena. I told them I'd cooperate. I had no choice."

"Good holy garters, Alden, here's what you don't seem to realize. This is probably already all over town. You've cast a blind eye, and it's making you look like a fool. And as your wife, it makes me look like one, too. Next thing you know, kids will be taunting our children at school, all because you haven't wanted to own up to reality."

"I'll remind you to show proper respect, Neena. I am the bishop. I have priesthood powers and I'm still the head of this family!"

"Yes. Well, I have some news about those Hardys. I talked to Sister Brown and Sister Christensen today after the Relief Society quilting bee. They're sure the Hardy family is hiding out polygamists and they're not shy about spreading the news. Sister Brown said her son, Enoch, saw women in those trailers."

A diesel truck roared by and drowned out the voices. Cowering in the shrubs, searing fear and anger rushed through Karen.

Sister Neena continued. "—visiting teaching there today. But that's when the Brown kids got caught in the sanctuary plunking on the organ. They didn't want spankin's, and they ran off like a house-a-fire. But they knocked one of Viva's younguns down the stairs. The baby was screaming and her nose was bleeding. That's all I could find out."

"For crying out loud!" The bishop pounded his knees. "I don't give a cat's meow about spankings or nose-bleedings. The point is clear as day, we're not the only ones to notice the Hardys are up to no good."

"Alden, the fact is my baby sister got too big for her britch-es the minute she moved into town. Now that her husband calls himself a police chief and a stake president, she's the Queen of Sheba. Truth be told, the man is a loudmouth and a bully. I know as a rule, church leaders are called by Godly priesthood revelations. Well, he's the exception that proves the rule. He's so dumb he couldn't even keep his victory garden alive during the war. We've got the whole federal government and all of Zion breathing down our necks and he couldn't protect us if he tried. Goodness knows he probably wouldn't know the difference between stinging nettles and a watermelon patch."

"Neena, all evening I've been saying a silent prayer that this would somehow work out to our advantage, and I think the Lord has revealed it to me. It's that word you just said, 'watermelon.'"

"What? Are you plumb crazy?"

"Like I've been saying, it's too doggone hard to put a stop to watermelon thieving when that Hardy farm is blotting out twelve acres in the middle of my holdings."

"I know. It's that Edward Hardy," Neena screeched. "The man refuses to listen to reason!"

"Right. Edward is a hothead. The son-of-a-gun won't even discuss selling. But now the feds are on to him, he'll have to come around. Leastwise, when he knows I'm in league with them."

"Oh, Alden, honey! If only you would've tried harder to come up with the money for this house without selling my inheritance. But now you're saying you think we can get the farm back from Edward Hardy? My dear father left it to me, in spite of baby sister wanting it. I planted the rhubarb and the asparagus, the daisies, and the raspberries. Those Hardys don't appreciate it, don't take care of it right. You must know how I've yearned to get it back."

"Of course I know, Neena. You talk about it day and night. Your happiness is all I care about. I'm thinking this mess is a blessing in disguise. The feds might be our best friends in getting what we deserve. And your police chief brother-in-law can gosh darn like it or lump it!"

"Oh, Alden. The Lord is reaching out a hand in our behalf. I feel His spirit. You do have it in you to stand up for what's right, to protect the kids and me. We all love and admire you more than I can say, dear."

"Shoot," the bishop said, "if we play this right, it might be that police chief who looks the fool. If he loses his calling as stake president, I could have a chance at it, and you'd be at my side."

"Oh, just imagine, me, a stake president's wife. Think of it. I can hardly breathe."

"You deserve it, honey, and so do I. I'm going inside right this minute and get on that telephone. I'll direct Sister Christensen and Sister Brown to get themselves inside that Hardy house at the crack of dawn. I'll say they have to get the goods on them for the Lord's sake. And they better not take no for an answer."

Karen was furious. Her chest heaved and she felt Lucinda's grip on her arm restraining her. She must hold it in, keep still, wait.

Sister Neena slapped a mosquito. "You have every right to know about whatever's happening in this ward. After all, you are called of God to lead it. With luck and the Lord's help, the sky's the limit."

"Let's go in, Neena. I feel pent up tonight."

"Would a little conjugal comfort help you? It has been quite a spell."

He gasped. "Good heavens, woman. It's times like this when we need to avoid all thoughts of the flesh. We can't let Satan have his influence. Let's look to the Lord. We've never needed Him more. You must know that."

"Oh, Alden, dear. I do uphold your priesthood. Women can be weak creatures. The feds will go away in due course, and with the help of the Lord, you could be the new stake president and some day, a Church General Authority and then maybe even…"

"Let's not get carried away."

For the girls in the bushes, the next minutes were long as they waited for the Taylors to fold the chairs and haul them inside.

"I think I hate that man," Karen whispered. She felt like a mouse in a tom cat's claws.

The girls sprinted back to Lucinda's house.

Karen twisted her fingers and fretted on a chair at the kitchen table. Lucinda finished the dishes. They carried their shapely bottles of orange Nehi pop in by the television. In the background, the TV blared out a movie about Charlie Chan.

"Karen, Bishop Taylor knows about the polygamy folks at your house."

"Well, yeah. No one is supposed to know, Lucinda, not even you."

"But I can't just keep playing dumb now, can I?"

"I guess not," Karen said. "I wish I could be just a normal kid living in a normal place out in the world somewhere."

"This *is* the normal world for us," Lucinda said. "Me, in this little house. You, in your big one with polygamists who always hop in and out like crickets."

"You know, Lucinda, somehow, it feels good to have someone else know about this. I feel torn and lonely keeping so many secrets stuffed inside." One fence inside of Karen now had an open gate. It might be a bad thing, but it felt better at least for one night.

Karen's night in Lucinda's bed was fitful. She slept, but didn't rest.

The morning light filtered in. By six o'clock, Karen was dressed. She nudged Lucinda. "I have to go home."

Her arms roped around the carpet bag at her chest, she slipped outside.

CHAPTER 25

FALLING FENCES

From the fresh morning outdoors, Karen stepped into the stuffy kitchen with the smell of smoking toast and a barrage of squalling kids. She resisted the urge to retreat to her hayloft hideout.

Rosemary scraped burned toast over the kitchen sink. "It's past six. About time you got home."

Davy was sobbing over a broken toy army jeep. "Gered done it." He dumped plastic pieces into Karen's cupped hands.

"I'll try to fix this later." She hugged him and wiped his tears on her sleeve.

The two toddler girls chased LaNae around kitchen chairs and squealed down the hallway past Mother on the telephone. "Karen, keep those kids quiet!"

Karen herded the girls into a huddle and out onto the porch to play.

She stayed inside to listen to Mother, her voice as worn out as the knees on work pants. "Brother Roland, you need to come right away to pick up Eva and the kids. We've done all we can..." Mother's hand felt in the sacred garments under her blouse for a hanky to soak up tears.

Eva trailed after her girls on the porch to brush their hair and dress them. Her eyes were as swollen as Mother's. The strain of the situation must have precipitated harsh words between them.

Richard clattered in with the morning milk bucket.

"Where's Father?" Karen asked.

"Brother LeGrande's out there demanding water," Richard said. "The pump is dead as a doornail. He wants it fixed."

"Not that stupid pump, again."

"Yes, that stupid pump, again. Nobody's had Postum. They're as cranky as cats with their tails in doorjambs."

Richard spread a straining cloth over the wide mouth of a gallon jar. He drooped the fabric into a sagging pouch across the top, then he fished a rubber band from the cow-shaped cream pitcher on the windowsill. His deft fingers secured the cloth before he strained the milk.

"All these people and no flushing toilet," he said. "Holy Cow, it's gonna smell real bad, real fast."

They grimaced.

Gered whooped by with another of Davy's cars. "I'll take that," Karen said. "You go out on the porch with your mother."

Father stomped in without bothering to scrape mud and manure from his boots. He stopped muttering under his breath when he noticed Richard. "Get down there and prime that gosh-forsaken pump. Keep trying until you get it started. No excuses."

Karen knew she had to warn Father about Bishop Taylor. "Father, I heard the bishop last night talking about us."

Father's face twisted like he had gas pains.

"I have no time for female gossip. You're not on center stage today, missy."

Karen persisted. "But the visiting teachers told him we have polygamists here. Enoch spread the news we have trailers out back. The Bishop wants the feds to raid us. He wants to get the farm."

Karen stood back in case Father lashed out at her.

Color rose in his face. "Good heck! I'm not about to listen to flimflam fairytales. We have no water and this place is teaming with people who need it. I have a sick calf out there and my irrigation rights start in one hour. That scrawny bishop is too big a boob to run me out. Just help your mother with the female work around here and keep out of my business. I'm too busy to have to slap sense into your head today!"

Karen choked back panic. Between shudders, she peeled and sliced what were left of Grandma's peaches. The Hardy girls set up an informal table of toast, peaches, cream, and fried potatoes. Disgruntled family members and guests grabbed a bite of breakfast. No one noticed they'd forgotten to pray over the food.

"Edward," Mother said, "Roland phoned. He was waiting for stores to open before he left. He wanted to run errands on his way here. I told him to come right away to pick up his family."

"All right, Hosannah. Now what about your daughter claiming the bishop is sending the feds? That bantam rooster's worse than ever now that he made bishop."

Father raked fingers of both hands through his hair.

"Anyhow, the extra people inside this house'll be gone before noon. I'm going out back to see to that blasted pump."

"Karen," Mother asked, "are you sure you heard Bishop Taylor say that? What exactly happened?"

"Honest Injun, Mother, he said it. Lucinda and I were out in the yard and I heard him as clear as day."

Mother's lip quivered. "Why is the Lord testing me this way?" A new storm of tears rained down her face. "I'd give anything for a few minutes of peace and quiet." Her fingers wrung the skirt of her apron.

"And there's something else." Karen didn't allow the stab of panic to stop her. "The bishop said he would send the visiting teachers back. He wants them to tell him everything that's going on here. They're coming this morning, maybe any minute."

"Mercy gosh!" Mother's voice screeched. "They wouldn't be out a weekday so early. They have their own families to feed." She gnawed her lip until Karen worried it would bleed. "With luck and the Lord's help, we can get everybody out in time. We'll straighten up the house by ten. They never show up before that."

Mother smoothed her wrinkled smock and apron over her belly. She blew her nose. "We'll hope the Lord will see what we're up against and give us a hand."

"Listen," Rosemary said. They heard voices and clattering from the front porch, then, knocking. Karen and the little children ran a footrace to answer.

The kids won. Karen had sprinted in from the kitchen seconds too late to block the visiting teachers from entering.

The frightening figure of Sister Christensen pushed past Davy. She carried a basket with Spic and Span, Dutch Girl cleanser, and rags instead of her church woman handbook.

Sister Brown was a scarier sight. She hauled in a bucket, mop, and broom. Her usual fussy hairdo was wrapped with a polka-dotted scarf, tied in a fat, square knot over her eyebrows.

Karen struggled to make sense of the senseless. Did the intruders expect to clean the Hardy house?

"Hello," is all Karen could think to say.

Eva sat on the guest bed sofa unfolded into the middle of the floor. She wore her usual pioneer-style dress with her braids hung down her back, not yet looped up behind her neck. Anyone would think she had stepped off a cowboy movie set, unless they were familiar with Mormon polygamist fashions.

Bulging shopping bags were propped by the front door, ready to go, along with a mountain of blankets and pillows. Toy tanks and green plastic soldiers were in formation to defend the end table. Three baby dolls slept, tucked into bed in the magazine rack. Newspapers, combs, brushes, children's socks, shoes, underwear, and hairpins littered the floor, leaving only a narrow path to the kitchen.

The bishop's two spies bustled with military precision into the middle of guilty chaos. It struck Karen that they weren't half as friendly as the dolls littering the room and were as stiff and plastic as the toy soldiers.

"We're here to help." Sister Brown let her supplies clatter to the floor and grabbed her hips to survey the war zone. "It's our job to lend a hand with whatever problem is keeping your mother from hearing her monthly Relief Society lesson."

Sister Christensen fell into formation beside her. "We thought the difficulty must be that she is not able to keep up with the housework."

"That's right," Sister Brown barked out, "seeing as how she is so sick with the coming baby."

Heavy boot stomps and Father's loud voice saved Karen from answering. Brother LeGrande followed him inside and let the door bang violently. The two men froze at the sight of the unwelcome church ladies, surrounded by a tearful Mother, a humiliated Rosemary, and Karen, who had grabbed Davy and Judy. Eva sat on the edge of her bed, hiding her stricken face behind her young son and two daughters, who were vying for her lap.

Sister Christensen found her voice first and harrumphed. "Edward, I don't believe we've met your… guests."

Father jerked up his pants. "I don't believe dawn is an appropriate time for visiting teachers or introductions." His eyes narrowed. "Since when do Relief Society ladies get up with the chickens to do their visits?"

"It's obvious," Sister Christensen retorted, "that Sister Hardy needs our help this early. Look at this mess." Karen could see the corners of the sister's thin mouth twitching with the urge to prattle. The woman pursed her lips to hold in the gossip for the time being.

Rhonda called in from the back porch. "Hello, anybody in there? Don't you have just a little water we can have?"

She and Millie, who was chewing on a cinnamon roll, stepped into the room. "Don't you keep an extra bucketful for priming the pump?" Millie asked.

Everyone was too intent on gaping to answer Rhonda or Millie. Even the kids were stock-still for the first time in days.

A car crunching over the gravel in the driveway shattered the silence. It screeched to a stop. The car door slammed.

Karen tried to catch a view through the window but couldn't see who had arrived. She could only hear heavy footsteps bounding up the front stairs.

Karen took in everyone's gasps around the room and stricken faces. Were feds about to smash in through the door? The sunny morning had turned dangerous.

Bam, bam, bam. The intruder waited a moment, then attacked the door again in a new barrage of pounding.

Everyone turned to stare, but no one moved. Karen stood nearest. She turned the knob and pulled open the door. Too late to avert the crisis, Roland Allred stepped inside. Already overwhelmed, Karen registered only slight relief that he wasn't a fed.

He stood transfixed at a sight which looked more like a battlefield than a family home. Karen wondered if he was counting the massed troops.

Before anyone could speak, the back door banged open. "Hey, I got that dang pump going," Richard shouted. "Geesh! That toilet needs flushing. It smells worse than the pig sty in here."

Rosemary slammed a hall door as a diversion. She bumped people and furniture in a rush to the kitchen to hush Richard. But she was too late to stop him from calling out, "The prophet's wives can get their Postum now!"

The tense faces in the room showed signs of terror.

Rosemary shoved Richard into the trap of the living room and she hid behind the kitchen door. His movements had turned slow and mechanical, like a robot winding down until he was transformed from announcer to background prop. Others in the living room came to life gradually with throat clearing and shuffling.

"We've heard all we need to hear!" Sister Christensen announced. "We'll be going. Goodbye." She pushed by everyone in her path to the door.

"Yes. Goodbye." Sister Brown picked up her bucket and strode after her friend. Her mop handle knocked Karen's head on the way out. Her foot crunched an errant plastic jeep as she left. The mishap barely slowed her pace. On the porch she dropped her pail and slammed the front door behind her.

Everyone turned to glare at Richard.

He stood motionless, his jaw hanging. "What's going on?"

"Just shut your yap," Father barked.

Davy scrambled to scoop up the pieces of another mangled toy. "Everybody's breakin' my army stuff today." He burst into tears against Karen's leg.

She watched through the window as the church women made a beeline across the highway. "They're heading over to the bishop's house."

Karen turned back to see her mother collapse into the gray chair, sobbing.

Eva bustled, picking up socks and hair clips.

Rosemary took center stage. "I've had it," she said, blubbering. "Why should I have to put up with all of this?" Her mouth contorted. She flung her arms and screeched.

"That Christensen woman lives next door to Hadley Johnson. I've only been out on one date with him. The minute his mother hears about this, he'll consider me nothing but garbage. And soon that's what I'll be to every other good LDS boy in this ward!" Her ranting dissolved into sobs.

Brother LeGrande stepped forward to take charge. "Everyone calm down. Rosemary, quiet down and get yourself a Kleenex." He softened his tone. "The same to you, Sister Hosannah." She was making hacking noises as she sobbed.

The prophet continued issuing orders. "Richard, you misspoke because you didn't know better. Help the Allreds pack up. Let's get them on their way and this place back to looking normal. Karen is showing her lovely sweet nature better than anyone here this morning."

He gave Karen several pats on the back.

"Humph!" Karen ducked away, shrugging off his hand.

Everyone fidgeted aimlessly. Richard and Roland hauled bags and bedding to the car. Rosemary and Karen folded the bed back into a sofa. Davy gathered his remaining toy vehicles into a shoebox. The girls grabbed their dolls from the magazine rack. Mother blew her nose on her soggy hankie. She went to fetch a fresh box of tissues.

In short order, the Allreds climbed into their car and left. Gered ran from the house yelling, "Wait! Come back. You forgot me." They backed up for him and as soon as he was in the car, they peeled rubber and sped off just as the car door slammed shut.

Davy hollered. "Leastwise the pump's working. Gered flushed the toilet afore he ran off."

Brother LeGrande smiled fondly and gave an exaggerated shrug to show the simplicity of God's plan. "Pray for the Lord's blessings and have faith."

Karen went to the kitchen sink for a good hand washing as she imagined the fences of secrecy collapsing around her.

CHAPTER 26

WE GATHER TOGETHER

The next day, the family was busy preparing for a gathering of Brother LeGrande's followers. Karen lugged a basket of laundry from the clothesline. She knew she had to put the clean clothes away before they could set up chairs in the living room.

Brother LeGrande's short, erect form stepped onto the path near Rhonda's trailer. Karen dodged behind the tool shop in hopes he wouldn't spot her.

"Karen, you're not trying to avoid me, are you?"

She groaned to herself. "I'm really busy."

"Stop a moment and listen. I'm impressed of the spirit to provide you with counsel this fine morning."

Karen resisted the urge to throw the basket. Instead, she rested it beside the path.

"You've been well brought up with ideals of female modesty and prohibitions against lustful desires of the flesh. Have you not?"

Karen nodded and turned away. "Uhh, I think I need to go…"

"No. You need to show proper respect by listening." He gripped her elbow and continued. "What I'm telling you will set you free. There's no freedom without obedience and you have much to learn. I've been told you're now physically, a woman. Your monthly cycle has begun. But you're unschooled and uninitiated in the duties of that role."

Karen felt a lump growing in her throat. She tried to pull away in the direction of the house. The prophet blocked her.

"You see, my dear, there are two ways of expressing physical intimacy between a male and a female. Your parents have rightly taught you to avoid the wanton worldly way. But there's a holy and most worthy attitude that wives must learn in marriage. Once the Lord sanctifies a union, wives are to give themselves to their husbands. A worthy husband's requests are not worldly or lewd. They are an expression of the Lord's plan to build His kingdom on earth. I've been commanded of the Lord to take you as a wife and to teach you these lessons. You are indeed special to be chosen of the Lord through me, to be a part of His noble plan of procreation in these last days."

Outraged, Karen jerked violently trying to break his hold. She screamed at him. "You called this meeting at our house tonight! Mother is too sick to get ready for it!"

Stunned, the prophet's body turned to steel. His hand felt like a wrench tightening around her arm. "Karen, you need to be of more help to your mother. She is burdened with trials and tribulations in these vexing times. We chosen people must gather together in fellowship. I command you to take your place as a sweet sister. You are to cheerfully put your shoulder to the wheel. We'll continue this discussion later on when you've had time to think better of your stiff-necked female stubbornness."

"Look here," Karen said, "the baby's coming any minute. The feds are breathing down our necks. And what do we do?

Have a polygamy meeting!" She spat the words like a hissing cat. "Good gosh!"

Brother LeGrande's hands were strong and rough. He grasped her shoulders. She wrested one from his grip but couldn't pull away. "Watch yourself," he said. "The Lord doesn't take kindly to young girls with spitfire mouths, girls who have lessons to learn before they are worth my closer attentions."

"Wait…"

"No, you wait. Bite your tongue, and wait for the Lord to bless you with womanly grace. You will learn humbleness and obedience. The Lord would not have called you as my future wife if you could not rise to that lofty goal."

Karen struggled. The prophet gripped tighter.

"You will prepare for my meeting. You will curb your errant speech. And…" His blue eyes bore into hers. "You will wear that birthday locket to the meeting. If not, you'll learn obedience the hard way." He gave her a shove and stormed off.

Karen retreated, but turned to scream back. "Don't call on me to play the piano tonight. I'll say no."

She took refuge inside the house. Her heart beat like an eighteen wheeler rumbling down the highway. Normal, manageable chaos had fractured and felt like a deadly threat. Tears burned her eyes and she wiped them away. All she could think to do was lock the door behind her, something the Hardys never did.

Still stunned, she endured Rosemary's bossiness as they dusted and scrubbed all day. Finally, the house was immaculate, unlike Karen's feelings. The three older Hardy siblings dragged two dozen metal chairs up from the basement and set them wherever they could around the living room.

As Karen swept the front walkway, Lucinda dashed across the highway.

"You look scared or upset or something." She patted Karen's back and looked anxiously into her face. "Do you wish we could just run off and play, like when we wuz little?"

"Yes, I wish that a lot lately." It was a comfort knowing Lucinda cared about how she felt.

"Know what? There's something funny going on at Bishop Taylor's house. I can't figure it out. I jus' know I have the goose pimples all over me lately."

"Me, too." Karen had finished the walkway and was sweeping the bridge across the front irrigation ditch.

"Shh!" Lucinda hissed. "Listen. Do you hear that? Somebody's a-squabbling."

"I think," Karen said, "Father's angry at someone. They're behind the corner of the house."

"I'm gonna go," Lucinda said. "Maybe you can spy here, and I'll spy on what's going on at the bishop's house. I feel real curious about that."

"Lucinda, you're a good friend. I don't care what anybody says." Karen swept a spiderweb off the white board fence between her yard and the highway. Finally, everything was ready for the gathering.

Returning to the house, she heard Father and Brother LeGrande from under the apple tree around the corner. She paused to listen.

"What have you done?" Father snarled like a polecat.

"Edward, calm down. Listen to reason. This gathering will be a healing balm on troubled waters. I feel impressed of the Lord in this endeavor. If we have faith, He will protect us from evil."

"I'm the head of this household," Father bellowed. "I have a bishop across the street. He's chomping at the bit to get my farm. Feds are tailing polygamist sympathizers all over the state. Now, you've demanded this meeting. Every one of your followers will be here. That includes four of your five wives."

Karen had often heard Father bark that way at the family, but never at the prophet.

"Yes," Brother LeGrande said. "Solidarity is our key to victory over oppression. I only regret that Miriam, my first love, refused to participate tonight. First wives can be such a trial."

"That's another subject, and you know it!" Father was trapped and lashing out. "What am I supposed to do if the feds show up to this shebang?"

"Edward, Edward, the Lord and His One Mighty and Strong servant are an all-powerful team. All the feds and bishops on earth can't hold a candle to the will of God. Be at peace. Think of the words of the hymn, 'All is well. All is well.'"

Karen, raw with worry, hurried inside to bathe and change. What to do about the locket? Wear it, but under her clothes. Her fingers fumbled with the clasp as she dressed.

Rhonda and Millie arrived first from their trailers for the meeting. Rhonda lugged jugs of cider for refreshments. Millie carried plates of her favorite homemade taffy and fudge.

Father paced and fidgeted. His eyes darted, and he mumbled, his usual reaction to stressful times. Two cars turned into the driveway. Father bolted out to supervise the parking.

Pickups and other cars followed as dusk draped the sunset. After the wide driveway filled, Father directed vehicles to line the back fence that separated the family yard and gardens from the outlying farm buildings and barnyard.

Wiry little Brother Thompson and his three wives and five sons picked their way through the weeds up to the house. They barely spoke and let their eyes dart everywhere at random, but not at anyone in particular. As the Butler and Billingsley families filed in, Karen could see that they were stiff and taciturn without their usual hugs and how-do-you-dos. The trying times were taking a toll not only within her family, but also on Brother LeGrande's other followers.

The crowd chose seats, mumbling under a damper of pent-up dread.

Mother finally dragged herself from the bedroom. She waved at the guests and attempted a brave smile. She heaved her body into the gray chair saved for her. The women each took a turn to stop and offer a word of comfort.

"These last few days of waiting are a trial. You'll soon have relief."

"Swollen ankles mean an easy delivery."

"The baby will be a welcome blessing."

"When the baby's here, you'll soon forget the pain."

"That young'un has dropped into birthing position."

"Won't be long now."

The assembled saints, starved for reassurance, turned to the prophet as he made his entrance. Brother LeGrande chatted up the crowd, smiling and hugging men, women, and children. "Have faith, the Lord is with us." Bubbling charm and warmth, he repeated the phrase again and again. His words caressed the troubled souls. His handshakes and his eyes soothed ragged feelings of anxious souls jammed into the living room. One by one, Karen watched followers perk up and smile from his attention. Friendlier chit-chat soon burbled from everyone's lips. Reassured looks followed him throughout the room.

He paused in front of Karen. "My dear, you look lovely. You're much more attractive when you're serene, like this evening." His eyes glimmered at her neckline. "I see your locket is caught inside your dress. Let me help." He slid a finger between the chain and the skin on her neck. "Very, very pretty," he whispered as he centered the locket on her bodice.

Karen stiffened. A shudder shot through her as his fingers lingered on her neck.

The prophet started the meeting with an authoritative air. "Welcome, ye elect saints of God. I sense fear and contention in this room tonight. So we will open the meeting in a special way by joining together in the Hosanna Shout. Perhaps our dearest Sister Hosannah Hardy is named for it. Most of you adults did it at special mainstream Mormon Church temple or tabernacle dedications. You'll each need to take out a pure white handkerchief." He produced a silk cloth with a flourish and swept the air with it.

Everyone with a handkerchief brought it out. Some men shrugged and held out empty hands. One sister reached for her diaper bag. "Would a bib or diaper do?"

Rosemary jumped up, "I'll find white dishtowels in the kitchen. Karen can find more hankies in the bedroom."

Rosemary returned and passed out two or three dishtowels and Karen had found four handkerchiefs in father's bureau and two lacy hankies in mother's special keepsake drawer.

"Good." Brother LeGrande dramatized the ritual whipping his cloth by one corner high above his head. His voice boomed. "'Hosanna, Hosanna, Hosanna to God and the Lamb.' We'll shout that three times and shake our cloth once for each word. Then, we'll say, 'Amen, Amen, and Amen.' This is God's way of sanctifying an edifice and keeping it safe from evil outside influences."

The prophet motioned for everyone to stand with their hankie, dishtowel, or diaper. At first they mumbled in an embarrassed tone. By the third go around, "Hosanna, Hosanna, Hosanna to God and the Lamb" was fervent and assaulted Karen's ears.

Karen turned away and saw that Lucinda stood outside the window motioning wildly to her. She was doing their alligator act with elbows touching and arms chomping like a wild cartoon character. Something terrible was happening.

Karen leaped up. She trampled toes and bumped the "Amen, Amen, and Amen" chanting congregants as she rushed out to meet Lucinda. On the porch, she grabbed her friend and waited to hear bad news.

"Karen, they're a-coming, maybe any minute. I seen a strange car out back of the silo. There's two guys sitting in the bishop's kitchen right now. They're eating chocolate cake. I know they're feds. I just know it." Lucinda's words spilled out faster than corn seed from a rotted gunny sack.

Karen squeezed her friend's arms in an attempt to calm them both. She craved details. She needed advice.

"I hafta go." Lucinda pulled away. "I'm high tailing it before the feds show up. You better be getting out fast, too," she called as she scurried into the darkness. "Run, Karen!" Lucinda hesitated only a moment to let a truck roar by before she sped across the highway.

Who to tell? Karen couldn't trust any of them to take her seriously.

Tell them all, she decided.

Inside the living room, she shouted. "Everyone! Please listen! The feds are coming. They're across the street right now. You need to leave! There's going to be a raid! Any minute! Hurry!"

The announcement was like opening the chicken coop to a weasel. Women screamed and flew out of their chairs. Men choked. Some of them kicked over folding chairs as they leaped to their feet. Children cried out for their mommies.

"Wait. Calm down!" Brother LeGrande's voice of authority boomed. "Don't listen to a silly girl! Karen can't know what the feds are doing."

"Yes," Karen screeched. "I do know. My friend saw their car across the highway. She saw the feds too, just this minute. Hurry!"

No one heard LeGrande's commands after that. Brother Butler and his wives were already in the kitchen, making a run for it, car keys and white hankies in hand, shirt tails flying. The Thompsons scrambled out on their heels, cramming themselves through the narrow door. Ladies snatched up their purses. Some remembered their sweaters and white Hosanna cloths and diapers. Most left them strewn on the floor. No one bothered with thank yous or goodbyes. The first car tore out of the driveway before many in the crowd could cram through the doorways. Brother LeGrande turned from one to another, but was unable to control the stampede.

Karen had the mixed-up feelings again of wanting to laugh and cry at the same time. Instead, she stood beside Rosemary, transfixed.

"What about us?" Rhonda grabbed Rosemary and Karen each by a hand. "Millie and I can't go back to our trailers. What can we do?"

Karen gasped. "You're right," she said. An idea was taking shape. "Hurry, I'll help you hide in the pump house."

"Yes," Rosemary said, "if the wives aren't here, we'll all be safer. They won't look down there."

Karen, Millie, and Rhonda snatched sweaters from back-porch coat hooks. The two wives followed Karen into the night away from the squawking mob and screeching cars.

Light from the house helped them find their way along the tool shop and around the coal shed. After that, they resorted to memory and feel.

Karen wished Spud were with them. He might be over at the Taylors with Topsy.

"Stop," Rhonda said. "We're in that field of horsetail."

The weeds scratched Karen's ankles. "Yes, we've gone too far."

Rhonda's trailer was parked near the underground pump house. "I think I can find it," she said. She led them out of the weed patch. "We're close now."

"There's a rise," Millie said, "over the pump house roof. Let's fan out and hunt for it."

"Wait," Karen called. "Over here. I think I've found it." She squatted and dug fingers into the dirt, searching for the iron pull-ring bolted to the pump house trapdoor. "I need a flashlight," she said.

"There's one in my trailer," Rhonda told her.

"Never mind. I've got it!" Karen lifted with both hands and slammed the door back over to the ground. She smelled the earthy passageway. "Watch it," she warned, "the steps are crumbling. And they might be slippery."

Karen headed down the stairs with Rhonda behind her.

Millie entered last and slammed the trapdoor as she descended the stairwell.

Karen felt for the grimy light bulb and twisted. The pit lit up in shadows. The three arranged gunny sacks on wooden pallets and sat huddled together. Dangling roots and mottled walls created an eerie mood. She had always primed the pump with the door gaping open to sunlight. It's like a grave she thought and grabbed Rhonda's arm. Karen tried but failed to think of something cheerful. "As much as I hate this place," she said, "I'm staying here with you. The feds could put me into the reform school if I go back."

"Do stay," Rhonda said. "Three heads are better than two."

Sitting silently for long, anxious minutes, Karen and the wives settled in to wait for the unknown.

"Thank you Karen," Millie said, "for thinking of this place. It's damp and disgusting. But I feel safer in here than in the middle of whatever is going on up at the house."

"I'm glad you're with me," Karen said. "I couldn't stand being down here alone."

"Karen," Rhonda said, "I saw the prophet finger that locket you're wearing tonight."

"I hate this locket," Karen said. "He gave it to me for my birthday. And ever since then, he acts like he owns me or something."

Millie shivered on the plank. "He gave you a locket? What's inside of it?"

"It says, 'MEANT TO BE.'" Karen heard the bitter tone of her voice.

"My bracelet charm says that too," Millie said. "He gave it to me when he said the Lord revealed I was his next intended."

"He engraved that message inside my wedding ring," Rhonda said. "Good grief! You mean he has his eye on twelve-year-olds now?"

"Looks like it," Millie said. "But we know he has Godly motives for what he does."

"Millie, how can you say that?"

"Well, he is the prophet, isn't he?"

Rhonda reached across Karen to feel for Millie's wrist. "We're down in a hole in the ground, Millie. We're scared to death of being dragged off to jail. We've been living in little tin houses, barely getting by. I grew up in a home with only one mother. That's how most people live. It isn't such a bad way."

"But it isn't the Lord's way." Crying now, Millie choked out her words.

"Think about it." Rhonda spoke in an angry whisper. "Five of us sister wives share one man. We each hope for a few crumbs of appreciation from him when our turn comes. Five wives, and that isn't enough for him. He's chasing a little twelve-year-old. And who knows? There could be others."

"I know it's a sin to hate," Karen said, "but I do hate the prophet. He grabbed me and yelled. I think he's mean, and I'd rather die than marry him. So there!"

"Yes," Rhonda said, "I understand. I don't blame you."

Millie let a few sobs escape before she answered. "We're being tried. The Lord knows best. He led us to wed this prophet for a reason. You're letting Satan tempt your faith. I won't listen. We mustn't be led astray." She sniffed and seemed to be fumbling to find a hankie. Finally, she wiped her nose on her sleeve.

Rhonda bristled. "I'm scared. I admit it. But I'm mad too. I want to escape."

"Me, too," Karen said. "I wish I had a place to go and some way to get there, and I'd leave in a minute."

"I know what you mean," Rhonda said. "When I get out of here, I think I want to get far away and never come back."

"Don't say that." Millie sniffed. "My mother made that mistake. She grew up in polygamy, but left it."

Rhonda shifted. "I don't understand. You've always said your mom was a polygamous wife. And that she's been happy with her life."

"I never told you this," Millie said, "but my mom ran off when she was sixteen. She was smitten by the temptations of Cedar City. She wanted to see the outside world. She worked in an ice cream parlor and met a gentile, my real father."

"Huh?" Rhonda shifted on the plank they shared. "What do you mean *real* father? You grew up in Short Creek. Everybody there is a polygamist."

"Yeah," Karen said. "Your father isn't your real father?"

"My grandfather found out where she'd gone. He went looking for her. He found her and brought her back to marry into the principle. Really, she shouldn't have run off. My real father doesn't even care about me. He sent me one little birthday card years ago. That's it! Nothing since I was a baby. You can never trust outsiders, Rhonda. Promise you won't."

"Shush," Rhonda whispered. "I think I hear someone up there." She shut off the light.

They shivered together on the damp boards in the earthen hole and waited in silence. Finally, they dozed.

CHAPTER 27

LAW AND DISORDER

From the passenger side of the car, Ben noticed Jack fiddling with his sister's photo as they watched the action at the Hardy house.

"That living room," Ben said, "must be jam packed with polygamists by now. Hey, look! There's that hired hand girl. The one who was nosing around us all afternoon. She's running home from the Hardy house. See her?"

A car, then another, peeled out onto the highway from the farm. "The kid tipped them off," Ben said. "Let's go."

Jack screeched to a stop near the Hardy's front gate as the third polygamist car sped away. The two cops bounded up to a passel of kids streaming out ahead of their mother and father who each had a tot slung over the shoulder. Inside they found other parents grabbing children and dodging overturned chairs in a mad dash to exit.

"Officers of the law!" Ben announced. "Who's in charge here?"

"I'm Edward Hardy." An agitated man with eyes bulging behind spectacles faced off with Ben. "I'm head of this household. Who do you think you are? No one called the police. This is a private family reunion. How dare you barge in!"

Jack had locked in on LeGrande and shoved a badge into his face before Edward Hardy finished lying. "Your name is Hyrum LeGrande? Are you the leader of this group?"

"Humph! Who do you think you are, big shot?" LeGrande stood up to him, his stiff pipsqueak body, belly bulge and all, bobbed with the cockiness of a featherweight boxer.

"You're under arrest," Jack spit out. "For violation of the Mann Act among other charges."

The remaining followers turned into stock-still wooden cutouts. A mousy man with a twitchy nose, who was poised in the kitchen doorway, backed out in slow motion. His family edged after him. They let the screen door bang, which woke everyone to the escape route.

The crowd fled faster than troops scrambling from a live grenade. Within seconds, Ben, Jack, LeGrande, Edward Hardy, and a woman and kids Ben presumed to be the Hardy family were the only holdouts, standing among a hodgepodge of toppled chairs shewn with white handkerchiefs, diapers, abandoned scriptures, sweaters, and a forgotten baby burp rag.

"Davy," a little girl, probably a Hardy child, piped up, "who're those bad mans?"

"Yeah," Davy said. "Who're you guys, anyhow?"

"Don't worry kids," Ben said. "Everything's okay." He pointed at their older sister, thinking she looked like a cheap prima donna. "Take the kids to bed and see they don't worry."

Her back stiffened and her nose turned up.

"Now!" Ben spoke with the authority of the Old Testament God and let his coat flap open, knowing the girl would see the revolver holster on his side. She picked up the kids, one under each arm, and hustled them into their bedroom.

Ben brushed past Edward Hardy and confronted LeGrande. "Here's my ID. You've seen my partner's. We have a warrant for your arrest. I suggest you cooperate. You'll wait in our car until we've had a look around."

Ben snapped handcuffs on the man, then led him, still posturing, to the car, with Jack backing him up.

"You have no right," LeGrande yelled.

"We're the law," Ben said. "We have a warrant. Stretch out over the trunk."

"You're just a punk kid, and a Jew boy." LeGrande sneered.

"Do it." Ben's hand jerked toward his gun.

LeGrande bent, his arms stretched across the back of the car, and Jack patted him down.

"We're going to cuff you in the back seat," Jack said. "Hold tight for the time being."

"My authority comes directly from God Almighty. You must not mock the Lord." LeGrande's impotent blustering reminded Ben of a tumbleweed sparring with a dust devil.

The officers secured him in the car, grabbed evidence bags and clicked on heavy black flashlights before they returned to the house.

"Release me, you slimy gentiles," LeGrande screamed. He pounded his head against the car window. "Do as I say! Beware, the wrath of God!"

Ben and Jack ignored him and climbed the front stairs.

Inside, a balloon-shaped woman who must be Mrs. Hardy sat weeping in a gray chair. She gasped and fanned herself with a children's picture book.

Mr. Hardy stopped pacing and snarled. "How dare you upset my guests and family. You've defiled this home."

"Mr. Hardy…" Ben held out paper. "This is a search warrant. You need to show us your outbuildings. It will be easier if you cooperate."

"Oh yeah? Scripture warned of your coming in these, the latter days. You're the embodiment of persecution." Edward Hardy's jaw and fists were clenched, but his eyes were wild with fear.

"Take it like a man." Ben tried to hide his smirk. "We're going out the back way in the direction most of your visitors took."

"Lead us to the trailer," Jack said, "the one out behind the barn next to the watermelon patch."

"I'll do it but not willingly. And I'll thank you to show some respect. You don't own this farm. I do."

The three men followed the lane beyond the barn, their flashlights sweeping the path to a darkened trailer house. "Who lives there?" Jack asked.

"Uh. It's a young cousin of mine. Her husband's in the Navy."

Ben rapped on the door. When no one responded, he yanked it open, and Mr. Hardy clicked the light in the compact room. The two officers opened every cupboard and drawer and filled bags with pictures, letters, and a purse.

At the double bed, Jack said, "Mr. Hardy, look back here."

Ben smiled to see a man's trousers on the floor rumpled over a pair of heavy boots, as if someone had undressed quickly.

"Is this clothing yours?" Jack held them up to Mr. Hardy.

"You lowdown dirty heel!" Hardy lifted his fists from his sides.

"Perhaps they belong to Mr. LeGrande?" Ben held out an evidence bag for them.

Hardy snorted.

"Let's go." Jack led them out. "Where's the other trailer?"

They retraced their steps until Mr. Hardy turned off to a second trailer. Inside, they repeated their search procedure. Ben checked the kitchen while Jack sat on the bed and rifled through a bureau.

"Good holy shit." Jack jerked up and thumped his head on the curved ceiling. He held a framed photo in both hands.

"Wait outside, Mr. Hardy," Jack ordered.

No one spoke until the door closed behind him.

"That motherfucking pervert!" Jack held up the picture of a middle-aged couple. Even with graying hair and sagging jowls, Ben noticed they resembled Jack. "Yes, my parents," Jack said, "mine and my sister Rhonda's."

"It's like we figured," Ben said.

"Yes. She's one of Hyrum LeGrande's polygamous child brides. I could kill that son of a bitch. And look." His hand rummaged in the drawer. "Here's the jewelry box I gave her for her twelfth birthday."

"We've got the bastard, Jack." Ben rested a hand on Jack's shoulder. "He'll soon be locked in a jail cell. If there's justice in the world, he can rot and die there."

They collected what they needed, including a soiled pair of men's Mormon undergarments and work socks. Jack shoved the door to leave.

"Good heck!" yelled a voice as the door whacked the side of the trailer and Mr. Hardy grabbed his head and stumbled out of its way.

"The door bump your ear, Mr. Hardy?" Jack asked.

"You're on my property. I have a right to hear what's going on."

"Help!" A voice screamed from the back porch steps. It sounded like the oldest Hardy daughter. "Father, hurry. Mother's having the baby."

A new flashlight beam weaved toward them. "Father," a young man called. "You there? I have the hospital suitcase in the car, but it won't start. I'm afraid it's flooded, real bad!"

The porch light showed Mrs. Hardy hobbling down the steps on her daughter's arm.

"Edward, it's time. Help me."

Edward Hardy charged toward the house. "I don't care what you two coppers say or do. You've snooped enough. I'm taking my wife to the hospital. Shoot me in the back if you want to!"

"Don't leave Weber County," Jack called to him.

They went to their undercover vehicle where Ben said, "We can put these bags into our car and finish searching the rest of the premises."

As he closed the trunk, Richard ran up. "Our car won't start." He panted. "Mother's screaming like a banshee. We need you to drive to the hospital."

"Shit!" Jack grimaced.

"It's like a Three Stooges movie," Ben mumbled. "Okay, we'll pull around back."

Jack drove up next to the car where Mr. Hardy sat blustering behind the wheel.

"Smell the gas?" Ben asked Jack.

Jack yelled from the police car into the Hardy's window, "Stop trying to crank it over. Get in."

Mr. Hardy and both kids struggled to help haul the panting woman from the family car into the front of the cop car beside Jack. Her husband crammed in on the passenger side beside her. Ben grudgingly slid in the back with LeGrande.

"Richard," Mr. Hardy yelled out the window, "come to the hospital as soon as the car starts."

Mrs. Hardy let out a yowl as Jack sped away.

"Hosannah," Mr. Hardy said. "You've done this five times before. Do you have to overreact every blessed time?"

"Shut up." She moaned. Her pain seemed spent.

Ben nudged Mr. Hardy's shoulder. "Your wife needs you to be strong. At least you can keep a civil tongue."

Ben shrugged at Jack's startled expression in the rear view mirror.

LeGrande leaned forward. "Brother Edward, I'll need you to come to the police station as soon as you can. You'll need to get me a lawyer, and the sooner, the better."

"Holy gosh!" Edward slapped his knee. "Don't blame me. I told you not to call that meeting."

"Explain the meeting," Ben said. "What exactly was its purpose?"

"None of your business," LeGrande bellowed. "You miserable Kike."

"Here's a question for you, Mr. LeGrande. Why don't you pick up your own dirty clothes when you cohabit in those two trailers?"

Jack stopped for a red light at Five Points. "We're going to the LDS Dee Hospital, I presume?"

Mrs. Hardy's voice was a thin scream. "Yes, Dee Hospital."

"And move it!" Mr. Hardy bellowed.

The car pulled up to a railroad crossing just as the arm dropped and alternating red lights and clanging bells heralded a freight train.

Impatient, Ben pitied the woman as he watched open cars of aggregate rumble by. "Mrs. Hardy," he said, "stay calm and rub your belly. It might help."

"Shut up! Men are brutes… every one of you… The baby's coming any minute. Hurry!"

They waited forever as train cars of sheet rock bumped along in front of them, followed by dozens of tank cars that rumbled lazily, and finally, a caboose. The black-and-white striped arm creaked up.

Jack's foot jammed the gas. All four passengers jerked as the car lurched forward, then slammed back against their seats.

"Fool… nitwit… imbecile…!" Hosannah screamed.

Ben kept silent, afraid of inciting more panic.

Jack killed the engine at the "Hospital Quiet" sign in front of the chunky brick building. Jack beat Ben out of the car in a blind dash to the front door. Within minutes, a starchy nurse, arrayed in white from cap to polished oxfords, marched out, maneuvering a wicker wheelchair. Ben wasn't sure how at last the expectant couple ended up outside the car and in professional care.

Jack pulled away from the hospital and they whizzed by darkened businesses and speed limit signs on their way to the police station. "It's a relief to be responsible for only one crackpot criminal. Doncha think?" he said to Ben.

"Yes, we'll process him into a cell then get back to the farm and finish our search."

CHAPTER 28

IT'S A BOY!

Rattle and spurt, inches from their pallet, jolted Karen, Rhonda, and Millie awake. *Chuka-chuka-chuka.* The pump came alive.

"What the…?" Millie sputtered.

They stirred and could make out the faint light of day rimming the trap door.

Karen shivered on the wet plank between the two polygamy wives. Mold and cobwebs conjured images of slime crawling over her skin.

Millie shuddered and stood. "I can't get my breath in here. I need air."

"Someone in the house is flushing the toilet or washing up," Karen said. "I think the raid is over. Maybe we can go inside."

"I'm turning the light on," Rhonda said. It illuminated the claustrophobic cavity.

"Let's go," Karen said. They clambered out and made their way to the house.

Rosemary met them at the back door. "Everybody's gone," she said.

"Are they all in jail?" Karen repeated and flopped into a chair. Rhonda and Millie's eyes widened adjusting to light and curious to find out what had happened.

"You hid out there in peace all night while the rest of us were dealing with the feds and with mother having to go to the hospital. The feds left and came back and poked around until almost sunup. That was after they arrested Brother LeGrande and locked him up.

Millie gasped, "Oh, no!"

"Good," Rhonda spit out.

Karen was too worn out to sort her feelings. She could see that Rosemary was as haggard as she was.

"Mother's having the baby. The feds took her and Father to the hospital."

"Baby? Mother might have had the baby?"

"Richard followed them into town in our car." Rosemary burst into tears. "My life's ruined. I'll never get another date for the rest of my life. This has probably spread all over Cloverdale."

"Shut up," Karen whispered and headed up to bed. The wives looked worn out, too, and went to their trailers, probably to sleep.

*   *   *

Karen awoke and came back to the kitchen in time to see father return. "It's a boy," he announced. Father's clothes were rumpled from his sleepless night. Whiskers bristled on his slack jaw. He slumped into a kitchen chair. "Another boy in the world without freedom to take the wives the Lord provides." He folded his arms on the table and buried his face.

Rosemary wiped her dripping hands on a dishtowel and her tears on a wad of Kleenex. "Are Mother and the baby fine?" She sniffed.

"As far as I know. The baby came right soon after those two feds dropped us at the hospital. Richard drove in, and he and I went to the jail to see Brother LeGrande."

"Hello, hello." Rhonda and Millie tapped on the screen door before they sidled inside.

Millie's uncombed hair flew about her shoulders. Both women's eyes were bloodshot embers and their backs looked crooked and pained. Rhonda's voice was soft but raspy. "Someone rifled through our trailers and stole things," she said.

"We heard your car," Millie said. "What happened?"

"Where's Hyrum?" Rhonda eased into a chair.

"What's the baby's name?" Karen asked. "When's Mother bringing him home?"

"I want a dolly baby," Judy chanted a tuneless song.

Davy joined in, but sang, "I want a golly maybe."

Father threw out his arms and slapped the table. "Hold your horses! Can't you see we haven't had a wink of sleep all night? This place is teeming with women. Can one of you get me a cup of Postum?" He rubbed both palms over his sandpaper face. "Listen up. I'm too flappin' tired to say any of this twice."

Rosemary poured water from the kettle into a mug and stirred in bitter-smelling Postum granules. Richard turned over the empty milk bucket for a perch. Everyone gathered around the table.

"Mother started hollering with the labor pains while the feds were prodding and poking around the farm."

"Wait." Karen couldn't help herself. "Did those police say we'd have to go to a gentile foster home?"

"Good gosh!" Father exploded. "Where do you get your crazy ideas? Be quiet and listen for a change."

Rosemary and Richard nodded.

"We finally had Mother in the car and the dang thing wouldn't start. The engine was moaning and groaning to beat the band."

Father gulped from the mug Rosemary handed him. He scowled and stuck his spoon into the honey, lost the thread of his story for a moment, as he stirred the brew.

"The feds finally ended up driving us to the hospital."

Karen pulled Judy onto her lap.

Father raked uncombed hair off his forehead. "They had locked LeGrande in the back of the fed car. After they left us at the hospital, they drove him off to the city jail." Father yawned and rubbed his eyes. "I need to get some sack time. I'll go to work a few hours this afternoon."

"But wait," Rhonda said, "what about Hyrum? He's still in jail?"

"Yes, Richard and I just left there. They finally let me in to see him. He thinks he can beat the charges. I'm not so sure."

Millie and Rhonda exchanged looks, Millie's worried, and Rhonda's defiant.

Father dripped scalding liquid on his lap. "Criminy!" He pinched the spattered pants fabric and plucked it off his skin. Karen handed him a napkin and he continued to talk. "Brother LaGrande seems to think I should take care of seeing about a lawyer. He expects me to watch out for his wives and kids until he gets out. I never bargained for that. Not after all I've already done for him! I have my own worries. What if I'd been thrown into jail with him? It would have been his fault. He's brought this on all of us. Sorry, Rhonda and Millie. I warned him not to call that blasted meeting. He wouldn't listen. A true prophet would have known better. He wouldn't be locked in a cell, sitting on a flea-bitten cot. Sounds more like a chump than a prophet."

"I'm feeling like a chump too," Rhonda said.

"Rhonda." Father glared at her. "I'm going to get something settled here and now. Is one of your brothers a cop?"

"What? I haven't seen my family since I married Hyrum. You know he won't let us mix with non-believing relatives."

"Well," Father said, "one of those guys was the spittin' image of you. I heard him talking about you in the trailer. He took your parents' picture with him. And the name on his badge said Jack Blackburn. That's your last name too."

Karen gasped and waited for Rhonda's answer.

Rhonda reached for the mug Rosemary offered, but her hand shook and she splashed Postum across the table. "Jack was here last night? While we were hiding in the pump house?"

"He was here, all right."

"Is he okay? Did he ask about me?"

"Sure, he's okay. That is if you think it's okay for cops to bully honest citizens."

"Did he say anything about Mom and Dad or the other kids?"

"You can ask him all of that tomorrow. I'm driving you to the police station. First off, though, you have to tell him to drop the charges. He hasta give up this whole dang-burn investigation."

"Did Hyrum say that?"

"I don't care what Hyrum LeGrande says. Tomorrow morning you're going to the police station. Go in and demand to talk to your brother. Make him back off this case. You owe us that for hiding you out. You owe it to your husband. You owe it to God Almighty. Do you understand me?"

Father gave the table a swift crack with his knuckles to end his speech. He washed his face at the kitchen sink before he stumbled off to bed.

Karen also wanted sleep but was too curious to rest. Everyone sat, stunned for a moment, until they heard the bedroom door slam. "Dang it." Richard stood and picked up the milk pail. "I waved at the dance band leader when we drove by his house. Yesterday, he was practically my best friend. Today he just turned his back on me and walked away. How can word spread so fast? After this, I'll never get to play my sax in Cloverdale, or any other town where people have family here."

Rosemary shuddered. She wiped tears on a table napkin.

Richard's lip trembled like he wanted to cry too, but he couldn't because of being male. "Looks like I'm the one stuck doing all the morning chores today. Heck, I was awake most of the night too." He headed to the barn, pail in hand.

Karen ran a glass of water at the sink and saw the bishop strutting across their back garden. He had never been shy about using their property to get to and from his own, but this time he swaggered with more determination than ever. As she watched, he veered up to their porch, instead of toward his own house.

"Good heavens!" She spun from the window. "It's the bishop, at the door, right now!"

The man didn't stop to wipe his feet or slip off his muddy boots, just stomped up the stairs and started banging and shouting. "Open up! Hurry or I'm coming right in!"

Karen opened the door, but she didn't have a chance to greet him even if she had wanted to.

"Let me in. I need to talk to your father. Now!"

"He's sleeping. Mother had a baby last night and—"

"So what? How long have you Hardys and the plygs been in cahoots? You've made me a laughingstock on my own farm and with this whole ward. Go get your dang-blasted father, and get him now!"

"Bishop," Rosemary called out, her voice like cracking glass, "you'll have to talk to him some other time. Can't you understand?"

"I understand that he and this whole blasted family could be excommunicated any minute. He's lucky he isn't rotting in jail like that false prophet you've been hiding out. You tell your father he'll be lucky if I pay two bits on the dollar for this worthless piece of dirt after all the trouble your family's caused."

Karen waited for him to turn and leave before she allowed herself to groan and latch the door.

Rosemary dissolved into mush on a kitchen chair. Her face was drawn and pallid like when she'd been down and out with the Hong Kong flu. "This is it. My life is destroyed," she wailed. "I can never hold my head up again."

Her tears dampened the table cloth next to the uneaten fudge and cider from the night before. She grabbed another napkin to blow her nose and still another for a new rush of tears. No one mentioned how wasting is a sin.

Millie picked up her untouched homemade candy. "Guess I'll take this back. No use letting it go stale," she said before she and Rhonda slipped outside.

As if on cue, the Hardy phone jangled two long rings, and a short. Both girls jumped to answer it. Karen picked it up. "It's Bradley, for you."

Rosemary took the receiver. Her voice sounded almost normal, but Karen knew her well enough to hear trepidation. "Oh, sorry about your mother, Bradley. Yes, okay. Goodbye."

Again she fell to sobbing. "He broke our date for the youth fireside chat meeting Sunday after church. He told a lie about having to drive his mother to Salt Lake City for some stupid dental surgery. What a joke. I'm a joke."

"But you can't much care about Bradley when you've been mooning over Ralph and Hadley and who knows what other guys."

"What can you know? You've never had a date and probably never will." Rosemary's eyes blazed. She picked up the sofa cushion and heaved it at Karen. "You can't know how public humiliation feels to a popular girl like me."

"You shut up!" Karen picked up the cushion to hit Rosemary, who ducked the first blow but suffered a couple of smacks. "My friends will hate me too! I'm going outdoors. Don't dare come looking for me. I'll be back whenever I'm good and ready!"

Karen stomped down the porch stairs.

She hated polygamy and Brother LeGrande. She felt as if she were still trapped in the house with the door shut overhead. Her stomach retched at the thought of it.

She wandered in a daze halfway to the barn, and then broke into a mad dash. The wind in her face cleared her thinking.

Two unfamiliar sets of boots had trampled the ground around the bottom of her ladder. One set was as large as Richard's, the other, smaller. A glint of silver caught her eye from one of the heel marks. She squatted, then, picked out the remains of a wrapper and words, Pep-O-Mint Life Savers. Feds must have invaded her barn last night. Karen felt as if a stranger had caught her naked. Anger and humiliation hastened her up the ladder.

One of those feds was Rhonda's brother.

Karen curled into the hay. Frightful feelings of violation melded into grudging respect for the intrusive feds. She breathed in the scent of hay, relieved that Brother LeGrande couldn't stalk her from his jail cell.

CHAPTER 29

REUNION

Ben hunched over Jack's desk at the police station.

Pen in hand, Jack glanced at him. "Does Millie's father know what's up? That his daughter's one of LeGrande's polygamy wives?"

"Not yet. I did report it to the office in Denver. I'll talk to him today. He's a good guy. I met with him before I left. He'll want a phone number for the Hardys."

Ben signed the form. "Looks done. The last carbon's faint, but who looks past the second one, anyhow?" He slid the paperwork back to Jack and caught sight of a young woman in a faded dress talking to Julie. Her tousled curls reminded him of someone.

"Stay calm, buddy, but you need to take a look at that girl."

Jack turned. "Dear God. It's Rhonda! She's here!" Jack's jaw dropped wide enough to catch a baseball.

He stood for a moment, incredulous, then, bounded across the room and swept her into a rough hug. "Sis, honey, you're here, out of the clear blue sky!" He laughed but looked close to tears. "I've been searching everywhere for you, and here you are waltzing right in before my very eyes."

"Oh Jack." She clung to him. "I'm so glad to see you." Her voice was shaky, her face, overwhelmed but radiant. "Dear me,

I can't believe it." She gasped. "And you're glad to see me. What a relief." She pressed her face against his chest.

"Relief? Hell, yes. I'm dyin' to see you! Thrilled to death in fact!"

He swung her in a circle and noticed Julie had left her desk and was standing at his elbow. "Rhonda, meet Julie. She runs this whole shebang. 'Course she has the good sense not to tell the chief that fact."

"Happy to meet you." Julie squeezed Rhonda's arm with one hand and Jack's with the other. "Your brother's kept you a secret."

"And," Jack said, "meet Ben, my partner."

Ben smiled. "Jack did tell me about you. I'm almost as glad to see you as he is."

"Julie?" Jack gripped his sister's hand as if afraid to let it go. "Is the conference room free?"

"Yes, all morning. I didn't know what to think when Rhonda asked for you. I guess I didn't quite believe her at first when she said you were her brother. Sorry, Jack."

"Not a problem. And no need to tell anyone where we are. We have some catching up to do. Come along, Ben."

Ben shook his head. "Are you sure you want me in on this reunion."

"Sure do. If it wasn't for you, it wouldn't be happenin'."

Julie held out a box to Rhonda. How about taking this with you to the conference room. It's fudge from one of your brother's admirers."

She clutched her brother's arm and looked into his face. "No thanks. I'm way too excited. I couldn't eat a thing."

With a flourish, Jack ushered Rhonda and Ben down the hall.

Ben had never seen Jack so animated. The three stepped into a carpeted room, crammed with an oval conference table and armchairs.

Jack sat between the two, staring at his sister, not blinking, at a loss for words. Ben kept quiet, sensing Jack couldn't get enough of seeing her.

Finally, Jack blurted, "Did you escape? Are you out of that mess for good?"

"I, uh… Edward Hardy drove me here today." Ben strained to hear Rhonda's soft voice. "I'm supposed to insist you drop the charges against Hyrum LeGrande. Edward told me to make you end the investigation. Until yesterday, I didn't even know you were in law enforcement. Hyrum forbade me to contact the family after they left fundamentalism. And that went double for you since you were never in it in the first place. He says nonbelievers erode the faith."

Rhonda was older than the photo, but her voice was that of a child. Ben thought she must be anxious about relating to anyone outside the compound.

"Ha!" Jack reared up in his chair. "That pervert had no right to claim to be a prophet. How dare he tell you to shun your own flesh and blood. Right, Ben?"

"Yes. I'm proud we locked him up. No offense, Rhonda."

A wan smile crossed Rhonda's face, like she was trying to muster flagging courage. "Well," she said, looking down at her folded hands, "he told me my family moved away and wouldn't want to see me again, me, being a polygamist wife."

Jack slapped the table. "It crushed me that you left. Since then, all I've wanted to do is find you and shake you loose from there. You're no longer a polygamist wife. You're a free woman. I'll see that you get a new start. You want one… don't you?"

Rhonda fiddled with her collar, then a curl over her ear, like she couldn't grapple with Jack's question. "What about Mom and Dad? And the other kids? Are they okay?"

"They're sure as hell better off than you've been. They're worried sick about you. We'll phone them tonight as soon as Dad gets off work. They're in Nevada now. Still Mormon. But at least they got over believing in plyg prophets."

"I want to see them. I'll visit as soon as I can." Her fingers pressed against her temples. "But how?" She crossed her arms. "I have nothing. No job. No money. No way to get to them." Tears filled her eyes, but she was able to dam their flow with convulsive gasps and sniffs.

"Good God!" The outburst startled Ben.

"I have a nest egg!" Jack's words rushed out in a torrent. "I'll help you! I can certainly buy you a bus ticket. The folks lost everything after falling in with religious crackpots. The family's not going to have room to keep you there forever. They're crowded into a two-bedroom rental." Hope glinted off Jack's face, but anger tinged his voice.

"At least they're okay. I'm real glad of that."

"The first hurdle is getting you out and safe from LeGrande and creeps like him. Are you willing?" Jack's eyes probed hers.

"Well, at first, I didn't mind it at the Hardys. I thought it meant eternal glory with The One Mighty and Strong. But there should be more to life than scrimping and doing without."

Rhonda's head hung. She smoothed the skirt of her simple dress, so thin and faded.

"And…" she squared her shoulders, "more than having an old man blame me for not giving him children. Jack, he had diphtheria just before I met him. None of his wives has had a baby since. It isn't any of us who have problems. It's him! But he blames us and scouts around for younger, more fertile wives."

"That God-damned pervert!" Jack thumped his fist on the polished tabletop. "Rhonda, you can't go back, even if he beats this charge. I can't let you. Do you understand?"

"But where would I go? Who would hire me? I didn't even finish high school."

"I'll help you." Jack bounced with enthusiasm. "We can go shopping this afternoon. You'll need new clothes, enough to fill a suitcase." He grabbed her arm. "Hey, I just got a swell idea. Listen! I'm going to call Aunt Nell in Piedmont, California. You remember her? That aunt who drank coffee and smoked? We stayed at her house one time. It was on that trip when we drove through a redwood tree. I talked to Nell after Uncle Albert died a coupla' months back. She's lonely. I'll see what I can do. I have a feeling she needs you as much as you need her. You can finish high school and go for some training." Jack's eyes pleaded with her.

"But, Jack." Rhonda held up a hand. "Wait. This is too fast. What about the charges? What about Hyrum? I'll have to go back to the trailer, at least to pack up."

"Okay, Rhonda. I'll humor you." Jack waved off her worries. "The charges? They probably won't stick. This is Utah. This state doesn't want to bother with the plygs they picked up at the big Short Creek raid last month. Kicking and screaming, they've convicted one or two independent polygamists. But authorities here are brushing all of this back under the carpet. A carpet with a lump the size of an elephant. No one around here will notice. Right, Ben?"

"I'm afraid you're right."

"And Hyrum LeGrande?" Jack pressed on, leaning back in his chair, "He'll cool his heels in jail until the system unravels and he gets out. By then, I hope to have you safe in another state. Can you handle that?"

"I guess I'm ready to leave Hyrum's polygamy group. With a place to stay, I could manage somehow." Her voice turned to a frightened whisper. "But I'm not used to being out in the world. I hate it where I am, but I'm scared to leave." Drained, Rhonda examined her folded hands.

"Don't be scared." Jack tilted her chin with his finger to look into her eyes. "You can bunk at my place until you're up to it. Then visit the folks. And then on to California. I'll get the bus tickets."

"But what about the Hardys?"

"Ben and I will collect your things at the trailer. The Hardys have to treat us nice. Their bishop's cooperating with us."

"Never going back." Rhonda's thin shoulders rose in a sigh. "That will take some getting used to."

"I'm thinking I'll have to leave, too," Jack said. "My job here has turned to puke. I barely got promoted, then, I left the church. That was bad enough. Now, I'm persecuting polygamists. Around here, those aren't considered smart career moves."

"And," Ben said, "your brother and I went against the chief to pull that raid in the first place."

"Jack, please don't lose your job because of me. I'm just so sorry for everything." Her faint voice cracked and tears drenched her cheeks. Jack hunted for a handkerchief and couldn't find one. Ben handed her his monogrammed one.

"Thanks." She slumped in her chair and cried. Her hand fumbled for Jack's and she cried harder. "I'm ashamed you two have to see me this way."

Ben tried to cover his discomfort by focusing on the light fixture centered in the ceiling. Jack gave her an awkward hug, then, twiddled a ballpoint pen, tapping it against the table. He dropped it, retrieved it, and stuffed it in his pocket. Rhonda's tears continued to flow and soak the handkerchief. A train whistle sounded somewhere outside and the men fidgeted and waited.

She blew her nose. "Thank you for taking Hosannah to the hospital. She had a baby boy. And thank you for not gunning us down in the pump house. I'm glad you didn't drag us out of there that night. We were ready to pee our pants."

Ben snickered. Jack threw his head back and laughed. "You're sounding almost like you did in the good old days," he said. "LeGrande is the one who shoulda been holed up down there, not you."

*   *   *

Ben still felt the interloper later that day when he met Jack and Rhonda next to the merry-go-round at City Park. Rhonda wore a new dress as bright as the carousel horses and organ music. After finishing a note in a new spiral note book, she tore it out and folded it.

"Looks like the two of you emptied the stores." Ben gestured toward packages heaped beside Rhonda on the park bench and at her feet. "You look very pretty. That dress seems to have cheered you up. Must be the latest fashion, my girlfriend has one something like it."

"Thanks. Blue's my color. I feel like a new woman. And thank you too, Jack. It's wonderful to wear something pretty for a change." Rhonda caressed the stack of boxes and bags beside her, as if to be certain they hadn't disappeared.

"You'll be fine." Jack patted her arm. "You have enough clothes to start life in the outside world. Ben and I will pack up everything in the trailer for you."

"What will I tell Brother Edward when he shows up to take me back?"

"Tell him you're not going. If he gives you any flak, I'll step in."

"I see the car. Here goes nothing." Rhonda's spine stiffened. The merry-go-round music ended.

The Hardy's Rambler rattled up and stopped. Rhonda hurried to the edge of the lawn. She stepped over a log which delineated the graveled street-side parking. She tapped on Hardy's window motioning for him to roll it down.

"I'm not coming back, Brother Edward. I need you to give this note to Millie for me." She dropped the folded notepaper through the window. "Jack's going to help me get a new start."

Hardy's arm shot out and whacked the door. "Rhonda, get in this car now, I don't have time for this kind of foolishness."

Jack strode from behind a clump of lilacs. "You heard her, Mr. Hardy. My partner and I'll be stoppin' by for her things. You can run on home to your family now. Goodbye."

"Wait just a doggone minute!"

Hardy's face contorted as if from a sudden attack of sour stomach. "May the three of you wallow for eternity in Outer Darkness."

"Sounds better than other fates I could name," Ben said.

He, Jack, and Rhonda turned away as the Rambler's engine choked and stalled.

"Do we have to give him a hand if it's flooded?" Ben asked.

"No," Jack answered. "That's a benefit of being damned to Outer Darkness."

Hardy tried again and again until the engine finally turned over. The melody of a new carousel tune burst out to the beat of backfires from the Rambler. The car lurched and rattled off toward Cloverdale.

CHAPTER 30

HERE WE GO

Karen bounced in the bus seat, headed to her first day of school at Wilford Woodruff Junior High. A few weeks earlier this bus had transported her to and from the nightmarish experience in the temple where she had gone to do baptisms for the dead. Instead of thinking about that humiliating day, she decided to focus on the exuberant kids bouncing in seats around her. They reeked of soap and Wildroot hair oil, smells which contrasted with dust in floorboards and cracking leather seats and stale lunches and sweat from last school year. The jabbering sounded like a horde of excited magpies.

Karen felt jittery about starting in a new bigger school, but this was nothing compared to what she'd been dealing with at home, the polygamy raid, her worn-out anxious mother, barely back from the hospital with baby brother Larry, father who was distraught over possibly losing his farm to Bishop Taylor. All in all, starting school was mild and normal in comparison.

The bus screeched to a stop for Camille, who preened as she waited, a fitting adornment, in front of her stunning white home and groomed grounds. She flounced into the bus in a double-circle poodle skirt spread over starched layers of pink crinolines.

"Hi Karen," she said bending so her mouth was an inch from Karen's ear, "Absolutely everyone is talking about that trouble at your house. You must have just died. Sheesh!"

Karen patted the empty seat beside her, inviting Camille to sit.

"I promised to sit with Randy." A deep breath puffed out her developing chest, sheathed in a thin pink sweater. "See you later." She looked away and added the word, "Maybe," as an afterthought.

She straightened to her perfect posture and waved off Karen's problems. "R-a-n-d-y!" She called the name, embellishing it with an enchanting grin, and savoring every singular sound, as if the name dripped with melting chocolate. Karen knew not to count on Camille's friendship in tough times.

Karen had often wished she could ride the same bus with Amy. This morning she wanted this more than ever. At least the two would eat together. She checked her purse for the quarter and dime she'd saved to buy a hot lunch. She and Amy had been celebrating the first day of school that way since starting grade school together.

The bus jerked and pitched into the circle drive in front of the rambling yellow brick Woodruff School. It was ten times the size of her friendly old Plain City Grammar School and outfitted with baseball and softball diamonds and official track and football fields.

Students shoved their way into the aisle before the brakes quit squealing. Impatient youth wedged into the jammed space and started a chant. "C'mon. Move it. Move it. Move it." The voices swelled.

Karen knew they were anxious to escape for a whiff of free air before again submitting to confinement of stuffy classrooms.

The flow of bodies trapped Karen and pitched her down the aisle, then over the deep steps to the ground. She jumped to the curb, arranged her hair, brushed at creases in her navy dress, and checked her flats for scuff marks. She sent a mental thank you to the saleslady who had helped her shop for her precious few presentable school clothes, knowing better than to "fall for fads," as mother liked to say, and wish for a poodle skirt like Camille's.

Trying to appear calm, she pulled out the official envelope she'd received in the mail. She pinned on the name tag from it and reviewed the schedule for her first class, home economics. The hall was packed with strangers and she entered the classroom hoping to find a few familiar faces.

The future homemakers already huddled into established groups. When Karen spotted Cloverdale and Plain City girls, she smiled and spoke to them. They glanced past her and continued talking as if she weren't there. Karen held in the hurt. She settled for a chrome dinette chair at the only empty table with her loose-leaf notebook in front of her for security.

"Good morning, students. I'm Mrs. Jackson." The teacher looked like a twin of the *Father Knows Best* mother Karen had glimpsed Tuesday night on Lucinda's TV. Both wore crisp shirtwaists and pearl chokers and had fashionable crowns of dark permanent-waved curls around their faces.

Mrs. Jackson held a pointer as long as her arm and tapped a chart of class rules and expectations that she read to the girls. Pride glowed in her face as she raved over the seven modern kitchenettes along one wall, each compact enough to fit in a trailer. "Please notice that every kitchen bears a sign, like a house number, one to seven." Home addresses were a big-city touch for a community accustomed only to rural routes and slapdash mailbox numbers.

"You'll find we're equipped with electric pop-up toasters and plug-in electric skillets and Mixmasters. Also notice that we have an electric mangle ironing machine for our table linens. Within a few years, no modern home will be complete without one." She walked over to caress a chair that was attached to a contraption that consisted of a padded roller about the size of an un-split fireplace log hooked to a tabletop. "The board of education has high expectations of you. That's why they invested so much money to train you as wives in Zion." Mrs. Jackson was as slick as Betty White filming a General Electric TV advertisement.

The teacher smoothed her starched collar before she continued.

"You fortunate girls will benefit from the newest advances in the modern science of electricity. You'll learn to make homes for your future husbands and children." Karen thought Mrs. Jackson must not know about or believe the end-of-the-world predictions that would certainly cut their lives short before they could realize such overblown dreams.

"And next term you're in for a real treat. We have a sewing room across the hall with lovely Singer electric zigzag sewing machines."

Karen cringed. She'd prefer to shovel cow manure than sew for school credit.

"Your first class assignment—" Mrs. Jackson's tone was brisk— "is to form groups for the term, four girls to each of the seven tables. I see that some tables have five and we have this one lonesome girl sitting all by herself." She tapped Karen's table with the rubber point on her stick. "Then I want to see which group can come up with the longest list of good reasons to attract husbands and embrace modern homemaking skills."

Karen's stomach lurched when she saw three of her friends—Camille, Anne Marie, and Nancy—inviting a stranger to finish out their group. Camille was taking charge and listing ideas before Karen could think how to proceed.

"Here you go, young lady." Mrs. Jackson motioned Karen to a group of unfamiliar girls. "Kitchen Number 7 has space available for you. And you four standing here waiting for a table may now take hers."

Karen grudgingly moved in with the three strangers. Two of them wore ordinary print skirts, not the expensive appliquéd circle ones with crinolines, the kind Camille and other richer girls sported. Another name tag read Honoka. She looked Oriental. Karen had seen pictures of people like her with glossy black hair and almond eyes, but she had never met one in real life. The third had on a simple dress like Karen's and the name "Betty Lou" on her tag. She looked taller than Richard and had a facial tic. The last girl was Carolina, a tiny freckled thing, whose yellow duck down hair fluttered around a pinched face. Karen had never considered herself a solid citizen of the most popular set. She was afraid this turn of events sealed her fate forever into the outer darkness category at Wilford Woodruff.

Honoka, a slight smile teasing her lips, ripped a sheet of paper from her notebook. "Does anyone think we can make a list even though none of us thought to wear the required poodle skirt?" They giggled. Carolina's high-pitched tittering turned her face red.

"Guess what?" Carolina lowered her voice from a squeal to a squeak. "I heard that Mrs. Jackson is a flawed and pitiful woman. She can't have children. She stays true to The Church by inspiring young girls to be housewives."

"Wow," Karen said, "I want to talk about this later. Maybe after we do our assignment."

"It's nearly done." Honoka was perfecting a tidy list. "But don't expect me to do all of the work every time. By the way, can anyone here cook? I can't even pour cornflakes in a bowl."

"Sure," Karen said. "No problem."

Betty Lou grinned, looking proud. "I'm a better cook than Betty Crocker."

"And," Carolina chirped, "I know all the juicy gossip."

"Good. We're a team," Honoka said. "Quiet. The teach' is about to speak."

"I see Kitchen Number One has a lengthy list." Mrs. Jackson adjusted her glasses. "The other groups may sign their work and turn it in at the end of class." She nodded at Camille. "Please come up to report."

Camille accomplished the required giggling blush before she read with recovered pride and poise. "We need to know how to set an attractive table to make our husbands proud…"

As she read the list, Karen noticed that Honoka was right. Her table was the only one with no poodles present. At the end of Camille's list the bell rang.

Karen hurried to second-period science with Mr. Heiner. He also gave a class overview. "Any questions?" he asked at the conclusion.

A boy with a butch haircut and no discernable lashes or brows held up the text from his desk. "I thought we wuz gettin' new science books, Brother Heiner."

"Ike, you and everyone else need to be reminded, to use 'Mr.,' not 'Brother' at school. And yes, Ike, new books are on order. The board of education had trouble finding an edition with no mention of evolution. They had to comply with community standards. So for now, we'll start out with the old books."

Karen sat alone and mute in science. She tried her best to act nonchalant to cover the empty feeling she had when her Cloverdale friends continued to shun her.

In the rush to the next class, Karen bumped into Brian. Relieved to find an ally and defender, Karen dug deep to come up with a smile and cheery hello.

"Sorry, Karen. I guess we can't be friends this year. I hope you understand. Nothing personal."

"Huh? No. I… uh… *don't* understand, Brian." She fumbled for words. "I thought you didn't blame me for what… uh… happened at the temple. I was going to thank you for that."

Brian blushed. "No, it isn't that. Well, it might be a little that. It's the raid and how everybody's talking. If I have to, I can poke Enoch in the nose, but not my parents and not every kid at church and school. Sorry, I have to go."

Finding no words, not even goodbye, Karen scuttled away, feeling lonelier than Robinson Crusoe. A solitary island home would be better than this, living in the middle of a sea of spite.

With grim determination, Karen propelled herself through the hateful crowds to her next class, general math with Mr. Taylor, who was one of the bishop's nephews.

Karen felt as reviled as a pimple on the tip of a bishop's nose. She wondered if the bishop had told his math-teacher relative all about the polygamy raid. Did every Mormon everywhere know each horrifying detail?

Phys ed, was the last class before lunch. As she came into the gym Karen was thrilled to see Amy, rushed over to her best friend. "Oh, Amy, I've been watching for you everywhere."

"Well." Amy hesitated and for the first time ever, she stuttered. "I... I... I... I've been around."

Karen felt a bad taste fill her throat. Was something wrong? Certainly, Amy, unlike the others, would not turn against her.

The girls stood in line at a sports supply storage room to pick up white gym shorts and shirts from a ninth-grade monitor.

Karen grasped her friend's arm and whispered, "Aren't you so embarrassed to have to get undressed in front of strangers here?"

Amy gently pulled her arm out of Karen's grasp. She talked to the row of green lockers along the wall beyond Karen's shoulder. "Don't feel bad Karen. It's so hectic and confusing here. I won't be able to see you much this year. Or have lunch together. Things change in Junior High."

That did it. Her last and best school friend was deserting her. Karen felt sick. She took a breath and stiffened, wishing to transform into an inanimate object. If only she could crawl into one of the metal lockers and hide.

Amy told the monitor her name, picked up her suit, and turned to leave.

"Wait," Karen said. "What are you saying?" Karen commanded herself to hold her tears in check.

Amy fidgeted and nudged up her glasses to wipe away a tear from under each eye. "Well, maybe we can pal around later in the year. Things might calm down eventually." Amy's remorse was a spurt of cool water on a searing scald.

"Your name?" the monitor demanded.

Karen choked out, "Karen Hardy," even though it occurred to her that a better name would be Mud.

Recognition dawned on the older girl's face, and she pulled back a step. "Watch out," she said. "Everybody's talking about you but they say your name is "Karen Hardy-har-har!"

The girl shoved the gym suit toward Karen and looked to the girl next in line.

Karen, still holding in her tears, took the suit. She scanned the row of lockers for her assigned number. She was a mechanical doll as she dressed, too dazed to be embarrassed about changing her clothes in front of strangers.

When lunchtime came, she dreaded having to face the cafeteria alone. It was loud, confusing, and smelly. She sniffed hot grease, burned beef, and baking bread, along with the smells of summer deep cleaning, bleach and floor wax. Two lines weaved from the hall outside the cafeteria and along the walls on either side to a counter and cashiers across the room. Kids at tables, in line and milling around with trays seemed to shriek at the tops of their lungs.

Karen let the crowd propel her into one of the lines. She checked again in her purse for her lunch money. Now that Amy had snubbed her, she wished she could skip lunch and hide out in a closet somewhere.

The line moved quickly. From the din, she overheard the word *polygamy*. When she focused on the boy she thought had said it, he turned his back.

She picked up one of the trays of roast beef, mashed potatoes, gravy, carrots and a canned pineapple ring, then took a roll from an oversized dishpan and a cup-sized milk bottle from a cooler, as she saw others doing. After paying, Karen looked for her friends and saw them huddled together at the most crowded table in the room. They saw her and turned away. She decided to wedge between two girls she didn't know.

"Hello, I'm Karen."

They looked up, but didn't answer and didn't seem to want to know her. Ordinarily, she would have relished the lunch but could choke down only a few bites.

English and Social Studies finished the day. The teachers in each class asked everyone to introduce themselves and tell about their summer adventures. Twice Karen said, "We have a new baby in our house, a little boy named Larry. I guess that's all that happened this summer." Both times she heard derisive throat clearing and choked snickers.

In spite of being in crowds all day, she had never felt so alone. As if through the lens of a telescope, she longingly viewed others who were detached from her, reuniting and flirting, meeting new friends. The home economics class, which this morning had been so daunting, now seemed like a cheerful wingding compared to the rest of the day.

Let me out of this madhouse, she screamed inside her head. I want to go home.

CHAPTER 31

HOME SWEET HOME

K aren shoved along the bus aisle toward the open door and home. Dwayne, from a front seat, jammed his leg in her path and blocked her. "Make way for the plyg pig," he said with a snort as he withdrew it.

"Shut up! You're the pig!" Karen stumbled through the door and jumped to the ground. Dwayne's face appeared at the window, his nose smeared against the glass, pig-like. Karen crossed her eyes and shot her tongue out in time for him to see before the bus pulled away. She raged across the highway. On the footbridge she resisted the urge to hurl her school books into the stream.

From there, she saw the bishop marching toward her through rows of corn stubble blackened by frost rot. He wore his irrigation uniform: hip boots, turned down and flapping, and a shovel on his shoulder. He advanced directly through the faded zinnias, brutally crushing the blooms as if they were pigweed. Karen retreated up the front porch steps.

"Young lady! Hold your horses!" In a commanding gesture, he slid the shovel to the ground. The blade cut deep into the tilled earth of the flower bed. He stood soldier-like, ready for battle, and barked, "Karen, you tell your father that I'm sick and tired of his scared rabbit act. He has until tonight to agree to my terms on this farm. Otherwise, I'll convene a church court. Your whole family will be excommunicated. I'll still get the farm. It was ours before you came, and we mean to have it back, one way or another."

Karen longed to be a man at that moment. She'd wrench that shovel from his mud-caked hand and plant it in his gizzard.

*   *   *

Father's rants preceded him into the house that night. "Richard, get your sorry carcass in here before I beat the living daylights out of you!" Father kicked the milk bucket. The blow jostled the table leg and sent a stack of tin stew bowls clattering to the floor.

Davy and Judy scampered into the living room and hid behind Karen's legs. She shooed them into their bedroom where they all cowered and waited, unable to ignore Father's rampage.

"I did like you told me." Richard's voice was loud but tinged with fear. "I turned the water on our field at four o'clock sharp. The bishop shut it off. He knows the schedule, but he went right ahead and switched the water to his field. I couldn't stop him."

"The bishop?" Father's rage veered. "That nasty, no-good worthless skunk now thinks he can steal water from me? Men have been shot deader than doornails for stealing a man's water rights. It's every bit as bad as stealing a wife."

A loud crash shook the wall.

From the bedroom, it sounded as if Father had thrown a chair across the room into the washing machine. "I'm going to take care of that Taylor, right now." The door slammed.

Karen hugged the little ones to her until they calmed down. She knew she wouldn't have to give Father the bishop's message. He'd head across the highway to hear it firsthand.

"Come on, kids. I'll help you find some crayons and paper."

"What's Father gonna do?" Davy's standard bravado had escaped him.

"I think he's going to see the bishop about water rights. And the bishop will be ready. Guess they'll yell and figure something out." Karen's hand shook as she dumped crayons from a juice can and gave the kids paper.

She went to the kitchen where Mother sliced carrots into a steaming stewpot. Millie sat at the table, her chin propped on her fists.

"Karen," Mother said, "take the baby until I can get dinner going."

Karen lifted the whimpering Larry from his bassinette in the corner. It felt comforting to cuddle him as she settled into the giant wooden rocker and creaked.

"This note—" Millie rattled a page of paper, "—came from Rhonda. She's staying with her brother now. She's never coming back. I've always been committed to the principle of polygamy." She wiped a tear from her pudgy cheek. "But Hyrum's in jail. Rhonda's gone. There's no one to turn to. What can I do?"

"What about your parents?" Mother asked.

"Yes," Millie said. "I might have to go there. Maybe they can find me a new priesthood holder. Rhonda and I saved a little nest egg from our sewing. She said I could have it. It's plenty for a bus ticket." Millie dabbed another tear. "I'm going out to pack up. I can't stay here."

"Good luck to you Millie," Mother said, resting her hand on Millie's shoulder. "Maybe Edward can drop you at the depot on his way to work tomorrow. Buses run often of a weekday morning."

"Guess I better get busy." Millie stood to leave. "The Lord will provide if I have the faith. I'll be going now."

"Sorry, Millie," Karen said. As Millie reached the door, the two shared a sympathetic glance. Mother turned away to peel potatoes.

Karen rocked the baby and ignored the phone ringing. Rosemary could get it.

"Telephone for you." Rosemary came into the room and called to Millie on the back stairs.

"For me?" Millie bustled back inside.

Karen couldn't make out what Millie said after she answered, only that she at first sounded confused, then excited.

Back in the kitchen, Millie looked flushed. "That was my real father. I haven't seen him since I was Judy's age. He asked me to come to Colorado and meet him."

"Your real father?" Mother sat down to listen.

"Yes, I have a real father. I'm going to meet him. It might actually work out in Colorado. I won't know if I don't try it. And I can always find another fundamentalist to marry if the Lord leads me in that direction later." She told mother the story she'd revealed to Karen and Rhonda down in the pump dugout. Mother listened as she worked and finally stopped and stared. "You'll have to pray and do what the Lord tells you."

Millie nodded. "That's all I've been doing is praying. This phone call may be the answer to those prayers."

Karen had seen Millie as always being a polygamist wife. Even so, her eyes suddenly brightened to new possibilities. Karen felt the flame of hope. "Do it. Millie. Try the outside world. It can't be as bad as this one."

Karen rested Larry in his bassinette. She and Millie might have been sister wives but now they might never see one another again. Millie hesitated at the door. The two hugged.

*   *   *

Father returned, still fuming. The family ate in silence, except for Davy and Judy, who poked each other and talked about which kinds of animals the homemade noodles resembled. When the younger kids were in bed, Father called the others to a family meeting in the living room.

He didn't bother to begin with a prayer.

"I gave that high and mighty bishop a piece of my mind," Father blurted. "He relented on the water, but…" Father raked his hair, stood up and paced, "but we're going to have to give up the farm."

"But…" Richard looked incredulous.

Mother and Rosemary gasped and slapped palms to their faces.

Karen waited, feeling stricken. Where would they live? How could they get by?

"I worked out terms," Father said. He's holding excommunication over our heads."

"Good gracious, anything but that," Mother said.

"I told 'im a church court would make him look bad, like he couldn't keep normal control over his own ward. He as much as admitted I was right, but said, 'business is business,' whatever that means."

"You're saying we have to just pick up and move?" Mother cried quietly into her hanky.

"Yes, but it could have been worse. The bishop thought I was played out. What he didn't know is that I hit pay dirt the other day. I've been late for work because of the baby and the stupid feds and everything. So I had to park on 25th Street. Getting into my car, I caught sight of the bishop leaving a bar."

"No!" Mother sniffed back tears, too scandalized to continue crying. Karen saw her own horror reflected in Rosemary's ghostly face and Richard's shocked eyes, as wide as owl eyes unblinking in the dark. The women clucked and Richard gasped. The family tensed in their seats and turned to Father for priesthood leadership.

"Don't say anything about this to your friends, but—" Father's chest heaved.

"I have no friends." Rosemary's face was drawn and haggard.

Richard nodded.

"None of us do." Karen, for once, agreed with her older siblings.

Father waved them off. "That fricken bishop," he went on, "came out of a place called Ko Ko Mo Saloon or something like that. I asked around. There's no food served in there, just alcohol."

"Oh, good golly!" Mother dropped her hankie.

"There's more. And this is far worse. I sat and watched that bow-legged banty strut across the street to a worse place. They don't even bother with the sin of drinking there. It's a place of ill repute. There've been murders there. But perversities worse than that happen there every night."

"Oh! You don't say!" Mother never held back her opinions on sin. Her righteous indignation blew like an exploding pressure cooker lid. "Well, I never!" Mother's eyes bulged. "This takes the cake." Her words sputtered like water in burning grease. "The out and out bare-boned gall of that man." She shook her fists, then, stopped herself. "Edward, the children shouldn't be hearing such things."

"Can't be helped," Father said. "I told 'im I'd keep mum around the ward. But my own family needs to know what a lowdown skunk he is."

"You children will have to look elsewhere for examples to live by," Mother said. "Just as well we don't live in a ward with a lowdown bishop like that."

"His folly is our gain," Father said. "All told, I agreed he can give us what we paid him for the farm. It could be considered a bargain seeing as how we've been making improvements every year we've lived here."

"Yes, I've put in flower beds and wallpaper. You've rotated the crops and kept up the fruit trees and berry bushes."

"Well, the bishop didn't care about any of that. But he was in no position to argue about the bottom line price."

"What'll we do though?" Richard asked, practical for a change.

Father looked quizzical, as if he hadn't fully thought it through. "Well, I guess we'll just pack up. Skip out. The bishop doesn't want the notoriety any more than we do. I think it's best if we clear out. We could settle in town where people don't know us." Father pulled off his glasses and rubbed his eyes, then his whole face. "Leastwise, I'll always have my government job."

CHAPTER 32

FIRED

In the kitchen rocking chair, Mother pulled her sacred garments aside under her blouse for Larry to feed. He snorted like a baby calf. "Girls, finish up your homework. You need to make dinner and do the dishes. I'm worn out. I have to rest as soon as Larry gets his fill."

"Can't Karen do dinner?" Rosemary tapped her stack of books on the kitchen table. "She's only in junior high. She can't possibly have as much schoolwork as I do."

"Well," Karen said, "then get it done. And quietly. So I can finish mine. It's hard enough to think with Richard in there playing 'Glow, Little Glowworm' like it's a Sousa march."

Karen filled in answers on her home economics worksheet. "What leavening is used for cakes? Rolls? Muffins?" Karen wrote in the blanks: first "baking powder and soda," next "yeast," and again, "baking powder."

"Oh, good golly." Mother was patting Larry, urging him to burp on her shoulder. "I hear a car." She tucked the baby into the kitchen-corner bassinette. "If it's those visiting teachers, tell them—"

"No, Father's home early!" Rosemary stood up, alarmed.

"Oh, no." Karen stiffened. "What now? He looks madder than a hornet."

"Dunderheads! Gall-blast all of 'em!" They heard Father's epithets rumbling up the back porch, where he banged the door with so much force that a stack of flowerpots shattered in the doorway.

"Those lily-livered ignoramuses! Those stinkin' rotten walking piles of cow manure!"

Father threw his car keys on the table. They clunked over the salt and pepper shakers shaped like smiling ears of corn.

No one moved to pick up the broken pots or spilled shakers. Richard glanced around the doorway, his sax in hand. Davy and Judy peered out between their brother's long legs. They all cowered, not asking the obvious. Father paced and clenched his fists with as much animosity as Karen could remember.

Finally he snarled. "Doesn't anyone care what's going on? Aren't any of your female brains the least little bit curious?"

"What's happened, Edward?" Mother shielded herself behind the rocking chair.

"I'll tell you. Those red-deviled sons of Satan have fired me. That's what!"

Only then did Father thud onto a chair. He buried his head on the table under his arms in a room of stunned silence.

He finally sat up. Frustration in the form of tears glistened in his eyes. It was one of the few times Karen had seen a grown man cry.

Father rocked in his straight-backed chair. "I thought we could move to town, away from the shunning, and live off my government paychecks. Now that's out too. I have a month to 'vacate,' is the word they used. They claim I'm ineffective because of absenteeism and a distracted attitude. It's pure politics. They got word of the raid. How dare they treat me this way! Those slime bags!"

Mother's face trembled. "You'll keep going to work, won't you, Edward? I mean for the month?"

"I have half a mind to chuck it. To tell 'em the truth about their stupid low-down worthless hides."

"Edward, you have to go back. We barely make it month to month. And you have to start right away looking for another job. Do you see that?" Mother's face contorted like her wrung out handkerchief.

Rosemary sniffed, then sobbed. "I told all of you my life was over. This proves it. I'll never feel joy again. Everyone hates me. Now I won't even have food to eat or a place to sleep."

"You're not the only one." Karen kept her tone hushed, but she could tell she sounded ragged and spiteful. She didn't care.

Richard eased into the room. He wore his short sleeved shirt with sleeves in tight rolls to his shoulders. Distraught, neither Father nor Mother bothered to chastise him for copying Hollywood immodesty. "I could quit school and start a band. We could go to Salt Lake City where they pay more. No one down there knows anything about this. Talented musicians bring in big bucks."

The comment elicited no responses. Davy and Judy crept in and hid behind Karen's chair.

"You can sell my cars and trucks," Davy said.

"You can have my dollies," Judy added.

"And," Davy said, "we'll only use three toilet papers to wipe with."

Again, none of them answered. The telephone rang.

Father jumped. "Did they change their minds?"

"It might be a date," Rosemary said.

"Maybe someone wants me to play my sax." Richard won the race to the phone. "Who? You want Karen?" He handed the receiver to her.

"Hello?"

"Hi, this is Enoch."

Flabbergasted, Karen sputtered, "Huh? What do you want?"

"Well, Karen. I heard that you're a polygamy girl. I want to be friends. I thought you could meet me in your barn for a little tumble in the hay."

"What? How dare you! Listen to me! I hate your stupid freckles! Your warts make me sick! And when I saw that birthmark you sit on, I wanted to throw up! Don't ever speak to me again, Zurflew! Because if you do, I'll tell my police friends to haul you in for watermelon thieving! Goodbye." She slammed down the receiver.

"Karen," Mother said, "Shame on you! Don't you dare speak that way ever again! And certainly not to any nice LDS boy, one who's taking an interest in you. Maybe the ward is starting to forgive and forget. If so, you've ruined it with that smart mouth of yours! Who is Zurflew? Is he Mormon?"

Again, the phone jangled two longs and a short.

"Zurflew is Enoch," Karen said. "If that's him, I'm not speaking to him!"

Father grabbed the phone. "Oh, hello, Mom. I know you haven't seen the new baby. This is a very bad time to talk." Father tapped his toe anxiously.

"Huh? Well, I hate to have to tell you this. I was laid off today. I'm out of work."

Everyone in the room exchanged glances.

"Mom, it was nothing I did. Just politics."

Father's face twitched with impatience.

"Yes, I'll be there a month. By then, I'll find something else."

Father raked his hair and paced as far as the phone wire would allow.

"Thank you. I'm just too worn out to talk right now. I have to go. What? You want to talk to Karen? Okay. Whatever." He held out the receiver.

"Me?" She took it. "Hello, Grandma." Karen wished she could fly through the phone line to be there in person.

"Yes. We're pretty upset." Karen listened carefully as she ran her pinkie through the coiled phone wire.

"Well, okay. I'll try. Goodbye."

The family ate a quick, sad meal of bread and milk and applesauce. Then they wandered into the living room. No one dared speak. They fidgeted in their usual seats with their eyes darting everywhere but at each other.

Karen broke the silence. "Grandma says it might be good to try for a government transfer job in Arizona or Colorado. She said we could make a new start in a new state. Maybe the bosses here would write a good recommendation because of all your years of service. At least that's what she told me to say."

"Good holy gosh!" Father bristled. "I'm still the head of this household. I make the decisions. Did you tell 'er that, Miss Smartypants?"

Karen dissolved back into the gray chair, determined not to say another word.

The room gradually turned dusky as the sun dipped behind the mountains. Richard reached over to pull the chain on the floor lamp.

"Stop that!" Mother screamed. "What have I been saying about wasting electricity? That counts double now. Don't anyone use a light without permission until this job emergency is over!"

Life seemed darker than the pump house with the door slammed shut.

CHAPTER 33

DEALING WITH THE DEVIL

That night, the gloom of the evening ruled Karen's sleep. A nightmare plunged her outdoors into the black currant vines, a place she had never gone after dark. Confused, but not alone, she first heard, then felt, a legion of beings converge on her, amorphous forms, veiled in darkness.

"Karen," they pleaded, "we've come to rescue you." The voices, perhaps familiar, maybe not, coaxed, implored, cajoled. "We love you. Come with us, sweet spirit."

"No," she answered, "stay away from me."

The entities circled and joined for an embrace, pressing ghastly bodies against her. Spindly fingers caressed her nightgown folds and hair.

Louder than a trumpet, she heard, "You will come with us now!"

The leader's voice blared with the authority of the holy priesthood.

The mob of Mormons, now, seeming familiar from other dreams, pawed over her. Voices wheedled or berated, too many to resist. They propelled Karen along the house and down the path. Her toes dragged over ruts and through weeds, past the coal shed in a swift current, she flowed with them toward a square of light, which glowed from the earth.

"Stop!" Karen didn't know if she thought the word or spoke it. "I will not go into the pump house!"

She kicked and struggled against the rush, but she was no more than a twisting leaf, buffeted between river rapids, rushing onward.

Eyes tight, she jolted from one step to the next down the crumbling pump house stairway. She felt slime laden air crawl over her skin, smelled the stench, heard the throb of the pump. She opened her eyes to see the bare light bulb and the same moldy walls she knew, the cob-webs, lichen scales, the hook and cheese knife. But the center of the room was transformed into surgical white and stainless steel, like the room she'd glimpsed before her tonsils were removed.

Hands, sheathed in rubber, lifted her onto a gleaming table. Others restrained her there.

The priesthood giant arose before the assembled congregation. He was the size of Goliath, and his voice rang out like that of The Almighty God, Himself. "Behold!"

Karen's pores pulsed, as if electric current, not blood, coursed through her veins.

"I hereby command you, Karen! Cast your eyes heavenward!"

Looking up she watched the room grow tall. Rows of twisted, misshapen mummy cases materialized on shelves above her. Somehow, she knew they'd been crafted as places for living beings to dwell. These were destinations for the likes of obstinate and wicked souls, forced into submission.

"Questions torment you, Karen. They cause rancor among the faithful, and disdain from on high. At long last every troublesome question shall be silenced. Your great gift will be a final opportunity. You can yet achieve peace and exaltation. You need only simple faith and obedience." Goliath's voice mellowed, took on the tinge of rehearsed warmth and charity.

"The precious souls above are happy, eternally as you shall be. I have the power to transform you into their likeness." The light bulb flickered. His hand whipped out in a dramatic arch and seized the butcher knife from the wall, then, he wielded it over Karen.

Her insides raged with a pulsing word. The sound rumbled through her chest and throat, gained force, and tore from her lips. "No, no, no!"

It stunned Goliath. He shrank back, as did the others.

Karen flew off the table and up the stairs. Instinct told her she had practiced long and hard on her ladder for this escape. Strong and graceful, she sprang out of the cavity and into the open air.

This, just as Spud, emerged from the darkness and tore by her. A barking, snarling wild thing, he lunged down the cellar steps.

Goliath's voice bellowed from the hole. "Press on. Go after her."

Karen heard Spud's frenzied growls, and she ran on. She heard him rip through their clothes, and heard the screams as he tore into their flesh. She continued to flee.

Safety beckoned through a gold streak of sunrise painting the pinnacle of a hilltop. On the slope, she turned to glimpse the swiftest pursuer reach for her heels. A few long strides carried her over the crest, and into the rising sun. Spud panted to the top after her. Winded, they embraced, stood, and faced those still struggling in pursuit. Karen saw them in the faint light of sunrise. She marveled that until that moment, she hadn't seen them clearly. They were mutilated humans, stunted and grotesque, distorted into the shapes of the mummy cases.

She examined her own trunk and limbs, found them strong and perfect. Triumphant, she shouted, "I won."

The creatures pleaded, but had no power in the light. They struggled, fell back, wallowed in the dirt of a hill, too daunting to mount. Her pity couldn't detain her. Time to leave.

She awoke in her bed. The creatures were a memory. The sunshine was real. She absorbed warmth, let it continue to uplift her.

But also with it came an abrasive sound, difficult to place. She puzzled over a rhythmic back-and-forth grate, like a saw, the size of Goliath. Going to the window she saw the apple tree below fall to ruin. Its best climbing branch crashed to the lawn. Bishop Taylor and Lucinda's father worked at opposite ends of a cross-cut saw, mutilating the harmless tree.

She tore open the window. "Shame on you! You're murderers!"

The men gaped at her audacity.

She scurried down the stairs in time to see Father storm out the front door.

"What do you think you're doing?" Father yelled.

Bishop Taylor stood toe-to-toe with him. "Edward, I bought this property, fair and square. Your signature is on the bill of sale. You have until the end of the month to vacate. I won't have these worthless, worn-out trees cluttering the view and soaking up my precious water. I suggest you start packing up and liquidating. I don't have time to discuss trivialities with you."

"Listen up, buster! This transaction hasn't cleared escrow. Back away or the deal is off. Do you hear me?"

"Whatever. We're done here for now anyhow. See you in church."

Inside the living room, Father's ire escalated. "That blasted snake-belly! Dang! I havta go do the milking. Then, I'm going to make the rounds and see who wants to buy the livestock and the farm equipment. Hosannah, I guess you and the kids better start packing."

He stomped out, slamming the door, which rattled the porch frame and the now empty pottery shelf.

Rosemary sat folding laundry from a basket, making neat stacks of underwear, socks, towels, and baby clothes across the sofa. "Karen," she said. "Take over here. I've broken a nail and need to get a file."

Karen, still awash in triumph from her dream, looked at Rosemary with new eyes. She had failed to notice, until now, Rosemary's cold glare, her pinched nose, and those selfish pursed lips, always issuing orders, never offering praise, or spreading cheer.

"No, Rosemary. Not today."

Mother looked in from the kitchen. "Karen, run on over to Lucinda's. Find out what the bishop's up to."

"Does that mean I get to associate with farmhands?"

"Get going!"

In the front yard, she passed Richard raking leaves. Seeing her, he went into the rude clown impersonation he used to annoy her. Instead, she was amused and laughed out loud.

She spun away, not noticing his reaction, and bounded over to the Crumms' little box house.

Lucinda answered her knock. "Hi, let's go sit on the Taylors' lawn to talk. I'm sorry about the apple trees. Dad didn't want to cut 'em while you wuz still living there."

"What's up with the bishop? Does he have other stunts up his sleeve?"

"Boy, does he! He's going to move us into your house. I'll get to have your room."

"Huh? You're taking my room?"

"And he plans to turn our house into a fruit stand. He wants to sell corn, and watermelons, and raspberries, maybe tomatoes and cucumbers too. People on the highway need things like that."

"Your family's taking our house, and you'll be in my room?"

"Yeah, but I won't hafta share it like you do. 'Cuz we only have three kids. Ain't that somethin'?"

"Yeah. That's really something all right." Karen heard bitterness tingeing her words. She was in no mood to stave it off today.

"Sheesh, Karen, you ain't mad, are you? And guess what else? Next summer he might let me make cash money working at the fruit stand. And he's going to put up a nifty sign, taller than the house. It will be shaped like a giant watermelon slice with seeds spelling out 'Taylor's Farm Fresh Produce.' Ain't that real classy?"

"He's moving you into our house? And you're taking over my room? And our family won't have any place to live?" Karen felt hot tears welling.

"Yeah. But, Karen, you've always been rich. Your family'll find a way to get by."

"I'm going now. You were my last friend in Cloverdale. Goodbye, Lucinda."

"But, Karen…"

Karen ran back across the highway without stopping. Desperate to let off steam, she tore around the house the long way to the back door. Winded, she trudged in to spread the news.

Mother turned pale. "That farmhand family will have my own dear house? They'll live here, tracking over my carpets? They'll dirty up my drapes and wallpaper? I'm glad we're leaving Cloverdale. This place can go to the devil for all I care. Find as many cardboard boxes as you can down in the basement. Bring them up here as fast as you can. We have to pack."

They stopped only to tend to the children and once to grab a quick bite of lunch. Karen, Rosemary, and Mother worked through the day, sorting, discarding and packing.

"I'm worn out," Mother said in the late afternoon. She dusted her hands on her apron skirt. "I'm going to sleep while Larry naps."

Karen and Rosemary continued to work until the telephone rang. Karen was standing nearby.

"Hello?"

"Hello, this is detective Jack Blackburn from the Ogden Police Department. May I please speak with Mr. Hardy?"

"He's gone now. Sorry."

"Well then, your mother?"

"She just had a baby. She's sleeping. I'm not allowed to wake her up for phone calls."

"I'll ask you this then and call them later. Have you seen Hyrum LeGrande today?"

"Huh? No, he's in jail."

"No, he isn't. That's why I'm calling. Mr. LeGrande is at large."

"You mean he flew the coop?!"

"That's right. He got out in the night. He's gone. Tell your parents we'll be in touch."

Karen dashed into her sleeping mother's room.

"Mother, the prophet's on the loose. He escaped."

CHAPTER 34

MEANT TO BE

Karen, still dressed in nightclothes, stirred a pot of oatmeal. Mother and Father sipped Postum at the table.

"Karen," Mother said, "bring over the rolled oats for us. We need to eat fast and get ready for Sunday school."

Father cradled his mug. "We're moving out in a couple of weeks. I see no reason to go to church today. Or ever again in this dang-burned ward."

"Fine by me," Mother said, "though it'll sure seem strange to stay home of a Sunday."

"No one's in the office. I think I'll go in while I still have a key."

"What? You're working on the Sabbath?"

"I think the Lord'll understand. I'll get some catch-up work done. And I want to check the files for jobs."

"Good. Can Richard drive you? I need him to drop off a load of castoffs at Deseret Industries. The neighbors are treating us like dirt, and I refuse to give one scrap of anything to them."

"Okay by me."

After they left, Karen went to the porch for Spud's food and water bowls. "Please, Mother, can't we take Spud with us when we move?"

"We've been over this a hundred times. He's a farm dog. He'll be better off staying with Lucinda."

Karen scraped leftover hamburger gravy into his feeding dish. She would miss Spud when they moved. He'd kept her company and protected her better than the adults who were forcing her to give him up.

She snatched a pork chop to smuggle to him with the gravy. Then she twisted the water faucet to fill his water dish. The tap emitted gurgles, a dribble, then a blast of air.

"Mother, the stupid pump's broken down again."

"Stupid is a bad word. Don't use it. Run upstairs and put on some old clothes. Then hurry out and prime the pump."

Karen controlled the urge to stamp her foot. "Why do I always have to be the one? It's Rosemary's turn."

Rosemary strolled in, blowing on her newly manicured nails. "That isn't fair. I work as hard as anyone around this house."

"Karen!" Mother put down her mug and shook a finger. "Quit complaining. Don't get me started. Get your clothes on and fix that pump. Hurry it up. We all need water."

"At least," Karen said, "when we move, that nasty pump stays behind."

After dressing in her detestable everyday floursack shirt and pedal pushers, Karen grabbed the half-full priming bucket on her way out the door. She nuzzled with Spud and fed him his breakfast before continuing to the pump house.

As she lifted the trap door, she held her breath against the dank odor. The crumbling steps and sloshing bucket kept her attention as she descended. At the bottom, she turned on the light. The cheese knife was missing from its hook. Mother must have packed it. Thankfully, this might be the last time she'd have to breathe the underground stench. Bending over the pump, she exhaled.

Something was wrong.

The knife was wedged through the crook in the main arm of the pump mechanism. Her mind spun.

"Yes, I jammed the pump." The voice echoed from the shadows.

Brother LeGrande rose out of the darkness. He stepped around her, went up the first steps, and slammed the door above their heads. "I knew you'd be down to prime the pump."

Karen shielded herself with the bucket. Her heart pounded into her throat. Words were impossible.

"You're my intended. They let me escape because the Lord wanted me to come back for you. It was pre-ordained. I've been to the trailers. Rhonda and Millie are gone. They're weak women. You're not weak, Karen. You just need to learn faith and obedience. It's my job to teach you."

She was trapped. Too fast, Karen thought. He'd moved too fast. He was also babbling too fast. Nothing made sense.

"No, no, no!" she screamed, and shoved the pail into his belly. The cold water splashed both of them.

He caught the bucket and banged it to the floor. With one hand, he wiped his face, the other hand grabbed Karen's arm. It happened in double time.

LeGrande slipped off his suspenders, unsnapped his pants. He unbuttoned his sacred garments. His swollen member lopped out in full view.

"No!" Karen wrenched under his grip. He squeezed tighter.

"Karen, my dear, this was meant to be. The Lord has revealed it to me. I'll be gentle, but my patience has limits."

"No!" Karen kicked at his shins and beat his arms with her fists, dug her fingernails into his face.

He laughed, sending tremors down her spine.

Spud growled above them. He leaped on the door in a frenzy of barking. His pawing and scratching dislodged dirt, which sifted through the cracks onto their heads.

"Let me go. Spud won't give up. He'll tear you apart if you hurt me."

LeGrande laughed again. "The knife can put a stop to that cur dog quicker than it shut off the pump."

"Down, boy." It was a stranger's voice. The door lifted and thudded to the ground. Light flooded the cavity.

Sunshine meant escape and safety.

The snarling dog pummeled down the stairwell and latched onto LeGrande's leg.

Karen struggled up the steps. A glint of sun flashed off the knife in LeGrande's hand.

She leaped toward the square of light. The prophet caught her ankle and dragged her back. He kicked the dog against the wall. Stunned, Spud whimpered on the floor.

LeGrande poised the knife at Karen's throat.

Karen gasped and fought off the urge to struggle.

"FBI." A dark-haired man peered down at them. "Come out of there! Now!"

"You're Ben, the Jew boy. Aren't you?" LeGrande snorted. "Put the gun down, or I'll use this knife on the girl."

Like *Dragnet* on the radio, Ben yelled, "Hurt her, and you die." He thrust out a snub-nosed revolver.

"Drop the gun."

"You drop the knife. Or you're a dead man!"

LeGrande jerked Karen's arm at an unnatural angle. She gasped.

He shoved her up the stairs, keeping the knife poised.

"Get out of my way, you punk kid," he said to Ben. "I'm clearing off this farm. I'm taking her with me."

Karen's mind recoiled at the memory of the prophet's pickup parked by Rhonda's trailer. She knew she must not get into it.

"Let her go," Ben snarled.

LeGrande tripped on a broken step. "Fuck!"

Karen twisted almost free. He wrenched her arm, not letting her go. She emerged to the open shaft of light and onto solid ground.

The prophet clambered out after her, slipping an arm back under a suspender. He grabbed a handful of Karen's hair and placed the blade to her neck. "Stand back, Jew boy. We're going to my truck."

"Let her go," Ben yelled.

Karen saw the truck bumper through the box elder trees. She gasped and LeGrande's knife hand wobbled. He shoved her. It hurt. In spite of dragging her feet, he was able to push her toward the truck.

"Hold it!" Ben crept after them, his gun leveled with both hands.

Karen's eye caught sight of a male figure crouched behind Rhonda's trailer and hoped he was on her side.

At the truck, LeGrande's fingers curled over the chrome door handle.

The couched figure stood. A rock shattered the windshield.

Karen stomped on LeGrande's foot and jumped out of his grasp. At that instant, she heard sounds like tire blow-outs. The tall stranger leaped from behind the trailer. His hand held a gun.

LeGrande crumpled into a patch of dry foxtails. His shirt and the nearby weeds turned gooey red. Blood streamed from his chest and formed a pool around him. His billowy white head changed to sodden red. The crimson flow trickled around stones, dead stems, and leaves. It floated bits of dirt and dry grass, twirled a cocklebur into a red puddle that broke into a stream which meandered through the foxtail toward the mouth of the cellar.

"He had a knife," the second man said. Tall and blonde, he looked and sounded somehow familiar.

"Well done, Jack." Ben lowered his gun.

Karen sank to the ground. Time stood still. Her sputtering heart slowed to a point of sluggishness. Her breath turned shallow. She observed a box elder bug climbing a stick. It reared on its four back legs and aimlessly cocked the other two in front.

Strange, Karen thought. How time moves fast, slow, then fast again, and suddenly, stops. Where had she heard such an idea? LeGrande had once said that, back at a meeting when he was alive, eons ago.

Spud limped from the pump house. He settled into her lap on the ground and whined against her chest. He licked her face.

Karen wasn't back to the here and now, but at least she sensed that Spud was back. She clung to him.

The shorter dark man, named Ben, knelt by her. "Are you all right, Karen?"

"I don't know," she whispered. "Who're you?"

"I'm FBI. My partner, Jack, and I are here to help you. We took your mom to the hospital the other night. That guy"—he pointed to the one called Jack—"is Rhonda's brother."

Karen couldn't answer. Her mind was distant. She remained silent and didn't care.

The tall, blond man bent over LeGrande heaped in the weeds. The man's fingers pressed the throat. "He's gone. I'm glad of it."

The screen door banged. Mother scurried down the lane toward them. She froze at the scene. Then, gasped. Finally, she exclaimed, "I heard shooting! Oh, good golly! What have you done? I'm going to be sick."

The two younger Hardys trailed after her. Davy and Judy clung to Mother's skirt. Their eyes were bright with shock. For once, they were speechless.

"Oh no, oh, no!" Mother cried out. "Is Karen all right?"

"She'll be fine, Mrs. Hardy," Ben said. "LeGrande attacked her. She's spunky and brave. Gave him a fight. Fortunately, we were here to stop him before it got too bad. Take those children into the house."

Rosemary arrived. "Don't look, girl," Mother ordered, as she grabbed the little ones by the hand to lead them away.

"No, come here, Rosemary," Ben said. "Help your sister inside. Make her some tea… or something. Wrap her in a blanket. She's shivering."

"You again?" Rosemary asked. "Haven't you two guys caused enough trouble?" Her eyes focused on the fallen body. She screamed.

"Take your sister," Ben repeated. "Give her hot tea, like I said."

"We're Mormon. We don't drink your kind of tea."

"Do you hear me? Take care of your sister!"

Jack and Ben lifted Karen to her feet. Jack placed Rosemary's hand under Karen's arm for support. "Tell your mother we'll need to use the telephone. And tell her we'll need a bed sheet."

Spud whined and shadowed Karen's steps. "Take the dog inside with you," Ben said. He and Karen need to be together for now."

"He's an outdoor dog." Rosemary bristled.

"Do as I say!"

Karen leaned on Rosemary who guided her inside to the gray chair. Spud rested at her feet. "The fed said we had to let Spud in," Rosemary told Mother. "He said to cover her with a blanket. I don't understand. It's hot today." But still she fetched the blanket.

The girls, Davy, and Judy waited with Mother in the living room. Mother sniffed and rocked. "Oh, my. Oh, my. Karen, are you sure you haven't been defiled?"

"No. I haven't."

"Did the feds hurt you?"

Karen shook her head, no, too tired to speak.

"Did Brother LeGrande do what they claimed?"

"Huh?" With effort, Karen spoke, "He was mean. He tried to hurt me. I need a bath."

"What will we ever do?" Mother moaned.

"I don't know." Rosemary clutched at her chest. "I thought my life was as bad as it could get."

Mother sat beside her on the sofa. Both blotted their eyes and twisted Kleenex. The two younger children's eyes were wide as they looked into Karen's face. They hugged her and felt warm against her legs.

Karen slumped in the chair, silently reminding herself that she was safe. Hopefully, she'd soon believe it. She felt detached from her mother and sister. They fussed uselessly over her and at each other. They reminded her of Heckle and Jeckle cartoon characters on a movie screen, fretting and chattering foolishly and making no sense. Karen allowed her mind to retreat. She offered no notice or comment.

Karen's thoughts drifted aimlessly and finally wandered back to the pump house. She shivered, as if a blizzard shook her by the shoulders.

Jack called in through the back door. "Bring that sheet, would ya?"

Rosemary took it to him. Later, he returned to use the phone.

"Hello," he told the operator. "I'm Ogden Police Detective Jack Blackburn. This is an emergency. I need you to get me Chief Gordon Walker. He might be at the Fourth Ward LDS Church meetinghouse of Ogden."

While he waited, he told Rosemary, "Go make that tea for Karen."

"The only kind of tea we have is herb tea," Rosemary said. "It's in case somebody gets sick."

"Good for you." Jack shrugged and pointed toward the kitchen. "Go get it." She hurried through the door.

Jack finally reached the chief and went through a lengthy conversation. Karen gave up trying to follow what he said, like she'd given up listening to Mother and Rosemary.

When he finished the call, Jack squatted and looked into Karen's eyes. "I think you're going to be fine. What do you think?"

Karen nodded.

"When you're cleaned up and rested, we'll need to ask you a few questions. Think you'll be able to handle that?"

She nodded again and reached for the fragrant, hot mug Rosemary brought. Karen held the warm cup and shivered under the blanket. Spud nudged her ankles.

Jack turned to Rosemary. "Go run a hot bath for Karen. Can't you see those blood splotches all over her shirt?"

Karen gagged at the word blood. "Did I bleed?"

"Don't worry." Jack patted her shoulder. "That crackpot prophet was near you when I shot him. I'm afraid you got splattered, but you're fine."

Karen looked out at the highway to avoid gagging again from seeing LeGrande's blood down her front.

"Bring her some clean clothes." Jack's voice was insistent. "After she changes, we're taking those for evidence."

"There's no water," Rosemary said. "The pump's broken down, like usual. Karen didn't fix it."

"I think I hear your father and brother out back," Jack said. "I'll tell them to get it going."

As the Hardy men came through the door, Mother and Rosemary produced a new onslaught of tears. They dashed into the kitchen.

"Edward," Mother cried, "the feds are back. They've murdered the prophet. He's dead." The women sobbed in unison.

"Mr. Hardy," Jack said, "Mr. LeGrande attacked your daughter Karen. Luckily, my partner and I were here. We were able to take him down before he used a knife on her."

Father chopped his hand like a hatchet in Ben and Jack's direction. "You ignorant feds. You're here and you've shed blood! How dare you? I should have known better than to tempt the devil by working on the Sabbath." Father's eyes snapped. His scowl turned to a sneer.

"Mr. Hardy, you and your son need to repair the water pump. Your daughter needs to wash up. We need her stained clothing as evidence."

"You need? You need to clear out of here and never come back. You've done enough damage."

"Mr. Hardy," Jack went on, "this is a crime scene. I'm the law, and I'm telling ya' to fix yur pump!"

"That can wait!" Father leaned over to Karen and took her by the shoulders. "Did the prophet do what they said? Are you all right, girl?"

Karen nodded and cast her eyes on her feet. "I think I am. He's dead and I'm glad. I need a bath. I have to be clean."

"Look at yourself. Why are you covered with blood and muck if you're not hurt?"

"Why? There was no water. I went down to prime the pump." Karen knew she was confused, couldn't follow what father wanted.

"Pay attention, Karen! What exactly happened out there?" His arm flung out in the direction of the pump house.

Karen struggled, but surrendered to her thoughts, which were whirling and pitching beyond her control. Spud rumbled a warning growl at Father, who stepped back. Spud then turned to Karen. His eyes implored her to rein in ricocheting memories and form them into words. She cuddled him against her.

"I went down into the cellar. The knife was stuck through the pump. Then he jumped up and grabbed me." Karen whimpered and rubbed Spud's ears.

"He said bad things," she continued. "He laughed at me. It was a mean scary kind of laugh. He said he was taking me away, started pulling off his pants and his garments." She forgot what she was about to say next. Her chest heaved. Bent over Spud, she noticed tears dripping on his head and rubbed them away.

"Did you do something to lure him, Karen? Why didn't you just run off?"

No one had tried to hurt Father. Karen wondered why he wore such an agitated face, eyes popping, and spit at the corners of his mouth.

"Huh?" She tried to understand the question and fit it together with one of the ideas ping ponging inside her head. With effort, she picked up Father's thread about running away.

"I almost got away. He caught me. Held on tight. Wouldn't let go." Karen looked at the purple welt burning on her arm and wondered how she could have forgotten it. "My arm hurts."

"I guess," Father's face had been changing minute to minute from anger, to fear, to worry, and disgust.

"He grabbed the cheese knife," Karen continued when she could, "and he held it on my throat. Like a Danite." She showed them where with the side of her hand, then shivered and pulled the blanket around her legs. "I know I'm never supposed to hate, but I do hate! Spud came to help."

On hearing his name, Spud lifted his head from her knee and let out a yelp.

"And that man called Ben came, too." Karen's hand went out to where Ben stood.

"That other one is Jack. He is somebody's brother, I think. He threw a rock and I think he's the one who shot a gun first and the other guy shot, too. Blood splashed all over me. I need to wash. I'm feeling sick." Karen folded her arms into her belly and rocked. It seemed to quell the taste of vomit rising in her throat.

"I see." Father wrung his hands. "You did the best you could, girl. I guess we didn't find the one true prophet after all. We'll have to look someplace else."

The praise helped. Karen was the center of attention, without being the one in trouble for a change. Father, and even Richard, looked stricken and confused.

Father kept talking, seemed upset, ranted about God and scripture and other subjects of no importance. Karen's thoughts floated outside the window and under the shade trees. She patted Spud's head, then, remembered she felt queasy and dirty.

"Holy cow!" Richard said. "I would have got my .22 rifle, shot him with it and beat him up. Sheesh, this all was going on while I was hauling stuff up to Deseret Industries!"

"Both of you!" Ben took control. "Listen up, and I mean now! There is a body outside. Inside, there's a need for running water. Repair that pump! The coroner will be here whenever he gets the word. There might be a wait. It's Sunday."

Father and Richard finally left.

"Good gosh almighty!" The screen door slammed behind Father.

"Holy cow. Sheesh. Holy, holy cow!" The screen door slammed again, this time behind Richard.

It seemed like forever before Karen heard the kitchen faucet groan and spurt air and water. She must have forgotten to turn it off earlier. "I can run my own bath," she said to no one in particular. She carried clean clothes. Spud gave a muffled cry as she entered the bathroom. She turned to hug him.

"Don't worry," Jack said. "I'll take him outside and see that he's all right."

Karen patted Spud and nodded at Jack.

Behind the bathroom door, she retched as she sloughed off the ghastly clothes. Long ago, she had blown her nose on that ugly shirt and called it a small justice in an unjust world. Cracking the door and throwing them onto the kitchen floor, she knew she'd never have to see the horrid shirt again, another small justice in a more unjust world.

Clean, I just want to be clean, she thought. She filled the tub higher than she had ever dared. In the tub, she lathered every pore of skin. She didn't care about wasting soap or water. She lathered her hair. She rinsed, drained the tub, and started over. The last dunk reminded her of baptism. She rose from the water feeling clean, finally.

Karen's mind wandered back to yesterday's phone call. "Wrong," she said out loud to herself as she dripped a puddle on the floor and toweled off. Dressing, she spoke more of her thoughts aloud. "Yesterday, the policeman told me LeGrande had escaped. That's wrong now. I'm the one who has escaped. From *him*."

CHAPTER 35

HIT THE ROAD

From a chair in front of the chief's desk, Ben watched autumn leaves flutter by the window toward his parked car. It was packed and headed east toward home. His mouth watered for a chunk of Sylvia's delicious yellow egg bread dipped in honey. He'd be with her and see her parents at Yom Kippur. He and Jack waited to speak.

The chief grasped the edge of his desk. His eyes were like lead slugs. "I'm not a man who suffers fools. I warned the two of you from the get-go to lay off the polygamists."

The words sounded as deadly as gunfire. "You disobeyed my direct orders by raiding that little farm. You are both insubordinate!"

"Sir," Ben said, "my job here was to investigate and help prosecute polygamy in this state."

The chief's hand flew up to cut him off. "Your assignment was within my jurisdiction. You're in my office now. I'll do the talking. You hauled in a no-account crackpot against my orders. I told you this department needs to fight *real* crime. I had the good sense to tell the guard on duty to look the other way, so LeGrande could take a hike. We were rid of him. Then you guys shoot him down dead. The two of you are responsible for a heap of bad publicity. You've thrown me into a political snake pit!"

"Hold on." Jack leaned in and tapped the desk for emphasis. "You teamed me up with Ben. We did our jobs. You, sir, obstructed justice when you allowed that lunatic to escape. He went back and assaulted a young girl. You want *real* crime and *real* bad publicity? That's what you'd have if that slimeball had raped and kidnapped a twelve-year-old kid. You fail to note that his pants were half off and he was dragging her by her hair to his pickup at knifepoint. We wouldn't want anyone thinking that you, Chief, were an accessory to attempted child rape."

The chief's fist thudded the desk. "This department works because everyone here follows my orders. You guys are nothing but trouble. I want you out of my hair and out of Ogden!"

"Sir," Jack said, "I've got applications in at four precincts in California and one in Arizona. You see that I get one of those jobs, and you'll get your wish. With that in mind, I won't mention how you thwarted justice."

"I'm more than ready to clear out," Ben said. "Jack is a good officer. We won't cause you further inconvenience, once you give your clearance. We'll both be out of state."

"Fine by me. Hit the road!" The chief snorted, sat back in his chair, a bull at bay.

*　　　*　　　*

Frost tinged the fall wind outdoors, and Ben looked forward to the cozy booth reserved for Jack and him at the Ko Ko Mo. They breezed in and greeted Eddie.

"You guys want your usual beers?"

"Sure do," Jack said. "Ben's about to hit the road."

"Thought I'd say goodbye," Ben said, as Eddie delivered foaming glasses. "What's with the glasses?" Where're the mugs?" Ben noticed a purple welt distorting Eddie's eyelid. "And what happened to your eye?"

"A rowdy customer and his mug did that to me." Eddie stepped behind the bar and brought out a bowling pin. "Live and learn. I now have self-defense." He lifted the pin overhead like a club. "The mugs, I donated to the Catholic Church. The clientele there will most likely use them for drinking, not for beating each other bloody like in here."

Jack and Ben nodded.

"I wanted to use your spittoon before I leave town," Ben said. He took out the end of a Life Saver roll and tossed. It hit the rim, but slid inside. "I'm no longer a smoker and I now hate peppermint as much as Jack does."

Jack laughed. "Glad you've come to your senses."

"Heck, Ben," Eddie said, "it's been nice having you. Late afternoons can be a bore. Most of my customers work this time of day."

"Here's to you," Jack said. The two raised their glasses to Eddie before he hurried off.

Jack asked, "Why'ja' hold back with the chief? You only called LeGrande a slimeball when we both know he's a Spam-sucking slimeball."

Ben laughed and said, "Spam isn't kosher. By the way, did it work out for Rhonda in California?"

"Yes. She's with the folks in Nevada. Our aunt in Piedmont said she'll be thrilled to have her. Rhonda will be on a bus to

California in a coupla days. Things look pretty good for me there. When I get a job, I'll help Rhonda until she's on her feet."

Ben shivered as Shortarm entered and held the door to let a sailor blow in with the chilly fall breeze.

"Shortarm," Jack called out to him. "You're looking great. What's up?"

Shortarm, beaming in crisp khaki pants and shirt, strode over to their booth.

Ben clicked his tongue at the spiffy appearance. "Going to a wedding?" he asked.

"Going to work." Shortarm stood for inspection. "Eddie and some of the other guys have hired me. My job'll be sumthin' like you guys do. Don't tell 'em at the precinct." He spoke in hushed tones. "But I'll be on the look out for undesirables around here."

Jack laughed. "Are you possibly calling cops, undesirables?"

"Well, some cops is up to no good. But I'll mostly notice any kind of troublemakers. An' I'll let Eddie and the others know who's a-coming."

"Good for you," Jack said. "I won't ask for specifics. This sounds like it might relate to the underground side of the street." He pointed down at the basement with the rumored connected tunnels snaking between establishments.

"Ben and I are about to go our separate ways, pal. I'm thrilled to see you looking good." Jack reached up to pat a crease on shortarm's shirt, fresh out of the package.

"Same here," Ben added. "Good luck to you, buddy." He shook Shortarm's hand.

"Thanks, guys. If it weren't fer pals like you two and Eddie, I don't know where I'd be. Take it from me, this street is the best place in Utah and that's a fact. You can't trust none of the Mormon riff raff out there." He absently pulled at his folded-up sleeve. "Got to go now."

"Keep your nose clean." Jack looked like a proud father whose kid hit a home run with bases loaded.

"Yes. Best of luck," Ben added. He was putting off having to say his final goodbyes and to facing the chill wind outside. I think I need another beer." Ben waved to Eddie. "No. Better make it coffee."

Eddie hustled over with a steaming cup and saucer and a fresh beer.

Ben wiped with a napkin at a wet circle on the table. "We didn't do too badly, did we? Utah is a strange situation. We fought city hall about as much as we could. Every one of us who learns about these cults and spreads the word will mean they'll ruin fewer lives. The Nazis took over Germany because good people did nothing to stop them. Let's hope that more good people speak out about polygamy. It devastates the lives of anyone it touches."

"Thanks, Ben." Jack studied the foam sliding down his glass. "I'm grateful we could get my sister outa there. And maybe Millie, too."

"And we saved Karen Hardy. She has a chance for a life."

CHAPTER 36

SEE YOU LATER, ALLIGATOR

"Karen," Mother said, "we're leaving right soon. "Hurry up and get Spud over to Lucinda's house."

"In a jiffy, Mother. But right now I'm helping Davy and Judy with their toys."

Karen might need Spud for a secret mission. She had to somehow destroy the silver locket. She fingered it in her pocket and shuddered. Should she smash it with a rock? Hide it in the pump cellar? Or barn? She wondered if wasting a locket was a sin she could never live down.

Father emerged in a cloud of steam from the bathroom. "I'm not worried about using up hot water today. The bishop owns this place. As of now, he pays for power and the pump and the water level are his problems."

"That's right," Mother said. "All the kids have had their baths this morning and washed their hair for the trip. Shouldn't we have a prayer before we leave, Edward?"

"Yes." Father set his shaving kit on the kitchen counter, the only surface left to put anything. The table, chairs, washing machine, and every movable thing had been packed. The house was an echoing cave. "Gather 'round, everyone."

Karen bowed her head in the family circle.

"Our Father in heaven, we pray for a safe and successful journey to Grandma Hardy's farm. We ask for Thy protection as we travel on to Phoenix tomorrow. Our hearts are grateful that we have survived the trials and tribulations of following a false prophet.

"We do thank Thee that Brother LeGrande was at least fortunate in his demise. Thy will was done in the name of thy Holy Principle of Blood Atonement. His blood did, indeed, spill freely into the soil of Thy earth. A true blessing if it atoned for his sins. Our fallen brother has now made amends for his wickedness. We are grateful that it is possible for Brother LeGrande to ascend into thy glory. Thou art a merciful God.

"More than ever, we are in need of Thy continued guidance in Arizona. Please, Father, this time help us to find the true and singular One Mighty and Strong. InthenameofJesusChrist. Amen."

After amens, Mother said, "Here, Karen, carry these boxes of food out. Put one in the car and the other in one of the trucks. It'll be enough to get us across the Arizona border after we leave Grandma's house. Then stop dragging your feet and get Spud over to Lucinda."

A faded but serviceable moving van was out front, packed with furniture and household necessities. Father was satisfied with the deal he'd made on the truck and thought he could resell it in Phoenix. The van led a convoy of Hardy vehicles starting near the driveway, stretching past the front yard and house, and ending at the ruined apple tree. Millie's Airstream bullet gleamed behind the van. Next, was LeGrande's truck which Richard would drive. The pickup sported a new trailer hitch, hooked to the square-topped trailer Brother LeGrande had built for Rhonda. Mother would drive the family Rambler which brought up the rear.

Karen wedged the carton, packed with cheese, canned peaches, bread, peanut butter, crackers, pears and pickles, on the floor in front of the backseat. She squinted to avoid seeing the pickles. Knowing they were there gave her a raging case of heebie-jeebies. Eating one was unthinkable.

When she returned for the second box, Mother made a final announcement. "Everyone, use the bathroom. I'm taking the toilet paper in the car for wiping mouths and noses."

Every word and footstep echoed through the hollow rooms. They had packed what they could and sold or donated the rest. The house was a vacant reminder of their past.

"Into the car," Mother commanded at the end of the flushing. "Let's get out of here while it's still early."

"Be right back," Karen said. "I have to take care of Spud."

Mother's fists snapped to her hips. "Sometimes, I could skin you alive. We'll all be waiting. So hurry it up."

Karen hustled out to Spud, but led him down the path to the pump house, not to Lucinda's. "Stay with me, boy. This is the last time we have to go down into that hole." Keeping her face turned away from the matted weeds where the prophet's body had fallen, she threw open the trapdoor.

She kicked over a rock the size of a cantaloupe near the mound. Blanched crawly things slithered in and out of slimy holes in the earth. With a stick, Karen scraped the wriggling muck off the dirt-caked side of the stone. She hefted the rock and noticed how heavy and rough it felt.

Spud whimpered and shied back.

"It's safe, boy. We're together. This is something I have to do, so you and I can go in peace, knowing we won."

They crept down the broken steps. Karen's skin prickled, and she held her breath, more from dread than a desire to shut out the oppressive stench. After flicking on the bulb, she peered into the empty corners. She heaved a relieved breath. Likely lurking entities were at least invisible.

The pump's largest mechanical arm cranked and creaked, pushing and pulling smaller levers in the eerie dance she'd so often seen. She stretched her own arms above her head and hurled the stone, crashing it into the mechanism.

The pump clunked and jangled, then died.

The arm of the pump flopped uselessly, half of it no longer connected to the mechanism. Again Karen lifted the stone. She took careful aim and smashed it near the rusty nut and bolt still holding it.

Spud let out a thin howl. Karen snatched up the bent and broken-off central pump piece and picked up the stone.

Her imagination wrestled control from her. She sensed a presence of the enraged unseen dead spirit of the pump, free now to rise up and merge with the dead prophet's soul. Their power pulsed and filled the space. Karen shivered as if an army of bleached centipedes and spiders scurried over her bare skin. "We'll leave the light on, Spud, That'll help fight 'em off and the bishop can pay the electric bill."

In two or three frantic leaps, she and Spud bounded out onto safe ground in the fall morning sunshine. She slammed the trapdoor and set the rock on it to lock in the destruction and the evil spirits once and for all.

Desperate to climb still higher, she urged Spud. "Let's go, boy." They made a mad dash to the hayloft ladder, Karen's fist still locked around the bent pump arm. Like an acrobat, she flew up the twenty-foot ladder, keeping her eyes squeezed tight to intensify her favorite ladder stunt.

She found the treasure box still nestled in its secret shelf. With it clutched in one hand, she slipped the pump piece into the hidden space. No one would notice it, perhaps forever.

The old pump was dead, never to be resurrected. It couldn't harm another person, not ever.

"I swear to God," she said with no one to hear, except Spud and the pump piece, "I will not go to a heaven where that evil prophet might be waiting. I hereby swear it!" She wedged the pump piece deeper into the secret hiding place. She lingered to remember the good times she'd shared with Lucinda in the loft. They'd laughed, cried, slept there a few nights, shared hopes and secrets, and watched kittens grow up there or sometimes, die. She'd miss the private time, the comforting sounds and smells, and especially, the solitude of the hayloft.

Holding tightly to the treasure box, she half-skipped down the ladder.

She and Spud didn't stop running until they both stood, panting at the edge of the highway. Lucinda waved to them from the other side. Karen waited for an eighteen-wheeler slowing up a string of pickups in every color and condition, then a Studebaker. They hurried over to Lucinda.

"Spud," Karen said, "say hi to your new owner."

He barked. Both girls hugged him. Then, they hugged each other.

"Lucinda, I'm sorry if I was mean to you. You know, because you're getting my room. I'm glad it's you and not some stuck-up snob, like Camille. And I'm glad you'll have Spud too. He likes you. He wouldn't be happy in Phoenix. And I know you'll watch out for the barn cats."

"Karen, I've been thinking. My wishes are coming true. I'm gettin' a big house. I'm gonna have a indoor bathroom and running hot water. And you're gettin' your wishes too. Remember when we wuz little? You know your wishes about getting out in the world?"

"Yes, I know." They hugged again.

Karen noticed Father and Richard climbing into the trucks. Behind them, the rest of the family piled into the car. "You're taking that dead guy's trailers and truck?" Lucinda asked. "Well, you might as well. His wives run off as soon as he went in the hoosegow. They sure don't need 'em."

Karen said, "His first wife, Miriam, came for the truck. First wives usually get everything. They're the only legal ones. The rest of them are high and dry.

"Father told her she didn't deserve the truck since she'd never honored the principle of plural marriage and she gave up on it for almost nothing."

"Having lots of wives is weird, ain't it?"

"Yes, it is."

"Father said we can live in the trailers until he gets a paycheck or two from his new government job. Then we can buy a house."

"Ya see? In a couple a days, your dad's already starting a new job with regular paychecks. I said you wuz rich. And you still are."

"Yes, you did."

"Before I go, I want to let you know that the old water pump died today. Bishop Taylor will have to buy you a new one."

"That shouldn't bother him none. He's rich."

The unfamiliar tinny sound of the moving van horn beeped at Karen. She waved at the family waiting for her. "Don't ever mess with plural marriage. That's one thing I've learned."

"Karen, I ain't dumb. I knew that all along."

Karen laughed. The family car horn trumpeted for her to hurry.

"Have to go. I won't forget you, Lucinda. Here's our treasure box." She placed it into Lucinda's safekeeping, then reached into her pocket for the blue velvet box. "This is for you, a locket." She snapped open the lid and showed it to Lucinda. "It says 'Meant to Be' because we were meant to be friends."

Karen crossed her fingers behind her back to cancel out the lie. It wouldn't bring Lucinda bad luck because Karen had washed the locket with hot water and soap to baptize away LeGrande's fingerprints and clean his memories from it, just as she'd washed them from her own body. It would be the last lie she'd have to tell a friend.

Lucinda lit up, speechless for a moment. "You'll always be my best friend, Karen." They shook hands like grownups.

All three horns lapsed into solid wailing. The trucks and car were warmed up and wasting gas.

Karen hurried across the highway and into the back seat of the car, beside Judy and Davy. Father pulled out first.

As Mother rolled onto the highway behind LeGrande's pickup, Karen leaned out of the window to her waist. Elbows locked, alligator jaws chomping, she signaled, "See you later, alligator."

Lucinda answered, "After awhile, crocodile" until the car was halfway to the ward house. A truck finally hid the view, leaving Lucinda and Spud behind Karen and the outside world looming ahead.

- End -

ACKNOWLEDGEMENTS

After retirement, I enrolled in writing classes and wrote children's books and stories. My husband encouraged me to write an adult novel based on my experiences with polygamy growing up, and I finally agreed. With trepidation I sidled into Peggy Lucke's writing class clutching my first chapter. She and my fellow budding writers bucked up my confidence. After that, Peggy has generously shared her expertise and professionalism to help me finish and polish my work.

I'm grateful to my ever supportive husband, Jerry, and to those original well-wishers who spurred me on my journey.

I also thank Eddie Simone and his spunky wife, Cindy, the owners of the Ko Ko Mo Club in Ogden, Utah. He's the only authentic name in the book. She stayed up one night to enjoy my completed book in one sitting, and she is brimming with her own tales of personal bravery. Eddie let me use his bar and his life as a backdrop for the Ogden police action in the plot. His experiences provide key elements for a side of Utah life I had missed.

I'm particularly appreciative of Jil Plummer, perhaps my favorite author, for her insight and suggestions as well as all of my other friends in the California Writers Club and the Mendocino Coast Writers Conferences.

I once believed that authors must be knowledgeable on every subject covered in their writing. Now I've learned to count on helpful experts to fill in whatever expertise I lack. I appreciate my collaborators, Bill Huffman, Harry Larson, Dave Howard, Bob O'Brian, Carol Perrin, Camille Minichino, my publisher Andrew Benzie, and others too numerous to list.

A heartfelt thank you must go to the Recovery from Mormonism Site (exmormon.org) for jogging my memories and providing me audience, and special thanks to RfM owner, Eric Kettunen and his lovely wife, Kathy. They have helped me publish and spread the word about the hidden crimes that continue in Utah and other states where little is done to curb the abuse of the victims of modern day polygamy.

www.ingramcontent.com/pod-product-compliance
Lightning Source LLC
Chambersburg PA
CBHW070803180626
46818CB00001B/79